NORSE VENGEANCE

JERRY AUTIERI

1

The shadow slid across Thorfast's face. Immediate cool relieved his left cheek from the lashing of the brilliant sun. Waves grumbled at his feet as if in warning, warm water tugging at the remnants of his pant legs. The gritty beach sand had pushed salty and earthen flavors thick on his tongue. He pressed his eyes shut, hoping to squeeze the blurs of brown and blue into something more distinct.

He heard breathing, felt the pressure as whoever hovered over his prone body reached for him.

Was it an Arab come to take him prisoner once more? Was it a villager come to pillage the wreckage washing ashore from the night's battle?

Or was it a Valkyrie come at last to carry him to Valhalla?

Whoever it was, Thorfast would be a victim no more. He would die fighting and join his brothers—Yngvar and his Wolves—in Odin's hall. He crushed sand into his left hand resting beside his face. He opened his eyes again, and the shadow had stretched beyond him into the churned beach around his head.

The world was clearer now that tears had washed the salt from his eyes. He would see his enemy's face before he died.

A rough, cold hand brushed his naked shoulder.

Thorfast flipped with explosive violence. He slammed his hand full of packed sand like a mallet into the hard bone of a man's head.

Whoever hovered over him howled in shock and pain.

Thorfast flooded with energy. He thrashed over like a landed fish. The bulky shadow of a man blotting out the sun had fallen back, one hand held to his face.

"Choke on your teeth, dog!" Thorfast shouted as he seized the moment to clamber to his feet. "I'll break you in two with my own hands."

Thorfast's vision blurred and he staggered backward. His enemy was as slow as he. He realized even a gnarled grandmother could have laid him out with all the time he had spent gaining his balance. The sand fell from his hand and he pressed his palms to both temples as if it could stabilize his sight.

"Peace! It is me, Hamar!"

Thorfast wobbled as his balance adjusted. Hamar sat on the beach, meaty hand clasped to his cheek. Even had he not named himself, Thorfast still would have recognized him from his square face. Though in every other way he was no longer the strong and confident pilot of memory. Like all of Yngvar's crew, he had spent too long in Prince Kalim's prison. His flesh was sickly pale, nearly indistinguishable from the gray rags clothing him. His head was shaved, leaving only a dome of brown stubble and scabs on his crown.

"You live? Or am I lost in a dream of death?" Thorfast rubbed his eyes, chasing out the last of the grit that still stung him.

"I asked myself the same," Hamar said, nursing the side of his head. "I thought I had surely drowned. But here I sit."

They would both have stories to tell of how they survived the violent, burning sea. But these tales would wait for a better day. As the excitement drained from Thorfast, he crumbled into a heap. Hamar seemed ready to tip over and sleep.

"Sorry about your head," Thorfast said, clapping the dirt from his palm. He sat beside Hamar, his waist and knees cracking painfully enough to draw a hiss from his lips.

"Aye, well, I thought you were dead or else I'd have warned you first."

2

They both sat staring at the sparkling, sickeningly cheerful water spread out before them. No sea was as dazzling as these waters. No sky was ever so blue. While salt hung in the air, a sweet and fair scent mingled with it. On the edges of sight, verdant hills climbed away into the haze. This was a paradise island filled with strange delights for even stranger people.

Thorfast wished the island and all upon it a miserable death.

"Have you found others?" he asked at length.

Hamar sighed and let his shoulders droop forward. Silence made his answer.

"I thought as much," Thorfast said, turning his eyes away from the blinding sparkle of the waves. Gulls whirled and called high above. Piles of shattered wood and tangled rigging rolled in the surf.

No bodies had yet found their way to shore.

"There is a woman not far from here," Hamar said. "A pretty girl, even if she's as wretched as we are. She hauled me out of the water before I drowned. A strong girl, or else I would have withered worse than I feared."

Thorfast gave a dry laugh and glanced at Hamar. "Only your cheeks defy the starvation you endured. Were it not for your square face I would think you a sack of husks. I expect you weigh as much."

Hamar shared the fleeting laugh, and returned Thorfast's critical glance.

"You've fared no better, Thorfast the Silent. And now I have learned how big your head is on that child's body of yours. It is like that berserk we sailed with to Ireland, Egil Skallagrimsson. What a head that beast possessed."

"I am not nearly as bad as he," Thorfast said, placing both hands on his head. "It is a trick of your eyes. Once I have eaten better, my body will find its proper shape again. Then we shall see if the maidens of this land prefer my strong arms over your square face."

They both laughed. Nothing else ever felt so refreshing. Thorfast had not realized how much he relished laughter, how he needed it as a man needs water.

"So little time to laugh," he said, his voice trailing off. "Tell me of this woman who saved you. Where is she now?"

3

"Down the shore," Hamar said. He pointed absently to the distance. "She dragged me to where my face was no longer in the water. She sat with me a long time, maybe all night. I think she was afraid and saw me as protection. Strange to think that, since she had found me close to death. She tried several languages with me. I believe she can speak Frankish. I named the place and it delighted her. But we could say no more to each other."

"A Frankish slave here?" Thorfast said. "I suppose the Franks are even closer to this land than we were to start. I don't know why finding a Frank here surprises me. So, why is she not with you?"

"In the twilight before dawn she left me for a time. When she returned, she used a stick to draw on the beach. She seems to have found a cave. I suppose she means for us to hide there." Hamar squinted into the sky. "If I am right, we should be in Sicily again. I do not know how far our slave ship had sailed before the Byzantines sank us. But the currents have taken us back to our enemies. It is well that we should hide from them."

Thorfast scratched the scabs on his scalp. "She waits at the cave, then?"

"I tried to tell her I would seek my companions and bring back any survivors. She seemed torn about going with me or flying off to her hiding place. You see how she chose. The morning is now in full strength. I must have spent an hour staggering along this beach. There is naught but jetsam and rocks the entire length of this strand. I was ready to turn back, but the gods showed you to me. A gull circled overhead. I suppose ravens do not live here. But a bird none-theless marked your spot."

"The gods are at work," Thorfast agreed. "They have put us together for a purpose, and they will not reveal it so soon. So let's use what strength is left to us and find this woman. If she is skilled, perhaps she will have found some food as well."

"You ask much," Hamar said, groaning as he stood.

"You cannot receive unless you first ask," Thorfast said. "For the gods will not extend their hands to silent men. What god does not yearn for prayers and sacrifices?"

"Then we shall walk and pray," Hamar said, extending his own hand to help Thorfast rise.

Again Thorfast's joints popped and cracked. He gritted his teeth in silence. The strain of his trials and imprisonment had aged him decades beyond his years. He feared if he ever survived to see the north again, he would return as one of those toothless sailors that sat wrapped in wool blankets by the hearth fire. They stared from milky, red-rimmed eyes with naked envy for the young and strong. They had no voice for song, no smile for jest, no hope but for death.

"I will die before that day," he said to himself. Hamar paused and stared, but Thorfast waved him off.

Their walk stuttered along the edge of the surf. The horizon remained clear of warships. The sea swallows all that it is fed without complaint. Yet where the water strokes the earth it belches out the undigested remains of its recent feasts. As Hamar had described, the shore was littered with every shape of debris. An entire warship could be rebuilt from the salvage they passed. Yet no corpse had rolled ashore. What the spirits of the drowned did not take to the sea floor, the creatures of the sea took to their lairs.

Thorfast realized how fortunate he had been to have survived. Worse still, he understood how likely it was he, Hamar, and this woman were the only survivors.

"My legs ache," Thorfast said. "How far away is this woman?"

Hamar shook his head. "I fear I may have forgotten where I left her."

A flash of anger passed through Thorfast, then left him. He sighed.

"It is enough that we live," he said. "We've no need of a woman anyway. She will only be a burden to us."

"I would swear that we have passed the spot already," Hamar said. "I must have walked too close to the waves. There are none of my footprints to follow."

"Think no more of it," Thorfast said. "Let us pause here. We have some time before we must move inland. I do not doubt Arab ships will come to these shores seeking lost companions. We cannot be seen or else we will have earned nothing against the fortune Fate has granted us."

They climbed into the grass and sat. Thorfast wrestled with the length of chain at his ankle and with a meager twist it broke away. Even the shackle bolt had loosened enough that the iron no longer chaffed.

"I wish I could shake this off," he said. "As weak as we are, even dragging this bit of iron tires me. And yours? How did you get free of your chains?"

"The bolt was not set right." Hamar rubbed his thin ankles. "From the start I thought I might break my chains in secret. When our ship was struck, the violence was enough to free me. I guess that is why I might have lived where others sank."

They sat listening to the waves and the grass rustle in the wind. Black rocks littered the length of the beach and white gulls perched atop them in flocks. Thorfast watched as a group suddenly took to the air.

"To be as free as those gulls," he said. "To fly over all the suffering we endure on the land. What greater gift could there be?"

Hamar shook his head in silent agreement.

Then another flock took to the air, screaming in anger. The rest followed.

Thorfast and Hamar both knew the sign.

"Get low," Thorfast hissed, pushing his arm to Hamar's chest. "Someone is about and the gulls know it."

From behind the rocks, a thin, dark-skinned man wearing only weather-beaten black pants waded out of the surf. He had a woven basket looped around one arm and he studied the water as he moved.

"Scavengers," Hamar said. "There must be a village nearby."

"The noise of battle and drowning men must have been loud enough in the night's quiet." Thorfast slithered onto his belly so that the man would not see him. Grass rose above his head, obscuring the scavenger picking through the debris accumulated around the rocks.

"He will pass soon enough," Hamar said. "His attention is on what he can gain. Half-naked as we are, he would still not prevail one against we two."

"I only hope he understands that," Thorfast said, watching the man fling a broken strake back into the surf. "We can ill afford even a light wound, at least not until we find safety and food. We can waste no more time looking for your woman. Perhaps you imagined her from the start."

"It may be so," Hamar agreed. "Let's get among the trees and hills. We are as easily picked as broken shells on the beach out here."

They scrabbled back from the scavenger toward the line of ridges and slopes. Strange trees and thick bushes waved there, beckoning them with shade and shelter.

Once Thorfast judged he had broken line of sight to the man on the beach, he sat up on his knees.

A dog began barking.

His hands went cold. He snapped around toward the sound.

A group of six men appeared from between the trees, following a thin path he might have otherwise missed. Leading them was a boxy dog with a shining brown coat. It strained against its rope, leaping toward them.

"This is not good," Hamar said.

"Well your brains are not so addled," Thorfast said. "Yes, I would call this an unfortunate meeting. Perhaps they have not seen us yet?"

Then the dark-haired natives called out and let their dog loose from his rope.

The beast sprinted off with a growl, bounding straight for them.

"Run!" Thorfast sprang to his naked feet and dashed toward the trees.

2

Thorfast sprinted with strength drawn from desperation. The slavering dog growled behind him, and the trees ahead offered peace. The men who had set the dog on him howled in excitement. The rough tones of Arabic were clear behind the dog.

His feet crashed painfully on rocks as he crashed through the stiff grass toward the hazy tree line. Behind him, Hamar's footfalls clomped against the earth and he cursed as he too fled.

"The beast is gaining," he said, gasping. "I cannot run farther."

"Nor can you fight," Thorfast said through his own gasps.

No matter how hard he strode, the trees seemed to flee him. His neck pulsed with fear. He gulped his breaths. His mouth tasted of stale spit. At last he whirled, scooping up a stone as he did.

"Odin, guide my cast!"

Hamar's square face loomed in his vision, red and sweating. His puffy eyes had widened with terror.

Thorfast let his rock fly.

It shot past Hamar and collided with the shoulder of the charging dog, that was now close enough to leap atop them.

The dog yelped and skidded aside. Hamar's eyes bulged ever wider.

"Come on, stone-legs!" Thorfast grabbed Hamar's sweat-slicked arm. He tugged him forward even as he slowed. "The trees are just ahead."

The Arabs were shouting war cries, but were still back far enough to be shaken off their trail. At least Thorfast hoped as much.

The dog had only been cowed, but now it shook its flat head and renewed its charge.

"Up a tree," Thorfast said, as he gained the first line. "I will lead it away."

"What?"

Hamar was not the clear-minded strategist that Yngvar was. Throughout dozens of battles, Thorfast could communicate an entire plan to Yngvar with such a simple statement. Unlike Yngvar, however, Hamar could not intuit that if he hid in a tree and Thorfast led the dog and Arabs away, then he would be free to escape. With luck, Thorfast himself would lose their enemies. They would have to trust the gods to put them together once more. Reckless, improbable, and weak, it was a plan nonetheless. The gods would aid no man without a plan, just as they ignored silent worshippers who waited on their notice.

"Get up a tree and keep silent," Thorfast said. "Run when I lead them away."

"But they can see us!"

Thorfast shoved Hamar against a tree. But the instant it had taken to explain the plan had left enough time for the dog to corner them.

The dog was thick and well fed. Its black eyes flashed malevolence and its yellow fangs shined with slaver. It leapt against Hamar, pinning him against the tree.

Thorfast backed away and searched for a rock or branch, but nothing showed in the underbrush.

The dog sank its teeth into the meat of Hamar's leg and began to savage him.

Hamar screamed in pain, batting at the dog with his fists.

The Arabs slowed their run, laughing and pointing, confident of their victory.

With a curse, Thorfast grabbed at the dog. It thrashed and clawed as Hamar wrestled against its jaws. Blood flowed over the dog's muzzle as it growled and tore Hamar's flesh.

"Don't struggle," Thorfast shouted. The resistance was only ripping away more of Hamar's flesh.

Thorfast turned the dog's attack against it. It had clamped onto Hamar and would not release. So Thorfast grabbed the dog's rear legs and pulled them apart.

He kept pulling until the legs could part no more.

The dog growled and twisted. Hamar slid down the tree, weeping with agony.

Thorfast pulled the legs wide until he heard them snap and shatter.

The dog released its jaws now with a great howl of pain. Thorfast kicked its belly for good measure and cast the animal aside. It whimpered and whined as it curled around its own broken legs.

"Hamar, lean on me." He pulled Hamar to his legs and draped his arm over his shoulder.

Hearing the mad calls of agony from their dog, the Arabs shouted and began running once more. Thorfast spared a glance back. The six Arabs were like a ball of black anger rolling across the blinding white of the beach. Their guttural curses flowed ahead of them.

"I can't make it," Hamar said. "Leave me. Find that girl. She is real."

"We are sword-brothers," Thorfast said. "Come, we have to try."

The words were hollow. The cursing Arabs were now close enough that each individual swear was clear.

They hobbled forward into the shade of the trees. He sloughed Hamar from his shoulder. The gods had set a heavy, dead branch amid the tree litter scattered around them.

"It's no sword," he said, turning to face the Arabs. "But I will stand over you, Hamar. We will greet each other in Valhalla."

"I will see you there." Hamar's voice was weak and trembling.

The six Arabs were not warriors. They were no more than villagers, dressed in faded, patched clothing. They wore no headdresses. Thorfast pulsed with strength now, excited for battle and death. This was far better than starvation claiming him. The Arabs had only daggers and curving knives that flashed in the spotted light beneath the trees. The sweet scent lingered thick in the air here, an unsettling contrast to the violence.

He ranged his branch at the Arabs as if it were a sword forged for a king.

"I killed your bitch," he said. "And I will brain you with this stick and piss in your broken skulls. Six shit farmers against a hero of the northlands. Ha! Perhaps you want to go back and get more help. I will wait for you. I swear it."

The diatribe had paused the Arabs' approach. While they did wield sharp iron, Thorfast had the reach with his club. He stood straight with all the cockiness of a young man with a bellyful of mead. If he broke two or three of them, the others might run. Despite their numbers, the fierceness in their dark eyes had already melted.

"So I killed your best warrior," he said, nodding to the dog whimpering and panting behind them. "No one to give you orders now that the bitch is dead? Here's a plan. Fight me, cowards. You fear death? I don't. See if I lie. Come."

He thrust the club forward and the Arabs shrank back. Their dark-bearded faces brightened in surprise and fear. Thorfast laughed.

"You outnumber me," he said. "You have real weapons. You should be encircling me, but you're afraid of a blunt stick. What a pack of cowards. Not worth my sweat to kill the lot of you."

He felt the heat of Hamar's blood pooling around his feet. If he did not prevail against these fools soon, Hamar would bleed out from his wounds. Yet Thorfast knew his limitations, even if the Arabs did not. Once he committed an attack to one, he would be exposed to the others. A dagger would find his back and he would be finished.

The Arabs murmured to themselves, yet each one marked Thorfast's every flinch with wide eyes. If they found their courage, they would swarm him. He thrust again with this branch, sending his erstwhile captors skipping backward.

"Look, you thought to find easy prey and let your dog do your evil. But here you have found me instead. Let us be, and I will let you go. Go back to your fields and fishing boats. Go on."

He waved them away with his club, and the cleverer of their

number seemed to catch the idea. One man, however, raised his voice. His eyes were heavily rimmed in thick, black lashes and tears streamed down his hollow cheeks. His words spilled out like a hail storm and he pointed at the dog that continued to whine and twist on the ground.

"Well, you set her on me," Thorfast explained. "Would it be better had it been your own legs? Now go before I lose my patience and show you where to stick those knives."

He was beginning to feel as confident as his own talk. Village scavengers, even when they outnumbered him six to one, lacked courage. They were opportunists pumped up with unwarranted belief in their own strength. He might actually brain all six and walk off without injury.

But Hamar moaned and shifted in the grass. Time was not his ally.

Then a flash beyond the Arabs caught his eye. Something small and pale swept through the bushes. Its passage left them shaking.

The Arabs sprang for him.

He had let his eyes off them for a heartbeat, and so had broken the glamor that had frozen them on the spot.

They screamed their desperate fear. Dagger points and white teeth flashed in the attack. Thorfast swiped up with his club, catching an Arab under his jaw.

He slipped back out of their striking range.

And tumbled over Hamar's body.

They piled atop him like emboldened children pouncing on an older bully. They had no precision or discipline to their attack. Their weight flattened him. Their weapons remained forgotten in white-knuckled hands. Had he been stronger, Thorfast might have slithered out of their pile and given them death.

But he was beaten and weak. His heart raced and his rage filled his limbs with strength. But it was the last burst of fight from a dying man. What felt like a surge strong enough to crack an iceberg in fact did nothing more than shake an Arab from the pile.

Then he was overcome.

They swarmed over him, punching and biting while their knives remained unused. Sparkles of pain traced the length of Thorfast's body. He head-butted the man atop him and he screamed. For a moment, sunlight showed, but another Arab fell into his companion's place.

He was smothered in the hot stench of sweat and stale breath. Dirty, rough hands pressed his face to the side to prevent another head-butt. Other hands grabbed his legs and arms. They jabbered and squawked their rough language like a flock of excited ravens.

Thorfast felt his left leg twisting and bending. He kicked hard and the Arab lost his grip before renewing his work. The bastard was trying to break his leg, probably in revenge for the bitch.

Rather than resist, Thorfast surrendered. He needed all he could muster for any potential for escape. With hands and legs pinned, he could not even wrest a dagger from these fools. Truly, he had been brought low. For these villagers would never had been a challenge otherwise.

The Arabs continued to squirm and shout atop of him, apparently unaware he had ceased resisting. Finally, one seemed to recover his wits and began shouting for the others to stop.

Finally, he saw the treetops and the speckles of blue sky through the leaves. Four Arabs pinned him, one for each limb. One other knelt beside his dog and wept, and the last glared down at Thorfast. He spit on the ground, then streamed insults at Thorfast until breathless.

Thorfast looked to Hamar, who lay beside him. His eyes stared up but still blinked with life.

"I suppose I should not have stood so directly over you," he said.

"I am ... no good to ... stand on." Hamar laughed, though it was weak and fleeting.

"Will you live?"

Hamar grunted. "I am cold and my heart ... it beats too fast. Breathing ... is hard."

Thorfast closed his eyes. His friend was losing too much blood. It did not gush from his leg but seeped steadily into the earth.

At last the Arab shouted at his brothers. They dragged Thorfast to his feet. Their grips on him were firm, but inexpert. These men had never held a prisoner before. He could turn into one of them, breaking their holds, and turn the fight in his favor. But the Arabs had learned he could be defeated. The next time they fought, they would remember to use their knives.

They prattled among themselves and Thorfast studied them. Someone produced a rope.

Then the white shape beyond them stirred again.

A woman with hair as strikingly blond as his own stared across the short distance. She huddled in the bushes. Only the crown of her head down to her shadowed eyes showed. Yet anyone could spot her had they turned behind. But the Arabs were focused on Thorfast.

Hamar's woman. She knew a place to hide. Now there was some hope.

He held her gaze but did nothing more to show he had seen her.

The Arab with the rope shuffled to Thorfast as if he might strike like a viper. He snarled at the man and laughed when he flinched. But the bindings would be tied nonetheless. His captors forced his arms to his back, and he complied.

Then the woman hiding in the bushes darted away.

In the next moment, more shouts came from the edge of the woods.

The Arabs drew still and stared at each other with gaping mouths.

Thorfast rolled his eyes.

"Gods, have you not shown me the worst of your abuses yet?"

But they had not. Shadows of more men filled the edge of the woods.

Iron flashed on their drawn blades.

3

Thorfast grinned at the new arrivals. Six more men, equal in number to the Arabs who had captured him, emerged through the thin tree line. These were Arabs as well, and unlike the others they wore head covers of white or blue. Their robes were cleaner and better mended. Three of them bore common spears with thin blades sharpened to a white edge. The others carried long daggers that tapered to grim points.

They were smirking, shaking their heads as if having caught their children in some offense.

Thorfast's captors began shouting at the new arrivals. They showed considerably more bravado to their own kind than they had him. They brandished their own daggers and swaggered around the newcomers. He remained nearly forgotten but for one Arab that held his arms back. This one at least had the sense to set his dagger edge to Thorfast's neck. He hissed some threat that was all foul breath and spit.

The new arrivals pointed at the crying dog and began laughing. Insults were cast between both groups, and the Arab who had wept for the bitch now picked up a rock. He threatened to fling it at the offending group, until one of his companions pulled his arm down.

"Is this a clash of old grandmothers with spears?" Thorfast could not believe the posturing and the reluctance of either side to fight. The Arab behind him tightened the dagger against his neck and growled a warning. Thorfast snorted in derision.

"You all shame yourselves," he said. No one spared him more than a glance. "You have spears! Run them through and be done with it. What does it take?"

Yet the Arabs' argument only whirled up into more shouting. Thorfast could not move his head freely with the dagger at his throat. Hamar shifted and moaned out of the corner of Thorfast's vision. He had an opportunity, if only a fight would start between the Arabs.

They gesticulated and pointed at landmarks beyond sight. At least three times men on both sides pointed at him. The dog continued to whimper enough that guilt began to filter into Thorfast's consciousness. He should have killed the dog and ended her suffering. Of all gathered under these trees, the dog was likely the most innocent of all.

One of the new arrivals must have felt the same. After a red-faced exchange with the other side, he stalked over to the dog and ran his spear through its side.

The crying Arab flung himself onto the dog's killer, shrieking with rage and grief.

Then the melee began.

Both sides launched at each other and neither forgot their weapons. Blades sank into flesh. Combatants screamed and cursed. Thorfast's captor backed away, dragging Thorfast with him.

"My friend," he said calmly. "I've never backed away from a fight. It's not happening today."

He twisted out of the hold. The cool dagger edge nicked his throat, but his captor had loosened his grip when he moved.

Thorfast locked the Arab's arm. Now full rage was upon him. Pleased to see their hero fighting again, the gods imbued him with strength that was not his own. He levered against the arm and snapped it at the elbow.

The Arab screamed and collapsed. Thorfast kneed his face as he fell, then scooped the dagger from the grass.

"Don't play with knives," he shouted, then slashed the dagger across the Arab's throat to draw a sparkling line of scarlet. "If you don't know how to use one."

The Arab collapsed and a wet gasp sucked through his severed windpipe. Thorfast turned back to Hamar.

He was lost amid the fight. Two Arabs already lay dead in the grass. Another two knelt over gut wounds that would surely kill them later.

The skirmish should have broken. But the place where Hamar lay was thick with men.

Others had arrived. How was that possible? Yet he guessed more than twelve still fought and had sprung upon the battle in the instant Thorfast had dispatched his captor.

"Hamar!" he yelled. "I come for you."

A single dagger against all these Arabs was a fool's dare. He knew it. But Hamar was the last survivor of his companions and crew. Could he go to Valhalla and look them in the eyes if he had fled a loyal friend in need? Would he even be allowed to Odin's feasting hall?

So, he pounced atop the first Arab in his way. He was tangled with another enemy and so had no defense against Thorfast's blade slipping into his ribs. But even as he collapsed, the opponent had no love for Thorfast. Rather than thank him for the aid, he simply plowed forward.

The blow knocked him back and he tripped over uneven earth. He crashed to his back and the wild-eyed Arab howled a crazed curse as he leapt with dagger poised to strike.

Thorfast rolled out of the attack to let the Arab crash onto hard earth. He scrabbled aside and brought his own dagger overhead. The blade flashed and stuck into the Arab's back. He arched and screamed. Blood splattered from the wound onto Thorfast's face, the ground, and the bushes.

A woman shrieked at the flying blood.

He looked aside to spot the white form of the woman kicking away from where she had hidden in the bushes.

"Wait!"

But his plea made no difference. He had shouted in Norse out of habit, only now remembering she might speak Frankish. The white shape of the woman melted away.

He heard the grass crunch and swish beneath charging feet. He instinctively leapt out of the strike. The spear instead stabbed the earth where he had stood.

The weapon was like a promise of freedom, buried in the ground before him. Thorfast grabbed the wood shaft as the Arab tried to pull back. The two wrestled for possession, chest to chest. He glared into the black eyes of his opponent. He had heavy features that shined with sweat. Thick brows were knotted in concentration as he struggled to prevail.

But Thorfast wrested the spear away. In the same instant he flicked the spear butt around to clip the Arab in the face. He shrank back, yielding the space for Thorfast to wield the spear correctly. He squared it to the Arab's torso and plunged it into his body just beneath the breastbone. The shocked Arab slapped both hands onto the spear as if he could not believe death had found him.

Thorfast shook him off the blade and swept him aside. Hamar was surrounded. More Arabs were filing into the forest. Only three of the original captors remained alive, and others were already kneeling in the grass.

"By the gods, how much are we worth to them?"

From behind, a woman hissed at him. He turned to see the woman standing amid bushes. Her features were thin and sharp. Her hair was bedraggled and stiff and nearly as white as a sheet. She pointed behind him.

Turning in time, he avoided the spear that might have ran him through. But he was out of position. His own spear held in his opposite hand could not bring the weapon around fast enough. His dagger sat on the grass, out of reach.

The Arab was swift. He spun in pace with Thorfast and struck again with his spear.

This time it struck flesh.

A lightning streak of hot pain ran up from his hip. The Arab's spear had plunged into his left side, where his hip bone protruded from his waist. The blade scored across the bone and sank into his flesh. He collapsed on his back. Hot blood welled up in his lap, flowing from his burning cut.

The Arab screamed again and raised his spear to slam it down into Thorfast's chest.

A rock collided with the Arab's head.

His strike faltered and he cursed.

Thorfast swept up his spear and flung it into the Arab's crotch. When it punctured flesh, he slapped the butt to drive the shaft in like a nail through wood.

Without a sound, the Arab staggered around and crashed into the bushes.

He clamped his hand over the puncture wound. Blood spread between his fingers, slick and hot. The spear had slipped into his lower belly. He had seen enough men lose their innards through a spear hole than he cared to remember. Any movement might unspool his guts into a stinking pile.

The woman peered out of the bushes. She stared at him, fear captured in her arched brows and bloodless lips. Her smooth and youthful skin was flecked with blood. She glanced across the field.

"Thank you," he said in Frankish. "But I think I am finished nonetheless."

The woman's face brightened. She looked like a child given a surprise gift.

"You are a Frank. God be praised! Come with me now. They are not watching."

Her accent was terrible, but he understood. She had clearly learned Frankish later in life. But rather than dwell on her, he tilted his head toward the knot of Arabs. Perhaps ten or more clustered together, examining each other for wounds or else sitting in the grass with their heads bowed. Two Arabs lifted Hamar off the ground. His arms swung limp at his sides.

"He is dead," the woman said. "They will search for you soon. We must leave now."

Thorfast shook his head. "Put a spear in my hand. I have killed my enemies. They have slain me, though I linger yet. Let me go to Valhalla."

"Valhalla?" The woman stepped from the bushes, holding up a long but ragged skirt. She wore fine clothes of green and brown. But they had been ruined with sea salt and the ravages of the shipwreck. She knelt beside him, producing a cloth from her blouse.

She brushed his hand from the wound and quickly jammed the cloth over the bleeding.

"If I move, my guts will fall out."

"I will sew it shut. But come. They are stirring again."

The Arabs were not soldiers and such violence had unnerved them. The sweet scent trapped under the trees was now fouled with the stink of blood and bile. The woods that had just echoed with curses and clattering blades were now shrouded with the mournful silence of a battle ended. The least shocked among the Arabs rubbed their faces. Their wits were returning and they would see him lying flat on the ground.

"I cannot run," he said.

"Crawl into the bushes," the woman said. "Follow me. There is a cave nearby."

The woman leapt into the bushes like a doe fleeing huntsmen. He looked back to Hamar, but he was already carried beyond sight. Perhaps he had only lost consciousness. But the dog had torn his leg bad enough to rip open an artery. He must have died.

Nothing more remained here other than his impending death. Rather than accept it, he instead collected the dagger lying by his hand. His other hand found the spear that had gouged him.

Rolling onto his side, the burning pain in his belly spread like hot oil across his waist. Yet he had suffered worse and years ago had nearly died from a gut wound. While not guaranteed this wound was less deadly, he did not feel the same as he did then. He was still warm and his heart, while pounding from desperation and fear, was not pumping so hard to keep up with loss of blood. Perhaps the spear had not sunk as deep as he feared.

Yet its position made the wound likely to tear from excess motion.

And he had to run. The victorious Arabs now mumbled among themselves.

He rolled into the bushes, spear tucked under arm and dagger held in the same hand that pressed the cloth to his wound. He would leave a blood trail any whelp could follow. But he had to attempt escape. To do less would shame him.

He caught on the trunk of the bush and had to twist painfully through to the opposite side. But once he had broken through, the blond-haired woman waited for him. She took him by the arm.

"Crawl," she said.

"No, I cannot flee these men. You must hide me well. Then come to find me when they have gone."

She stared at him, her expression severe and judgmental. The blood had dried on her face, lending a fierceness to her countenance. The nostrils of her thin nose flared.

"Crawl," she repeated. "I am not skilled enough to do all you ask. God has given us this chance. Do not squander it."

"I cannot run," Thorfast repeated.

The woman sat back on her feet. She reached into her brown skirt and unraveled another cloth. She slapped it to his chest.

"I will save you," she said, then pointed a thin finger toward the bushes. "They will kill you. Follow me, if you are wise."

She struggled to her feet, winced as she held her waist a moment, then sped into the bushes.

The voices of the Arabs grew louder beyond the bushes. Some began shouting anew.

4

The Arab voices grew louder behind Thorfast. He scrabbled along the ground on hands and knees. Warm blood soaked through the cloth he pressed to the wound that crossed his hip to his lower gut. He had not dared to look at it, fearing the sight of it would unnerve him. Yet the fiery pain seemed to shift as he crawled, leaving him to wonder how deeply he had been stabbed.

Rough branches slapped his face and scraped along his naked torso as he shoved through bushes. He pursued his rescuer, the woman with hair so pale as to be nearly white. She left no apparent trace of her passing, even with his face so close to the ground.

He paused to tuck the dagger into the waist of his pants. The long spear dragged on the ground, leaving a clear line to follow. He lifted it and decided to stand rather than mark his passing so prominently. A weapon was key to survival both against the immediate threat of Arabs and the longer-term prospect of defending himself. He would not abandon it even if it revealed him to his enemies.

A smile crossed his face. Strange to be counting breaths until death in one moment, then planning for survival days and weeks from now.

He stood, then clenched over his wound. Yet nothing spilled out of the puncture wound. The blood flow did not even increase. The pain had spread but he could manage it. Had he enough mead he could drink the pain away.

The trees and brush around him were sparse enough that he could see stripes of blue distance between them. He looked around for the woman, but did not see her.

The Arabs, however, saw him.

One shouted and others responded. Thorfast did not spot them, but instinctively crouched as he bolted directly away from the shouts.

Fear of capture replaced the worries of further injury and pain. He loped ahead of his pursuers, confident he had enough of a lead that he could disappear if the gods invested more of their favor in him.

He ran, aware his blood flowed faster with his exertions. The fresh cloth began to drip blood. Careful trackers could follow that, and a hound would easily sniff his trail from it. But the Arabs were not careful and their dog was no longer a threat.

The humid air drew more sweat from his brow. It trickled into his eyes to sting him and flowed salty wetness into the corners of his mouth. The branches of foreign bushes and small trees scored his body. Stones bit into his feet. Yet he continued directly away from the voices drawing nearer.

He had no plan to where he fled. For all he knew, he could be running toward the Arab village. He knew enough to follow the incline of the land. If there was a cave nearby, it must be in the side of these hills. The woman had left him no sign to follow, at least none that could be discerned in haste.

At last the wound began to tell on him. His legs weakened and his stride shortened. His feet throbbed from striking rocks and roots. His breath came short and ragged. His body had been tormented to its limits and now, even with the shouts drawing nearer, he had to stop.

He took a sharp angle against the approaching Arabs. Rather than shoot recklessly to the side, he moved with caution. A trail of snapped branches and footprints had trailed him thus far, but now if that trail stopped it might confound the Arabs. He stepped toward a thicker grouping of trees, then slipped among them. He hissed whenever his hip brushed against a trunk, both from pain and from leaving a stain of his passing. But otherwise he was confident his trail had become harder to follow.

The shouting Arabs arrived behind him at nearly the same moment he had climbed into a cluster of rocks and bushes up the steep incline. He looked down but could not see them from this vantage. Their shouting halted, as they evidently arrived at the end of his trail.

The rocks were rough and cool, splattered with milky green lichen and emerald moss. Three tall stones formed a crawl space and Thorfast paused to consider it. He could fit within, and if he pulled bushes to the entrance he might remain hidden.

"I can't run anymore," he muttered to himself. "This is it."

The Arabs renewed their loud talk, but they no longer shouted as if calling for his blood. They had lost his trail, but their sudden halt had called them to a more considered search for him.

He snapped a bush from its trunk. The white of the broken wood would be as good as a flag to experienced trackers. He had to trust to the Arabs' incompetence. Tucking into the crawl space beneath the rocks, he pulled the bush over the gap.

Despite the heat and humidity, the stone and earth enclosure was cool against his itching skin. He felt like a fox cowering in its den, hiding from the hunting dogs snuffing his trail. The spear was a poor fit. He set its blade down so that only the butt of it poked above. Again, the Arabs were fresh from a fight and likely still unbalanced from the death of friends and foe alike. With luck, they would give up and tend to their wounds before spotting the telltale spear butt exposed through the rocks.

He cowered in the shade, hearing nothing but distant calls back and forth. The Arabs either cared more for his capture or cared much less for their injured and dead. They sounded as if they had all come out in force to search for him. But thus far, none of the sounds of their searching drew near.

His wound burned hot and the blood leaked over his hand. The cloth wept blood to the ground. He had nothing left to stanch the flow, and his constant motion had not allowed the wound to clot. His heart continued to pound. Now he worried it was a sign of the blood he left on the floor of the woods rather than the excitement of pursuit. His eyelids began to flutter.

Don't let me faint now, he thought. Hear me, Odin, All-Father. See me, your desperate servant. There are greater deeds I can accomplish in your name if I may yet live. If you must give my life to these Arabs, then let me die fighting. Not asleep under a rock where they will plant their foreign blades in my back.

His eyes did not close, but his vision darkened. His heart raced against his ribs. His hand, pressed to his cut, slicked with blood that did not cease flowing from his wound. He had come to the verge of consciousness.

An Arab voice spoke close to him. He called out to companions that had fanned out elsewhere. His voice boomed like thunder. Thorfast jerked in surprise, and his spear clattered against the rocks.

He held his breath. Beyond his den of bushes and rocks, the Arab seemed to hold his as well.

Thorfast squeezed his eyes shut as if wishing away a bad dream. Yet he heard the distinctive crush of feet on the dead twigs and debris of the woods. Each step was considered and slow. The Arab seemed to pause with every step, waiting to hear more. Each step, he drew closer.

But Thorfast was now frozen as still as the hunted fox he imagined himself to be. Curled into his den, he willed himself to remain still.

More footfalls. In the distance, Arabs shouted.

This was a single man, separated from his companions. He had guessed Thorfast's hiding spot. It was too obvious, too convenient. The unnatural clatter of his spear shaft against the rock had been enough to alert the Arab.

He could see shadows of motion beyond the bush he had propped before his crawlspace. He was curled up so that even drawing his dagger would be useless. If the Arab pulled away his cover, he would be easy prey.

A wave of exhaustion flowed over him. He could not do more. He could not fight any longer. From imprisonment to shipwreck to wading ashore, all his strength and willpower had been sapped. This had been his best and last desperate attempt to avoid his fate.

It had not been enough.

The Arab lifted away the bush, casting light into Thorfast's den.

He looked up at an Arab in a blue head cover. His dark eyes widened with surprise and his teeth flashed in his opened mouth. Thorfast lay hemmed in by the rocks sheltering him, but enough space remained that a blade could easily slip through. Fortunately, the Arab held the bush in both hands and had unwisely stuck his drawn dagger into his belt.

In better days, Thorfast would spring to throttle the Arab before he could raise alarm. But now he weakly reached for his dagger. His arms trembled as he dragged it from his waistband.

The Arab threw aside the bush and snatched for his own dagger. But in the next instant his head snapped back in time to a loud thump.

He staggered around, holding his forehead. His foot caught a rut and he crashed to his side with a curse. More shouts echoed from the distance, but these were the same cadence as before. No one had yet been alerted.

Thorfast crawled out of his hole, crushing his hand around the dagger grip. The Arab moaned and rolled onto his back. Bright blood flowed down across his face.

The blond woman scurried out of the bushes, her face even paler than before. She crawled on hands and knees to keep her profile below the surrounding bushes. Stopping before the Arab, she looked between him and Thorfast.

"Kill him," she whispered. "I did not hit him hard enough."

Thorfast barely had the strength for speech. He clawed to where the Arab squirmed on his back. The rock had dazed him but not enough to keep him down. He understood his danger and was already fighting through his addled wits to regain his feet. When he did, Thorfast would be finished.

"Hurry," the woman said, casting her gaze down the slope. "Others are coming."

"You do it." Thorfast dropped the knife before her. "I cannot raise my arm."

He crashed face-first into the grass. Cold dirt pressed his cheek and dead leaves crackled around his face. The Arab groaned as he flipped onto his knees and began to raise himself.

"I've never killed a man," the woman said, her voice shaking.

But she would now, or else both of them were finished.

He closed his eyes. "Then, flee. I am ... dying."

The Arab growled as he collected himself. A curse hissed from his lips. Twigs and leaves crackled as he struggled to his feet.

Then he screamed.

Thorfast's eyes snapped open. The Arab lay on his stomach once more, bright blood blooming across his light gray robe. The blond woman hovered over him, bloodied dagger held in both hands like a spike. Blood had splashed across her pale hands. Her face was rigid with shock and horror.

But the Arab had not died, and his screaming continued.

"Again," Thorfast said hoarsely. "Cut his throat."

The woman shook her head.

"Then run," he said. "Leave me to die."

She grabbed the screaming Arab by his hair. He twisted against her, striking back with his arm. She fell aside with a squeal. The Arab might eventually die from his wound, but not soon enough. His hateful face, full of sweat and forest debris clinging to it, met Thorfast's gaze. Blood oozed from his mouth, but he continued to scream and curse.

More calls answered.

The woman flung down the dagger. Thorfast's hope died with the metallic chime of the blade hitting the hard earth. She fled, leaving Thorfast's sight.

The Arab squirmed and regained his feet. Blood drizzled from his mouth as he panted dark curses. He gathered his dagger in hand and sat up on his knees. He pointed it at Thorfast.

Then the Arab snapped his head up. The woman charged past Thorfast, leading with his spear. The blade plunged into the Arab's chest. She drove him onto his back, folding him over like a broken doll. He gasped and died, dropping his curved dagger.

Thorfast smiled. "A fine sight. It fills me with strength."

The woman stared at the dead body. She panted and leaned on her knees.

"I think I'm going to be sick."

"Later," Thorfast said. He summoned the last of his power to get to his feet. "We cannot outrun them now."

The Arabs shouted from all around, drawing closer to the last shout of their dead companion.

"We have to discourage them," he said. "Look aside and stand back."

The woman's courage had emboldened him. If she fought so valiantly for his life, he could not shame himself with surrender. His legs wobbled and his arms trembled. As he stood, unplugging the spear from the corpse beneath him, he saw flashes of white and blue as the distant Arabs rushed toward him.

The spear was sharp and sturdy. He cut across the Arab's face. He laid bare the skull beneath it. He dragged the point down to cut away the enemy's robe. He dragged again to lay bare the bones beneath the skin.

Had he strength, he'd have carved the blood eagle into his Arab, pulling the lungs from his body to set them like gory wings on his back. But he had neither strength nor time. He sliced across the belly to dump the Arab's guts into a stinking pile.

The woman gagged at the smell and sound. He turned from his grizzly work and took her by the arm.

"Lead me," he said. "I will go as fast as I can. Do not forget the dagger. Always, keep a dagger ready."

The woman looked at him, recoiled at the hot blood that had splattered his legs and feet. But she snatched the dagger from the ground, avoiding sight of the disfigured corpse.

Then they ran off as the first Arab arrived.

They had a minimal lead on the Arabs. But the first one to the scene screamed as Thorfast had hoped. These were farmers, not warriors. Spilled guts, poked eyes, and dismembered limbs were horrifying even to experienced warriors. How much worse would such a sight be to a common man?

He laughed as he shuffled after the woman. The Arabs would either renew their lust for revenge or, more likely, they would flee at the prospect of meeting the same fate.

Branches and bushes waved and snapped as the woman led him up into the slope. She never looked behind, nor did she ever release Thorfast's hand. Her grip was slick with sweat and tight as a rigging line. She navigated with confidence through the woods, until Thorfast was ready to beg for a pause.

Yet they found the small crevice in the side of the steep ridges. Bushes and trees obscured it from easy sight. Deep brown rocks had crumbled before it.

"Inside," she said, at last turning to him. "We have not gone so far that they can't follow us."

"Blood trails will be simple enough to follow," he said. "But we must trust to the gods. Do they love us still?"

He heard nothing but the rustle and crack of a forest at rest. The Arabs had lost their voices.

And at fore of this thin crevice in the rocks, Thorfast lost consciousness.

5

Rain. The patter and splash Thorfast heard was rain. Was he in the rain? His body felt damp, but not wet. Something covered him, soft and warm. He realized his eyes were open but he saw nothing. Panic and terror seized him. His first thoughts were for Prince Kalim's lightless prison. He had been recaptured? But there was no stink of rot and filth. He smelled dank earth and—fish?

He raised his head and his hip wound tugged with a flash of sharp pain.

His head dropped back down and crunched into a pile of leaves that had been made into a pillow. He rested a moment, scratching the stubble of his shaved head.

"Woman?" His voice was low and tentative. "Are you there?"

"Speak Frankish," she said. "Or else I cannot understand you."

"I asked if you are here," he said.

His voice echoed. He realized now that he was inside a cave and that a bare light seeped in from outside. Gray light outlined jagged edges of stone above his head. Sinuous forms crawled through that gloom, likely roots of trees. The rain hissed and splashed at the mouth of the cave.

"What do you think?" The woman's shape rose up from the darkness, a light gray wraith in the earthen black surrounding her. Her hair nearly glowed with the faint light.

"How bad is my wound? It burns and I am still weak."

The woman's clothing rustled as she approached. She had to crouch to keep her head from hitting the cave roof. Thorfast padded around his wound, encountering the smooth cloth that draped him. Despite its protection and the heat pervading this entire island of Sicily, he was cold at his core.

"I have not seen it properly," she said. "The rain came last night and I have been in the dark since. I cannot start a fire on my own, at least not without a striking iron."

"Last night?" Thorfast raised his torso on his elbows. The pain of his wound protested, but he wanted to see where he was. A jagged slash of diffused light beyond his feet and flashing rain was all he could see. The woman's ghostly shape now squatted at his side.

"You collapsed outside," she said, pointing a slender arm toward the entrance. "I had to drag you in. The cave is deeper and bigger down there, but this was as far as I could get you. You've been asleep since yesterday morning. I don't know what time it is now. Midday, I expect."

"And the weapons? You've kept them dry?"

Thorfast grabbed her arm. Her skin was yielding and her flesh soft. A pleasant warmth filled his palm. But she pulled back.

"Like a Norseman, you worry for your weapons before anything else. I put the spear deeper in the cave where it is dry and stood it against a wall." Her silhouette shifted away from him. "And I carry the dagger. So you mind your hands or you'll lose fingers."

"I will behave," Thorfast said. Did she not see he could barely raise his head? He smirked at her, trusting shadows to hide his expression. Then he lay flat again. The leaves folded around his ears. They both sat a moment listening to the rain spray rocks and earth.

"Why do I smell fish?"

The woman chuckled. "I had a look around while you were asleep. These were from a fisherman's catch. He had pulled ashore for some reason and I was able to snatch them from the barrel while he looked away. He was a lone man. By the time he noticed me, I was already far off."

"You went looking around after those Arabs drove us into this hole? You are either brave or foolish."

"Aren't those one in the same?" The woman shuffled aside. "No matter, we must eat and there are two fish here. I've no idea how to prepare them. Do you?"

"Most people cook with fire, but it seems we will cook only by the blessings of the gods. Anyway, did you see the Arabs?"

She shook her shadowed head. "We are alone in these hills, at least while this storm beats the coast."

"I will feel better once I eat," Thorfast said. "I am weak, but I do not bleed anymore. Meat is the best food for recovery. But those fish will soon spoil or bring animals. I'm surprised this cave was not some animal's den. Again, you were brave to enter here."

"You credit me much," she said, her voice lowering. "I was desperate to survive. What of your friend? Do you think he lives?"

Thorfast remembered Hamar and how his arms hung limp at his sides.

"I cannot be certain. That dog tore his leg badly. He was already looking into the next world before the Arabs caught us. I expect he did not survive. He was a great man, a Norse hero that will not be forgotten as long as I breathe."

The woman sighed. "I had hoped for two heroes. Now I must settle for you alone."

"Settle for me?" Thorfast raised his head again. "No one settles for me. Friends rejoice at my coming and enemies quail at my sight."

"And this shipwrecked woman hopes you will be useful enough to repay your debt."

Thorfast blinked, then forced himself back to elbows.

"Well, shipwrecked woman, I may lack the manners of the great jarls, but I am no scoundrel. You saved my life, and I will repay that debt."

"Jarls have manners?" The woman sniffed. "Do they bring gifts before burning the village and raping the women?"

"Yes," Thorfast said flatly. "They bring the gift of death. For if a man cannot hold on to what he has then it was never his, including his life and home. The strong take from the weak and the world is better for it."

"This talk sits ill with me." The woman stood, bumping her head against the low ceiling. She ducked with a short squeal. "You owe me your life, Norseman. I will heal you as best I know how. I will have a task for you when you are strong enough to fight."

"And what task would that be, shipwrecked woman?"

"In time," she said. "We will both soon starve. But at least we have clean water. Wait here."

He looked down his body. A brown cloth covered his stomach down to below his knees. "I was not considering a stroll through the hills, if you worried for it. And have you covered me in your skirts?"

"You were shivering," she said, her voice fighting the hissing rain.

She appeared in the light of crevice. She had stripped down to her underdress. As she knelt the hem rose up her leg to reveal the white of her calf. Even in his weakened state, he felt stirrings. After months at sea and all that time in the fetid blackness of Prince Kalim's cells, a woman's calf was a delight to see.

Yet he was too weak to remain propped up. He lay down again. The woman grunted and shuffled back to him. Water sloshed in a bucket, which she set down with a wooden thump. She settled on her knees beside his head.

"I found this bucket on the shore as well. It leaks but we could fix it. Here, I gathered these shells from the beach. They make poor mugs but will serve. Drink a little at a time or you will vomit it all out."

She dipped the shell into the bucket then propped his head up with her hand. She was still lost in shadow. He remembered thin and harsh features arranged pleasantly in an oval face. But now he imagined she smiled as she raised his head and offered him water. He was like a babe to his mother.

The water was cool and clean. As it slid down his throat a raging thirst erupted. He had forgotten the simple pleasure of clear water harvested from the clouds. He was eager for more, and the woman scooped to his eager lips as fast as she could. The salt and bile tastes coating his mouth washed away.

When she finished with him, she scooped more water for herself. She drank with as much relish as he had.

"That was wise of you," he said, his voice humbled. "Thank you."

The woman waved off his gratitude, but did not pause slurping from the water. He watched her. Now that his eyes adjusted to the light, he could study her shape. She was thin and her undergarments were wet with rain so that they clung to her body. It revealed a pleasing shape that brought heat to his face. How could he even notice such a thing under these conditions? But he had. He did owe this woman his life. It should have rankled his pride, but instead he smiled.

"Shipwrecked woman, what name may I know you by?"

"You cannot pronounce it," she said.

"I cannot make it worse than your Frankish. You speak swiftly, but your accent is a test of my will."

"Sophia," she said, placing both hands on her hips. "Sophia Palama."

"Sophia Palama," Thorfast repeated. "I said it perfectly."

She shook her head. "So-fee-jaa Pa-jaa-ma is hardly perfect. But I will accept it. And what is your name? Shall I guess? Thor Blood-Face? Harald Tooth-Breaker?"

"Fine names," he said. "But I feel you mock me, Sophia Palama. I am known as Thorfast the Silent. You may call me Thorfast, as we are now companions in this ill-fate."

"Sophia will be fine for me," she said. "Do you want more water? I must save some to wash your wound."

"The rain is plentiful," he said. "Let me drink my fill."

He sat up and pulled the bucket closer. He dipped his hands into the water and gulped it until his belly was tight. He sat back and let Sophia expose his wound to the cool air.

"If I could lie abed for a month, this wound would not trouble me," he said. "But I will not enjoy peace, I fear. For we must soon leave this place. We have made too many enemies to remain."

"Of course," Sophia said. "It was never my plan to remain in this horrid cave."

The dagger flashed in the low light. She cut a strip from the hem of her underskirt, then dipped it into the bucket. After wringing out the water, she gently wiped against the crusted blood on his torso.

"You have a plan? Well, you are a sight better than me. I was glad simply to have survived the attack."

The wet cloth assuaged the heat surrounding his cut. The pain was dull rather than sharp, a good sign. Still, he lay still as she padded around the edges of the cut.

"I must get back to the empire," she said. She folded the cloth to a clean side and continued to work around the wound. "I would have welcomed capture by the Roman ships. They would have recognized my family name, I am certain. Now I must get back to Roman territory on foot."

She put aside the blood-stained cloth, then cut a new piece.

"Where is Roman territory? Do you mean the Byzantine lands?"

"I don't know what that is," she said. "I am a citizen of the great Roman Empire. Rome itself is lost to us, but the emperor still rules from Constantinople."

"Those are too many foreign words for me," Thorfast said. "I have no care for any of these places. There are a few Arabs I must kill before I return north. Then I wish never to speak the names of these places again."

"You'll tend your business after you repay your debt to me. Can you raise your hips? I must tie this bandage in place. I can only cut so much of my garments before I am left naked."

"You are nearly so as it is. It is pleasing to see."

She smiled but did not answer. Faint light brushed smooth, high-boned cheeks as she did.

Thorfast raised his hips and found the pain sharper in this position. But Sophia worked swiftly to place the bandage and wrap salvaged cord around him. She pulled it taut then sat back.

"Rest," she said. "I will put the bucket out for more water."

The droning rain lulled him into sleep. But his dreams were troubled and he awoke with a start. Black wolves had chased him through a dreamland of snowy fields, running him down the moment he awakened. Sophia lay huddled beside him, and raised her head. His neck still pulsed from the imagined chase.

"Do not shout," she said. "The rain is slowing and you may be heard outside."

He blinked away his sleep. The light had grown stronger, and the rain pelted softly. Sophia now lay beside him, pressing her body to his.

"How long have I been asleep?"

"Less than an hour," she said. "These wet clothes and earth floor make me cold."

She pulled away as if embarrassed to have huddled against him. Thorfast sat up, testing his bandage.

"My stomach growls," he said. "We must eat those fish. Their scent is strong enough to reveal us to anyone passing near. If we had dried wood and kindling, we would be eating by now."

"I gathered that when your friend went looking for survivors," Sophia said. "I just have no means to start a fire."

Thorfast sat up straighter. The wound tugged painfully but such was his surprise that he ignored it.

"You are an efficient woman. Food, water, and now a fire. And here I am still addled from the shipwreck. Were it not for your wits, I believe I'd be in an Arab prison again."

Sophia brushed her platinum locks off her face. "Well, I have a plan and I must survive to see it through. Aren't those just the basics we need to survive?"

"They are," he agreed. "You just shame me in your forethought. I was eating beach sand while you were building a survival camp. For all my years a-viking and living far from home, I still am a laggard compared to you."

"But there is no fire yet," she said. "Unless you are hiding a lamp under these covers."

"That is no lamp, my lady, but something just as fiery."

Sophia tilted her head at first, then as realization grew she hissed in disgust. She slapped his shoulder.

"Your crude humor serves nothing. And remember I hold the dagger. I will use it if I must."

"I believe you will use it more than you wish. But not on me. Show me to this kindling and lend your dagger. I will strike a spark to bring us fire, and soon thereafter cooked fish."

"Oh no, I am not so simple as to surrender my only protection."

Thorfast sighed. "Really? That is what you think of me? Such words cut me deeper than that Arab's spear, truly. I will make our fire and return your dagger. Besides, I prefer the spear."

"You are a terrible poet," she said, then removed the dagger tucked into the waist of her skirt. "Do not dull the edge, unless you believe your cock is not only a lamp but a whetstone as well."

"There is more humor in that thought than you know," he said, taking the dagger. "But I have a task which requires my concentration. Help me up."

The flirtation with Sophia livened his spirit. Humorous banter was an aid to fighting men when their situation grew dire. He could not count how often his jesting had turned defeated men into warriors once more. This was a battle of a different kind but no less in need of something to raise the mood from the sullen desperation of reality.

For he could think of little more depressing than being trapped in a cave, injured and surrounded by vengeful enemies.

Moving came easier than he had expected. The spear wound pulled and twisted and he could not tell if the heat he felt was more blood squeezing from it. In fact, the wound was not bad despite all the bleeding he had suffered. The trauma of his situation had led his mind to take every setback as a mighty defeat.

Sophia offered him dried moss, leaves, and twigs. He gathered these together then used a stone and the iron dagger to scrape out sparks. The process was long and frustrating, and Sophia's impatience led her to wait by the cave mouth rather than continue to watch.

But soon Thorfast had a fire burning. He carried a burning twig to set a fire deeper in the cave. Without a word, Sophia accepted the dagger in return and gutted the fish.

By evening they were in the main pocket of the cave where the higher ceiling gathered white smoke away from their faces. The rain had stopped, but the dripping continued to echo through the entrance. The fish was soft and juicy, though without any seasoning it was plain fare. Still, he had not eaten anything as succulent as this since before Prince Kalim's prison.

"I am glad for clean food and water," he said. "I have too long eaten from buckets that served both my food and carted away my filth."

Sophia paused and wrinkled her nose. She looked aside. The yellow light had turned her pale figure to gold and deepened shadows in her eyes.

Thorfast laughed. "That is only the start of the start of the horrible stories I can tell you about the Arab prisons. When I am recovered, I will force Prince Kalim to eat shit that I cut from his own bowels. I will preserve his head in a bucket of piss. Don't think I—"

"Silence," she hissed. She held up a hand and tucked her head down as if wanting to hide. "Do you hear that?"

Thorfast stopped, following her gaze up the gentle slope toward the cave entrance.

Water dripped. Wind rustled leaves.

And something scraped and bumped inside the stone of the cave.

Voices whispered, fleeting echoes filtering down to them.

Thorfast reached for the spear he set beside the fire. He nodded to Sophia's dagger tucked into her waist.

Enemies had cornered them in the dead-end of their cave.

6

Thorfast stared across the fire but it obscured everything beyond in orange haze. The steady drip of rain water echoed down from the mouth of the cave. The white smoke crawled along the high ceiling and wove toward the exit up the rough slope. The scent of cooked fish was strong in the cave, but it would be lost in the wind outside. Had the campfire attracted attention? It seemed impossible given he had set it as far back in the cave as sensible.

Sofia's eyes widened. She pulled the dagger close to her chest. She had replaced her brown skirt, which appeared as orange in twisting firelight. Her legs unfolded beneath it with a soft rustle of cloth.

Thorfast gestured that she hand him the dagger. Their cave was spacious enough for two people at rest. But no spear or long sword would be of use within it.

Yet she did not remove her eyes from the single path into the cave. The dagger remained clutched in her white-knuckled hands.

No more whispering floated down the slope. The fire popped and the run-off from the rain outside continued to splash into puddles.

Perhaps the intruders had left. The flickering camp firelight would have warned them of occupants. They were probably Arabs out searching and now went to fetch reinforcements.

But if these were Arabs out searching at night, why would they not carry their own torches? The woods were dark and the cave darker still. Thorfast's hands itched for a weapon. He wrapped his palms round the cold and smooth spear shaft, if only to soothe his heart. The shaft leading down to this cave allowed only one person at a time. He might set himself at the exit and impale whoever appeared.

"I don't hear anything," Sophia whispered. It still sounded as loud as a shout to Thorfast, who winced at the sudden speech.

"The two of us heard something," he said. "Though whether it was voices I cannot be certain."

She shook her head, her matted hair falling across her face. She did not lower the dagger.

"Perhaps we imagined the voices," he said. "It might be an animal searching for a new den and our fire scared it off. People would've brought their own light."

"Unless they were also trying to remain unseen," she added.

Then Thorfast's heart lifted and all his fears fled.

"Survivors," he said. "Maybe Yngvar or Bjorn were saved as well, as impossible as it seems to me. I lived. They may have also."

"No one else survived," Sophia said. "I'm as sure of it. At least no one you want to meet."

Yet Thorfast paid her no heed. He was certain now that the tentative noises from the cave were survivors seeking shelter just as they did. He imagined Yngvar curled into a crack in the cave wall and straining to hear the whispers from deeper within. He would be wondering if he heard the familiar tones of Frankish and whether he should risk pushing deeper. Being Yngvar, by now he would have found a weapon for himself and held it ready to strike.

Thorfast used the spear to lever to his feet while pressing the cloth against his wound. A small brown stain had seeped through, but the bleeding was not as bad as expected. The pain burned deep beneath his flesh, but he could ignore it. He set the spear against the cave wall.

"Those are not friends," Sophia whispered. "Believe me."

"Then give me the dagger."

Nothing filled his extended hand while he stared at the dark passage out of the cave. When Sophia refused to release the weapon, he approached the passage.

The warm clasp of the campfire tore from him as he slipped into the passage. It was as wide as a strong man's shoulders but still low enough that he had to duck. His eyes revealed nothing but red impressions of the campfire while they adjusted. He turned sideways and slipped up the rock-strewn slope.

He was in darkness now but his shadow would be revealed from the light behind. If anyone watched the passage, they would see him. The smile broke over his face as he climbed out of the passage into the smaller room by the exit.

Nothing. The cave was dark, and the light from behind was not strong enough to penetrate this far. Outside the night showed through the crevice entrance a shade lighter than the blackness of the cave. Dripping water flashed as it caught moonlight that slipped past storm clouds.

He dropped his shoulders and sighed. Then something crunched on the gritty floor to his left.

A form detached from the darkness.

Another joined the first.

Each figure was a head shorter than him. Wavy hair broke up the outlines of their shadows. The folds of white cloth robes caught the thin light spilling through the entrance. The cloth seemed fresh and whole, nothing like the tatters of a shipwreck survivor.

A wave of regret passed over him, burning his face with shame. He had been cornered by enemies in a dead-end cave and now he walked into them without a weapon in hand.

Neither figure moved. He was unsure if they were men or women, so little light filled the small cave. He had a chance to either flee or speak. Given he was still in no shape for a fight, he raised his hand for peace.

"Friends," he said in Frankish. He had given up thoughts of anyone understanding Norse. "You must know this place well to have come by the light of a moon that hides behind clouds."

The two figures looked at each other, then back to him. Neither spoke nor changed his stance. Thorfast kept his hands raised.

"I am alone," he said, not knowing if they understood. "If you've come to capture me, well, here I am. The night is early yet. I will go with you to your leader. Come, take me if that is what you wish. We leave now."

One of the figures spoke. The hard Arabic words meant nothing to Thorfast, though they were delivered with uncharacteristic gentleness.

He shook his head. "I don't understand you, nor can I see you. Outside. We will discuss outside."

Gesturing them out, the two figures shook their heads as one. The other spoke, forcefully but not angrily. They shifted toward the entrance to block his escape. What light that reached into the cave revealed one carried a bulky object that had been tied with string. He held it in one hand.

They both began to rattle off their gibberish. Thorfast could live here for a hundred years but he would never learn their speech. He had no gift for languages like Yngvar or Alasdair had. He pointed to his ears.

"I hear but don't understand the words."

Yellow light began to creep around Thorfast's feet. The two Arabs stopped talking.

"By the gods, woman," he said. "I'm trying to lead them away from you."

He turned to see the glow of Sophia's brand as she came up the passage. The torchlight guttered but cast enough to reveal her crown of pale hair.

Turning back to the Arabs, the new light source shined on the drawn dagger held in one's hand.

So they were enemies after all. They were delaying for help, no doubt. Unless he broke through their blockade, both he and Sophia would be trapped against the rear of the cave.

Despite the pain of his wound and the weakness of his limbs, he struck for the one gripping the dagger. Though he had rested and eaten, it had not been half as much as he needed. Nevertheless, the desperation of their plight lent him strength.

He latched onto the arm holding the dagger and slammed the Arab against the stone wall. He and his friend called out in shock. The short Arab was surprisingly light and the crash against the stone drove out his breath.

Thorfast crushed him down, intent on wrestling the dagger free or else driving it into the Arab's body. Yet before he could achieve either aim, the other Arab leapt on his back.

Ragged nails raked across Thorfast's face as the second Arab screamed and clawed at him. He tried to drag Thorfast off his friend, but he was too light for the task. Despite the burning scratches, he did not feel outmatched by these two attackers.

Sophia began shouting as well, though he did not understand the language. Thorfast released the man with the dagger and he crumpled to the ground. Then he pushed backward against the other Arab clinging to him. The unexpected shift in weight drove them both across the short cave into the opposite wall. Thorfast drove with all his force, hoping to smear the Arab across the wall and dislodge him.

He cried out, relented, then fell away.

The other Arab had recovered and now sprung forward with his dagger raised to strike.

Sophia jumped before him, waving her flaming branch to ward the attacker away. But he was already in mid-strike and her sudden interception allowed no space to evade.

He collided with her and the torch she carried thumped straight into his face.

The branch snapped in flaming pieces and the hiss of searing flesh followed. The Arab screamed, clapped his hands to his face and fell back. Burning embers gurgled on the wet ground and died. The iron dagger clattered on the rocks as the wailing Arab stumbled out the entrance. Sophia had spun aside into the passage.

The Arab on Thorfast's back, however, screamed with pain equal to his friend's. He sprang up from the ground, but Thorfast was prepared. His eyes remained fixed on the dagger glimmering with points of the broken light from Sophia's dropped torch. The leather-wrapped grip was still warm as he snatched it into his hand.

He spun around as the Arab landed on him. Thorfast rammed the dagger into the Arab's ribs and forced it to its plain cross guard.

The Arab wailed like a child. His breath was ragged and wet as he slumped to the side. Thorfast shoved himself free, tried to pull the dagger but found it stuck, then got to his feet.

He turned to Sophia, who had recovered from her fall. She did not accept his extended hand, but went to the Arab's side. The shadowed figure of the man wept and gasped, but his strength had flowed out of him. Thorfast knew the sounds of the Arab's wound. The dagger had punctured his lungs and he was gasping his final breaths.

Sophia lowered her head when the Arab's death rattle echoed off the stone walls. For long moments, only the sound of dripping water filled the cave. The last of the torch embers hissed out, leaving smoke and a bitter stench.

"You act as if they were your friends," Thorfast said, his weak voice loud in the silence.

"No," Sophia said as she stood again. "They were just boys. It's unfortunate."

"Boys with weapons and a will to kill me," Thorfast said. "They chose to fight and so earned their fates. You cannot fret over every boy we will kill before we escape this place."

Sophia sighed and turned away. "You are right. I have not seen so much violence. I suppose I will have to accustom myself to it."

He ducked along the low ceiling as he moved to the dead Arab. He flipped over the corpse to reveal a smooth face obscured in shadow. He had no beard and only the wisps of a mustache. The dagger remained planted in his ribs, and a pull on the hilt revealed it would not budge.

"His clothes won't fit me," Thorfast said. "Though I have become so thin, maybe I should try."

Sophia went to the bundle that had been dropped and prodded it.

"It's bedding," she said. "This must be their cave."

Thorfast twisted and levered the dagger, but it bent as the flesh sucked around the blade. He sat back with a frustrated curse.

"Bedding? I will not think what they planned to do here this night. It is all strange to me, but what is not strange here? So now we have bedding. Maybe I can salvage this robe to protect my naked skin. At least we can make bandages from it."

"How did your wound fare?"

Thorfast sat up. "Did you need mention it? I felt nothing until you asked. Now it burns hot and painful."

He touched the cloth and blood came away on his fingertips.

"And it bleeds again." He also became aware of a dull pain on the back of his head. He touched the rough stubble there and also came away with blood.

"Gods, I think I hit my head on this low ceiling during the fight. I don't even remember it. I am a walking wound."

"The other one escaped with a burned face," Sophia said listlessly. "He will have to explain that to someone. He knows the path to this cave too well, I fear. The Arabs will come for us."

"You knew we couldn't stay here long," Thorfast said. He started to tear away the Arab's robes. Everything had a use and he would not waste any scrap the gods tossed before him.

"But I had hoped at least for one day of rest," she said. "You are bleeding again. I am cold to the depth of my heart. We are trapped here and I don't know where to go."

"Away," Thorfast said, tearing a strip of cloth. "Toward your Roman Empire. We have weapons, and so I am confident I can take what we need by my own strength. Such as it is."

She laughed without humor. "I wish I could be as confident of our future as you are."

"Despair is useless," he said. "In truth, I feel it as well. But what will crying about my lot bring me? My father taught me to fight. It is the only path. So the gods have given me a spear. If they had wanted me to cry they would have given me a cloth to dab my tears."

Sophia laughed again, now with real mirth. She pointed at him.

"And your hands are full of cloth."

He looked down and smiled.

"You have a sharp tongue, woman," he said. "And a strong wit. We will make a fine team."

Though he smiled, he looked out the cave to the world beyond and felt his heart grow cold. Nothing but enemies awaited him outside. He would face them with a dagger and spear, and a handful of cloth.

Somewhere, he knew, the gods laughed as well.

7

"Just up ahead," Thorfast said. "Then we can rest."

"I can't do it," Sophia said.

Thorfast thrust his hand down to her as she clung to a dark, wet rock with both arms. She was on the other side of a small gap that Thorfast had just leapt across. They had climbed for an hour, choosing the hardest paths into the mountains to prevent leaving an easy trail to follow. Looking down, he judged they had not climbed equal to the height of their efforts. Like everything about this horrid place called Sicily, the mountain terrain frustrated them and wasted their strength. Looking into the distance he saw clustered dots of fires, likely from the village where the Arabs lived. They were nothing but points of orange light that flickered in and out of the treetops as he had proceeded up the rocks.

Sophia's brown skirt and green blouse glowed with the silver moonlight. The storm clouds had parted to reveal the sky. The half-moon was powerful enough to show them where to place their feet as they climbed. But she had slipped and fallen no matter how sturdy a ledge Thorfast had found for her. So now she hugged to her rock, hesitating to grab his hand and make the short leap to his position.

"From here, it is a short climb to the top. We will be safe and can rest the night there." He tried to keep the impatience from his voice, but he heard its angry rasp. Sophia had saved his life and fed him. He needed to show her more gratitude. Still, her hesitation only increased the strain of their climb.

"I don't know if I can make it," she said.

"Woman, you can stretch your leg over here without any risk. It is like hopping a brook. Take my hand and I'll pull you over. But don't cling there forever. You are like a white flag for anyone to see from below."

Sophia swallowed then grabbed Thorfast's hand. Her palms were slick with the rainwater that coated everything, but warm and firm. He clasped his fingers over hers and hauled her across the short gap. She squealed, but fell easily into his arms. She pressed to him as if she might tumble off the mountain.

"Even if you fell, you would only bruise your hip," Thorfast said as he guided her ahead of himself.

"I've never been up so high. When I look down," she said, peering over the short stone wall they had scaled. "Dear Jesus, I'm falling!"

She seized Thorfast's arm and pressed her face to his chest.

"You are not even moving," he said. "Sophia, why did you not say you feared high places?"

"I did not know," she said, peeking up at him. "But what other choice do we have? Look to the sea. This is it."

Thorfast freed her well away from the edge. A scree-covered slope led up to the peaks of these so-called mountains. More accurately these were steep hills covered in rocks, grass, and the strange trees Sophia said were palm trees.

He glanced back toward the water, where the lamplight of patrolling ships shined. The triangular sails were trimmed, leaving three masts poking into the night. Doubtless these were Prince Kalim's ships sweeping the coast. The mountains were the only safe place to hide, but just like the cave they also created a dead-end.

The bale of bedding Thorfast had thrown across the short gap lay against a stone. He snatched it up along with his spear. He started up the slope, passing Sophia who stood frowning at the ships. Despite the warmth of the night air, his naked feet were cold against the scree.

With every rock that jabbed his soles he wished for a good pair of boots. At this point, he would take them over food.

They had eaten the fish Sophia had stolen, leaving nothing but the big bones. They had also gulped as much water as their guts could hold. For the moment, Thorfast's hunger was sated. But he knew the exertions of this climb would leave him hungering by morning. While the mountains were a good hide-out, he doubted finding food and water up here.

"See, a hidden camp," Thorfast said. He walked into a flat area surrounded by rocks and a stone wall that led up to a narrow peak. Small puddles reflected the moon. "We are at the top of the mountain. No one will find us up here as long as we do not set a fire."

He threw the bale of bedding into the center. Sophia trailed after him, looking about as if entering a new home.

"If it rains again, we will be drenched," she said.

"Nothing escapes your attention," Thorfast said. "But you may have noticed the sky is clearing."

"So it is," Sophia said, looking up. Her hair fell back as she gazed at the stars. The moonlight set it ablaze around the fringes with silver fire.

"Now I know why Yngvar insisted I wear my cowl all the time." He ran his hands along the stubble of his head. "You're like a beacon with that hair."

She smiled quizzically at him, then started to untie the bedding.

"You should've seen it on my wedding day. Nothing like this salt-matted mess. It was the envy of every woman who saw me, and they were not shy to let me know it."

"Wedding day?" Thorfast set his spear against the stone wall. The iron blade scraped as it slid to rest. "You are married?"

She nodded. "You have that tone in your voice of a man about to ask a score of questions about my past. Let us put that aside for another day. If we live through tomorrow, I will tell you more."

"Ah, so you wish to remain a mysterious woman. Perhaps so that I will fight harder to learn your secrets? You'll be disappointed to find I am not a curious man."

49

"Hardly," she said, shaking out the bedding on the driest patch of earth. "I'd rather you not pry. I will tell you what you need to know."

"And you are not curious?" Thorfast took up the other end of the bedding and helped pull it taut. "Do you wish to know more about the man you saved?"

"You are a Norseman and a slave," she said. She began to pull the large rocks from beneath the bedding and toss them aside. "You like killing and gold. I expect you like killing a bit more than gold. You're often drunk when you're not killing. You hate God and his messengers. You are fond of whoring and lose your gold thusly. So you find someone weaker than yourself and take his wealth. The story repeats until one day someone kills you. Did I misstate anything?"

Thorfast sat back and crossed his arms. "I am no longer a slave. I actually like gold a bit more than killing. And I only get drunk at feasts. It's Bjorn who's drunk on most days."

"Ah well," Sophia said, folding her arms in a reflection of Thorfast. "I am corrected."

"You're a bristly woman," he said. "But at least you are not whining."

"I detest whining," she said. She smoothed out the bed. "Come, we will lie together for warmth. I still have the dagger."

"A fact I will not forget."

Thorfast lay beside her and pressed his side to hers. The wound on his hip throbbed now that he lay still. Every inch of his body from his head to his heels throbbed. His full belly sloshed around and he gave a large belch that tasted of fish. Sophia turned aside and moaned.

"I suppose you will not tell me how you came to be an Arab slave," he said. He grabbed at her brown skirt and felt the stiff material in his hand. "This was once good quality. You are not poor."

Sophia remained on her side, facing the stone wall.

"But you can tell me how you survived the wreck at least. I was chained below decks, and when the Byzantine—"

"Roman," Sophia said.

"Ah, Roman ship rammed us I was broken free. I can swim,

though not with any skill. The gods sent me driftwood and a current to take me to shore. You know the rest. But what of you?"

She sighed then rolled onto her back to face the stars. Moonlight outlined her sharp features. Even in a neutral expression her face fell into an angry shape, but now that she reflected on whatever had happened to her the anger softened.

"I was not below decks," she said. "I was a prized captive. When the Arab captain realized he was trapped, he boarded a small boat with his officers and his wealth and abandoned his crew."

"Coward," Thorfast said with a scowl.

Sophia shrugged, the salt-stiffened fabric of her blouse rustling as she did.

"Or you could say he was practical. That's how I look at it. I was part of his wealth and so I went with him. They were already rowing away when the Roman ship crashed into his. The Arabs got us to shore safely. They cried when they saw the destruction at sea. I did as well, but not for their reasons. I'd have given anything to be taken aboard those Roman ships. But God has more tests for me."

She grew silent and closed her eyes. Thorfast simply waited. She clasped her hands over her stomach as if she were praying in the Christian way. At last, she sighed again before continuing.

"They were preparing to travel inland. There were twelve all together. They had weapons and shields and all of them looked like they knew battle. Even the captain. So they were probably going to some local outpost. I did not want go, obviously. So when they were not looking I slipped away. I found that cave and hid."

"You escaped them so easily?"

She unfolded her hand and slapped the bedding with both. "You call this easy? No, they chased me but I outran them. But they had been rowing and were already distressed from their losing their ship. They couldn't abandon their treasures for long. So eventually they let me go. I am valuable to them, but not beyond the gold they carried in their coffers."

"But valuable enough that if, let us say, a young Arab boy with a burned face should describe you to the locals that this captain may mount a stronger search for you than he otherwise would for two common slaves."

Sophia turned to him. Her eyes were wide.

"You see," he said. "This is why you must tell me about yourself. This news changes my plan."

He did not have much of a plan beyond hiding in the mountains until the searchers lost interest. Yet Sophia did not need to know this.

"Do you think the boy saw me well enough?"

Thorfast shrugged. "I doubt he saw much after getting flamed in the face. That sort of thing burns up a man's wits along with his flesh. What he saw before, that is the question. He was charging for me. So perhaps he only saw the glow of your torch. Up close."

He laughed at his poor jest. But Sophia now stared at the sky.

"I didn't think anyone would bother with me. But you might be right. They know this land better than either of us. They must know all the hiding places nearby. So they can flush us out in their own time."

She faced him again. Her already pale face was even whiter.

"What will we do, Thorfast?"

He smiled at her and took her hand. "Rest. I will protect you."

She tightened her grip on his hand, and stared back into the sky.

Thorfast closed his eyes and soon fell asleep with her hand in his.

He awakened to the dawn and the distant barking of dogs.

8

Thorfast remained lying on his back as Sophia shot out of their bedding.

"Dogs," she said breathlessly. "Can you hear them barking?"

Thorfast nodded and rubbed his face against the sleep that lay like a veil over him. The heat of the morning was already pricking his flesh and drawing sweat to his brow.

"Shouldn't you be more worried?" Sophia crouched low and waddled over to a stone by the ledge. She peered over the side.

"Dogs are not much for mountain climbing," Thorfast said. He yawned and stretched. "And they're not going to follow our scent up the rock walls we climbed to reach here."

"But the Arabs will know where we have gone."

"They already know where we've gone." Thorfast sat up. His spear wound ached but a good night of sleep beneath the stars had aided the healing. "I've got to piss."

Sophia remained studying the scene below. Thorfast streamed out all the water he had guzzled from the prior day. The splashing of his urine against the rocks was louder than the barking dogs. They probably weren't even barking for them. Sophia was just nervous.

"Look, I know I scared you last night," he called back over his shoulder. "But your Arab captain and his crew are likely answering for how they lost a ship and its whole crew and cargo. Knowing Prince Kalim, they'll all be whipped to death soon enough."

He pulled up the remains of his pants and turned to Sophia. She remained crouched behind the rock, staring intently.

"You can't see anything from there, can you?"

Sophia shook her head.

He laughed. "Well, let me scale to the top of this peak. I can have a better look around. We must head east to reach your Roman friends. But before we do, we need better clothing as well as food. I think water will be plentiful enough, but stealing some wine to see us through the journey is ideal."

"Let me check your wound," she said, abandoning her position. "A climb up that rock might worsen it."

Her hands were light and cold against his skin. He smiled at her as she untied the cord binding and lifted away the bandage. Working so near his body, her wet breath rushed over him. Her eyes nearly crossed as she inspected the wound up close.

"Am I dying?"

She threw the soiled bandage aside, then took fresh cloth they had cut from the Arab boy's robe. She sniffed as she folded it into a square.

"The flesh is holding together, but it can reopen with a good twist. You should have this sewn up."

"I thought you promised to do that?"

"I would've promised you anything to get you away from those Arabs." She pressed the new bandage in place and secured it with the cord. "Fine, make your climb. But know you could tear this wound and make it worse. It is not so deep now, but that could change."

"Unless I fall, I will not worsen it," he said, adjusting the cord to his liking. "Now, see if you can collect any water from these puddles. It is still fresh and we don't know where our next drink will come from."

He scaled the spire-like rock with ease. As a boy in Frankia he had loved to climb trees. He and Yngvar both loved it. Bjorn, who was too squat and heavy for anything but the lower branches, had called

54

them squirrels. While not the same as trees, scaling rocks came just as easily to him.

At the top of the spire, he clung to the rock with one hand and guarded his eyes against the sun with the other. A brown- and white-feathered hawk glided above him and called out as if in salute. This hill might not be a true mountain, but it was the highest point for a long ways. To the east, the green ridges climbed higher and thus blocked his sight. But before him green fields and palm trees spread out to blue haze. Behind him, the sea gleamed with morning sun. Double- and triple-masted ships now cruised along the waves as if no violence had ever visited the spot where Yngvar and the Wolves had all drowned.

He returned to surveying the land. Licata, the seat of Prince Kalim's power, lay in the haze of the west. Its walls traced irregular paths from one point on the shore to loop around to the other. He could not see beyond it, but behind it were stretches of small tree groves ordered in neat rows.

Closer to his position, a village of simple homes clustered amid a dozen or more fields. Smoke rose from these buildings, built from stone and plaster. Their roofs were made of deep red or brown tiles, something Thorfast could not imagine even on a jarl's mead hall.

"You were not wrong to seek riches here, Yngvar." Thorfast spoke softly to himself. "Even the farmers live in palaces."

"Do you see anything?" Sophia called up from below. He now hung two body lengths over her. She stared up at him with both hands shading her eyes.

"The dogs are not for us," he said. "We are perfectly—"

A flash caught his eye. He focused on the spot and glimpsed a second flash as it disappeared beneath the edge of the ridge. Sophia began calling up to him again. He held his hand out for silence.

Other gleams showed around the same point. A column of men with shouldered spears were heading into this hill. The angle of the hill prevented him from seeing where they entered, but it was opposite of his position. Nor could he count the men, but guessed at least a dozen with spears.

More small shapes followed.

"What is it?" Sophia asked, slapping her hands against her thighs in frustration.

He slid down the rock spire, then jumped down the last distance. His injury protested the jolt and his bony feet had not softened the impact. He grabbed the spear where he had set it against the wall last night.

"So I have another thought regarding your captain."

He smiled at Sophia even as his voice quavered. She pinched the bridge of her nose and started shaking her head.

"A dozen men with spears are climbing into this hill opposite us. As many more men follow, but I cannot see what weapons they carry. I wonder if your captain, rather than face Prince Kalim, has started a new life as a bandit. Wouldn't be a far-fetched idea. He has gold and fighting men. Why turn that over to the prince and face punishment? He knows you are up here and are worth something to him. So he gathered up his men and the villagers, and calls for us at first light."

"I liked your story about him being whipped to death," she said, rubbing her face. "What are we going to do? We're trapped up here."

"We are," Thorfast said, scratching the stubble of his head. His crown was still tender from bumping it on the cave roof. "But they can't fight us all at once in these mountains. There are only two of us and this is a long ridge. We have the lead on them. If we string them out, we can cut them down man by man as we head east."

"Well, you make it sound as easy as baking bread." Sophia bit the knuckle of her index finger and began to pace. "Do you think they'll line up nicely for you to cut them down?"

"I've never baked bread," Thorfast said. "But from the way the women complain, I don't think it is easy."

"Do not laugh now, you fool. We can't just stand here," she said. "You're at least right about fleeing."

"I'm right about all of it," he said. Sophia began to roll up the bedding. Thorfast stepped on it. "Forget this. It'll slow us down. Besides, unlike our pursuers, we will not sleep tonight. The moon will be bright again, and as long as these clouds stay high and thin, we will have plenty of light to travel by."

"And food?" Sophia asked.

Thorfast was already climbing over the next ledge. He paused to extend his hand to her.

"We only need water. We can do without food for a few days yet."

They picked their way along the ridges as they worked east. They saw no sign of pursuers throughout the morning. At last they had to pause to rest. Thorfast's naked torso streamed with sweat. He wished for a light shirt to at least soak it off his flesh. Sophia too was winded and her hair stuck flat to her head.

The rain of the prior day still sat in puddles and offered meager refreshment. This was the one benefit to the stifling humidity, though by the end of the day the puddles would disappear.

They sat together in the shade, neither speaking. Thorfast picked up every sound. When palm fronds rubbed, he knew it. When a pebble slid out of place, he knew it.

When the Arabs caught up to them, he knew it as well.

He sat up, grabbing his spear. The voices were indistinct and far off. Sophia sat up with him and rested against his shoulder.

"You hear them?" Her voice was small and warm against his ear. He nodded.

Keeping low, he climbed back to a position where he could view the path he had taken to this spot. The Arabs were easy to spot from their glinting spears. He saw three lingering on the last peak they had passed. They were distant enough that their faces were formed only of dark points of shadow. Their shouting had betrayed them. One called down the peak.

Below, two more men had paused to answer. They were even more distant and obscured by treetops and rock spurs. From what he glimpsed, they were not the armored Arabs. They were not on the correct trail, either. They seemed to be headed down the mountain.

"They haven't found us?" Sophia whispered, lightly touching Thorfast's arm as she crouched beside him.

"The men on the peak have the best chance to follow us. Though there are enemies below us, too. So we cannot risk descending here."

Sophia's grip tightened on his arm. "So we begin cutting them down now? Three against we two?"

He smirked and twisted to meet her eyes. "You'll be fighting alongside me?"

His smirk vanished, for he saw the earnestness in her eyes.

"You'll battle all three? You forget your condition. I am no Amazon, but I will fight. I have no other choice, it seems."

"Amazon?" Thorfast shook his head, dismissing his question. "It is true that I will need your help. But even the two of us cannot prevail against three healthy warriors in a straight fight. There is another way to bring down these wolves."

"You'll call down Thor's hammer to smash them off the mountain?"

He stifled his laughter and ducked back behind the rock. "You'd do well in the north. I would welcome the gods' aid, but they have extended their hands to me too many times. Today they will judge what I have made of their gifts. So we must make a good showing before they will aid me again."

He gathered his spear and crouched low as he studied their surroundings. He grunted in appreciation.

"They have set us in a position for an ambush. The trick is in luring just those three and not every enemy on this hill. If we can overcome them, then escape will be far easier."

Sophia shook her head. "How would it be easier?"

"For one, we will steal their clothes and weapons. From a distance we will seem as one of them. Their head covers are perfect disguises. Once we seem as one of them, we can pull ahead of the search before they realize who they should be chasing."

"This plan relies on luck alone," Sophia said.

Thorfast pulled up short. He had leveled the same accusation at Yngvar countless times. Now that the onus was on him to find the path out of the trap, he created the same reckless plans as his old friend.

A slow smile came to his lips. "So it does. But no man dies before the time Fate has chosen."

"Yes, but a man can be enslaved before Fate kills him," she said. She grabbed his arm and pulled him forward. "I will fight by your side, but only when there is no choice left. For now, we can escape."

Thorfast shrugged her off and returned to his hidden lookout. The three Arabs were on the move again, scrabbling over the rocks toward them.

"Whatever strength we have left is best preserved for this fight. These fresh-legged Arabs will catch us even if we run. See how far they've come compared to us? They are fed and rested."

Sophia pulled her dagger from the waist of her skirt. She stared at it as if unsure of its purpose.

"Get up on this ledge. Gather the heaviest stones you can throw. I will help you up and join you in a moment."

He set his hands to give Sophia a foothold, then pulled her up. She toppled inelegantly onto the ledge. After recovering herself, she looked across the long gap. She lurched behind a stone outcrop.

"They are drawing closer," she said. "But they seem to wonder where to go."

"They'll know soon enough. Gather those stones."

Thorfast took his spear and then slid up against the ledge facing the Arabs. The footing here was uneven and wide enough for three or four men only. If all the Arabs were lured into this place, they would be clustered tight enough that their rocks would not miss. They would not be killed unless their casts were guided by the gods. Yet they would be dazed. He could then stab down from above with his spear. Their necks would be exposed from that angle and he expected to slay at least one of them.

He raised his spear tip barely over the rock ledge. He rolled the shaft gently between his hands. The wood was smooth and warm from his grip. The butt of the spear crunched against the gritty earth beneath him. He continued until he heard an Arab shout.

They had seen the flash of iron. They were close enough that even if they called for help, others would not have time to reach this position before they did. He counted on their arrogance and bloody-minded lust.

Bending at his waist, pressing against his wound that burned and throbbed in protest, he reached the ledge. With a hand from Sophia, he leapt up.

"I must be all bones if a small woman like you can lift me." He nudged her to the side. The ledge was deep but not wide. Its greatest benefit was the large outcrop that provided cover from below. Sophia had piled fist-sized stones into a pyramid by the edge.

"That was the best I could find," she said. "There's not much space to search."

"Would you trade your dagger for my spear? Once the Arabs are below us, we will pelt them with stones. Then you must spear at least one through his neck. I will jump down and kill the rest. But a spear will be too long down there."

"No, this is my dagger," she said. "And I have no experience with a spear. The Arabs will just grab it from me."

Thorfast sighed. "Woman, I am no enemy. I owe you my life. What I ask is for the benefit of both—"

Sophia offered him the dagger. The severity of her features had softened and she bit her lip.

"Return it to me when we are safe again. If you do not survive, I will not fare better with a dagger. I will be already lost."

He accepted it with a curt nod.

Then the Arab shouts closed on them.

"Pick the heaviest stones first," he said. "And aim for their heads."

Sophia smiled. "They are doomed, aren't they?"

Thorfast saw the first dark hand seeking purchase along the ledge where he had just hidden.

"The gods wish to see a slaughter, and we shall give it to them."

He matched her falsely confident smile.

Blood began to leak from his wound, trickling down his skin in a thick line.

9

Thorfast gripped a stone in his right hand and his spear in his left. He quivered with anticipation. While not at peak strength, he had eaten and rested better than he had since being thrown into Prince Kalim's prison. He was prepared for this battle.

The Arab's hand padded along the ledge, then he hauled himself over with a grunt. He wore a long blue robe with a matching head cover. His body was padded out with armor beneath it, likely a quilted jerkin. Thorfast could not imagine anyone scaling mountains in this heat wearing mail. The Arab clutched his spear with both hands, crouched low and ranged his spear as if expecting attack. His dark eyes swept across the small space.

Thorfast backed into the cover of the rocks, barring Sophia with his arm. They stared at each other as they lay in wait. Thorfast held his breath. The enemy was close enough to touch but completely hidden by the rock ledge.

After a period of silence the Arab grunted and spoke in a low voice to his companions. Spear shafts clattered on stone. Their robes swished as they climbed into the small space. The first Arab had backed up to make way for his companions. He came into view, but was intent on helping the others regain their footing. Both of his hands were full with spears lent by his companions.

Sophia's eyes were bright and wide. He nodded to her that they should spring their attack.

He whirled into the gap, slinging the rock he carried with all his strength.

It slammed into the head of the Arab directly below. He shouted and stumbled aside, spears clacking to the ground as he fell. The thud was softened by the head cover, but the Arab's body slammed hard against the ridge.

Sophia shouldered up against him and flung her rock. Her cast hit the Arab who was already prone, thumping against his leg.

"Hit the others!" he shouted.

Now that he had swung out of hiding, he saw the other two Arabs. One had apparently hurt his ankle in the climb and sat on the ledge massaging it. The other hovered over him, hand extended as if offering aid. Both now stared in surprise at their fallen companion.

The prone Arab put his hand against his temple. Seeing he was not dead, Thorfast cast his spear. It sank into the enemy's side and he curled around it with a gasp of agony.

Drawing his dagger, Thorfast leapt into the battle.

Sophia's next cast thumped the standing Arab square in the back. It was enough to foil a grab for his sword. He grunted and twisted to face Thorfast.

He crashed into the Arab, forcing him against his seated companion. The force knocked the seated man over the ledge and bent the other Arab over the ledge.

Quick as a snake, Thorfast stabbed his dagger into the Arab's armpit. This both avoided armor and cut into a major artery. The enemy screamed, his voice echoing off the stone. With his free hand Thorfast covered the Arab's mouth while driving the blade deeper with his other.

He tore the blade away while stifling the Arab's pained screams. He forced the Arab's head down, his blue cover twisting over his face as he struggled. The next stab landed in his neck, and he gasped then fell limp.

Confident he had killed one, he looked back to the enemy he had speared. Sophia flung rocks at him, but his body remained curled around the spear through his side. A wide pool of dark blood spread out beneath him and flowed glistening into cracks in the rock floor.

Two dead. Now he looked to the one who had been knocked off the wall.

When he bent over, two hands grabbed him.

The Arab had only gone over the side and managed to cling to the steep slope that ran down from this position. Already off balance, Thorfast flung over with him. They landed in a pile and began to skid down the slope.

It was a long, scree-covered slide. Thorfast's naked torso cut on rocks and grit as he slid on his back. The Arab shouted as he too rolled down the slope.

They both crashed into the ditch at the bottom. Lying on his back, he tilted his head to see the ledge above. From a prone position it seemed like an endless slope reaching into the blue sky.

But he held his dagger still.

The ground crunched as the Arab wrestled to his knees. Thorfast's stomach burned with fear. The Arab's sword chimed from its sheath.

He rolled into the Arab, who now sat upright on his knees. His head cover had been lost on the slope, revealing wild black hair that framed a square, thickly bearded face. His skin gleamed with sweat.

Thorfast had reclaimed his advantage by closing the distance. The Arab fought to turn his sword, but Thorfast's dagger was faster. It punched into his enemy's belly.

The padded armor slowed the blade, but it was more protection against blunt or slashing strikes. A pointed blade ran through the jerkin as easily as a linen shirt.

The Arab doubled over, collapsing with a gasp atop Thorfast.

He felt hot blood seeping through the padding and running onto his hand. The Arab convulsed and coughed, but did not die. Yet his suffering scrambled his wits and he slapped at Thorfast's back with the wide part of his blade. The cold iron blows hurt but did not wound.

Thorfast shoved free, and when the Arab fell back he took Thorfast's dagger. Lying on his back, the hilt stuck out of his belly. It rose and fell as the Arab gasped in his final moments of life. Thorfast sat back and watched his enemy groan and claw at the air until he at last dropped his arms and slackened in death.

Now shouts came from below. The other two searchers were calling.

They were nearer now.

His heart leapt. The slope was steep and had been a difficult climb the first time. Now he was sore and bleeding.

Bleeding.

Blood flowed readily from his old spear wound. As Sophia had promised, it had torn open during the fight. The bandage was lost, leaving it to leak blood down his leg and into the dirt underfoot.

The calls came again. He grabbed the heavy sword and sheath from the slain Arab. He unplugged Sophia's dagger from the wound, having to brace with his foot to wrestle it out of the body. He had time to loot nothing more.

He scrambled up the steep slope. Sophia appeared above, her hair like a white blaze against the blue sky. She waved him forward.

"As if I don't know to hurry," he muttered. Every three steps up the slope sent him sliding farther down. The more he rushed the worse his climb went.

The other searchers were nearing, but without any reply they did not know exactly where to go. The trees and rocks below kept Thorfast hidden. He had time, but none to spare.

At last he made it to where Sophia held out her hand. She hauled him back, groaning with the effort. He popped over the ledge and Sophia crashed to the ground.

The two Arabs had already been disrobed. Their naked bodies were thinner than their armored appearance had made them appear. Their robes and padded jerkins had been tossed into a pile held down by their swords and daggers.

"You surprise me once more," Thorfast said, pointing at the prepared clothing. "You didn't fear when I went over the ledge?"

64

Sophia shook her head. "Alive or dead, your plan was all that remained to me."

She gathered a robe and head cover. Thorfast angled aside so she would not see his reopened wound. It was instinctual, more the reaction of a shamed child than a warrior.

"Your back is scraped up," she said. "Let's see your wound."

"Do you have more bandages? I think I will need one."

Her fingers were cold and hard as she dug them into his shoulder, then spun him around. She gasped at his wound.

"That is worse than before. I warned you."

"But I've always looked forward to sliding down a mountain on my bare back and nearly dying at the bottom. You can't deny me that."

She ignored his sarcasm and pulled a length of cloth stuffed in her blouse. "This is the last of it. We'll have to cut more from these robes."

"No time," he said. "The others are calling for their companions and are drawing toward us."

She pressed the bandage against his skin and began to wrap it with a rope belt taken from one of the dead. She muttered in a language Thorfast was glad he did not understand. The pressure of her hand brought sharp pain that he smiled through. Once she had secured the bandage, she turned to the pile of robes.

"They're all torn and blood-stained," she said. "We won't fool anyone up close. I'm not removing my clothes. So no need to stare like that. These are large enough to wear over my own clothes."

"That will be too bulky for easy movement," Thorfast said. "I'm not going to wear their padded armor."

"And I'm not going to wear their clothing any longer than I must," Sophia said. She fit the head cover on her head and adjusted the band to hold it down. The brilliance of her hair vanished into it.

"Rags and old weapons," Thorfast said. "But I feel like a rich man to claim them for myself."

The head covering cut his field of vision. The robe was soft and comfortable but wet with blood that caused it to cling to his side. The blue dye hid the blood stains well enough. He strapped on the heavy sword, tucked a dagger into his belt, then grabbed a spear.

"You make a fair Arab," Sophia said, smiling. "The robes are too long for me. I will trip at every step."

"No you won't," he said. He took her arm and began to lead them forward. "Use the spear to balance yourself."

An Arab shouted a single word from below, repeating it as a soft echo beneath the canopy of palms and leaves. It might have been a name.

"Gods willing, they won't find their dead companions soon," he said, casting a glance down the slope. The dead Arab lay stark against the stony earth. The red blood pooling beside him shimmered with the hard light of morning. "Let's be swift while we still have a lead."

They climbed into the peaks, hot sun beating their shoulders. They threaded narrow paths, squeezed between boulders, and traced ridges above the trees. Sweat flowed down their faces. Flies and gnats, even at this elevation, snapped to them at every pause.

Thorfast's feet throbbed. His soles, though toughened, were not accustomed to rocky ground. The Arab's sandals had not been sized for him. Better to go barefoot than risk stumbling with ill-fitting sandals. But with every stab of a sharp edge, he reconsidered his choice.

Sophia followed, one hand holding her robe and skirt up like a maid crossing a stream. The spear in her other hand lent her stability. She did not fall, but cursed twice as often as Thorfast.

"I must learn these foreign curses," he said. "What speech is it?"

"Greek," she said. "And if I must take another step, you will hear many more Greek curses. Can we not rest?"

He stopped, and during the pause, a fly landed on his cheek. He waved away its tickling dance, but the fat insect circled around and landed on his hip. The dark robe there glistened with fresh blood. His wound burned like a strap of fire encircling his waist. Weakness was seeping into his limbs.

"A short rest," he said. "The Arabs had water?"

Dropping her shoulder, Sophia unhooked the strap of a skin stoppered with an animal horn. She unplugged it and sipped, then pressed it to Thorfast's hand.

The cool fluid slid down his throat. Rather than refresh him, it left him burning for more. Yet he surrendered the skin still sloshing with water to Sophia.

"You found it, so you finish it."

She slung it over her shoulder. "We save it for whoever needs it most. I have not heard the Arabs for at least an hour. We must be safe enough to descend now?"

Thorfast nodded.

Then someone shouted.

He ducked his head as if he had been shot at. Sophia fell against a stone. They were standing on a small ledge. A single stone poked up here, covered with moss on one side. The other rocks around them were scattered and stout. To their left a sharp ridge led to the peak but was too steep to climb. Every other direction left them open.

Across the canopy and on a peak lower than his, Thorfast spotted two men waving at them. They wore the drab pants and shirts of farmers, and not the colorful robes of the Arab warriors. They clung to the bare rocks there as if they were two cats treed by hunting dogs. They waved frantically at Thorfast, shouting across the gap. Their voices were high and thin.

He shared a look with Sophia.

"Time to test our disguises," he said, smiling. He straightened up. His bandage shifted and he felt a gout of fresh blood run down his leg. He winced but otherwise tried to mask his pain.

The two men continued to wave, and Thorfast waved back. He took care to keep it brief and close to his body. Sophia extended her hand as well, but Thorfast pushed it down.

"Our skin is too fair," he said. "Let's not show them too much of it."

She nodded, and whispered an apology.

The two farmers seemed desperate enough to miss details. After the acknowledgement from Thorfast, they shouted another unintelligible stream of words then waited.

"What are you going to do?" Sophia whispered, standing still beside him.

"Answer them, of course," he said.

He stepped confidently to the edge and pointed with his spear toward the canopy and away from himself.

Then he began to bark orders in his best imitation of Arabic.

He had heard enough angry commands shouted at him since falling afoul of Prince Kalim. The shapes and rhythms of the words were cut into his memory. So he growled and barked the way his captors had, emphasizing his words with his spear.

The two stared at him, neither moving or answering. When they did not react, Thorfast feigned impatience by leaning on one leg and wiping his face. Then he continued to point with his spear and shouted more nonsense that sounded authoritative to his ears.

The farmers followed his pointing spear. One pointed in the same direction, then shouted back to him. The distance was such that their expressions could not be read. But he imagined their confusion and had to swallow his laughter.

One of the farmers shouted something like a question. Thorfast nodded his head and pointed them away once more. Then he waited while the two turned to each other and spoke.

Finally they waved and began to descend from the peak. Thorfast waved back as if dismissing them.

Sophia stared at him, her normally frowning expression replaced with gleaming eyes and raised brows. She slowly shook her head.

"You shouted nonsense at them."

"I did," he said. "But men hear what they want to hear, no matter the language. They clearly wanted someone to send them home. I was happy to give that order."

"That was magic," she said. "I know a handful of Arabic words. But nothing you said came close to anything I know. Yet they obeyed you."

"Perhaps they are not Arabs themselves and doubted their understanding," Thorfast said, watching as they disappeared under the canopy. "From this far away, I would not even understand Norse. They just wanted to be done with this wild hunt. As do I."

Descending the mountain was not as simple as Thorfast wished. While they could proceed across the ridges or skirt the steeper peaks, they did not find many paths that led down from their height. Not until late in the day did they reach the bottom, and by that time they had to concentrate on camping for the night.

Thorfast's body ached. Blood still seeped through his robe. His heart raced and his body trembled. At last at the bottom, whatever strength born of anxiety and need drained from him.

He looked at Sophia, whose double layers of clothing clung to her from prodigious sweating, and swallowed.

"I think my wound is worse than I thought."

"Let me see it," she said, wiping her brow with the back of her arm.

"Certainly."

Then the world went black and Thorfast knew no more.

10

Cold, black water engulfed Thorfast. Air bubbles rushed around his head. Thundering cracks and booms echoed darkness. He opened his eyes. Salt burned him. He saw nothing. Panic seized him. He started to paddle. Up. He had to swim up.

His head broke through the surface. A new world of sound assailed him. The crack and boom was sharper, clearer. Men screamed. Fire blazed on the water, hissing into steam. Something flat floated past him. He threw his arms over it and rested.

Smoke and salt water blurred his eyes. Waves shoved him from one side to the next, spinning him like a leaf on a pond. No matter his will, he exerted no control over his direction. Besides the brilliant columns of flame, he saw nothing but velvety darkness.

Then a ship sailed out of the unknown. It was a skiff, crewed by shadowy men raising spears. They leaned over the sides, impaling unseen victims floating alongside Thorfast. They screamed and gurgled as they sank beneath the water.

He tried to paddle away. But he could not escape. The skiff approached.

Yngvar, Alasdair, and Bjorn leaned over the side to glare at him. The burst of relief he felt retreated from the hateful glares of his kin.

"Why do you struggle?" Yngvar asked. "Lift yourself up to our ship!"

"Would you to forsake us?" Alasdair asked.

"A fucking traitor," Bjorn shouted. He stood, rocking the skiff, and raised his spear. His single eye glowed with the fire burning all around. "You are no wolf! If you must die, then die by my spear!"

Thorfast shouted, throwing both hands up to defend himself from Bjorn's mighty cast.

Then he stared up into gloom. Faint shadow danced with pale yellow light. Abstract patterns of light and dark resolved into rafters and beams. A roof was set over his head. Warmth seeped back into his limbs.

"Valhalla?" His voice was weak and his throat dry.

Something shifted in the darkness, the rustle of cloth. He felt hay prickling beneath him and scented the rank notes of animal fur.

"Not Valhalla yet."

A female voice answered in accented Frankish. Sophia. But when she slid across the darkness into the light of a candle set on a crude stool, Thorfast marveled at her appearance.

Her hair was brilliant as ever, but now clean and full. Her faded green blouse and brown skirt were flowing and brighter even in this gloom. Most incredibly, her face was clear and cleaned. Her brows furrowed over clear eyes that glittered with life that had not been there before. Her lips were thin but redder now. Her sharp nose wrinkled as she smiled.

"You are still weak," she said. "And it is late, yet. Sleep more."

"No," he said, trying to rise. Sophia set her warm, smooth palm over his bare chest.

He was naked beneath a heavy wool blanket. The damp air chilled his flesh, though the sweat that glistened on Sophia's brow showed the chill was his alone.

He was in a small barn fixed with two empty stalls. Whatever animals had been penned here were gone. A single door was barred shut, containing the weak light of a white candle that burned down to a stub in its iron holder.

"A candle in a barn," Thorfast said. "Is that not a fire soon to start?"

"I cannot see you otherwise," Sophia said. She pulled the blanket over his chest.

"I remember coming off the mountain." He lay back but looked around the tiny place. "What magic have you worked since?"

Sophia sighed. "I prayed and God answered me."

"Did your god deliver us to this barn? I cannot see how you would have had strength to carry me to wherever this place is."

"God's hand carries the faithful," she said. Then she tucked her chin down and looked aside. "He carries us even when He knows we will sin against His will. He loves us that much."

He listened to her breathing as she sat in thoughtful silence. No memory of events after descending the mountains came to him. Perhaps the Christian god had carried him.

"Where is this place? Where are our weapons? Are we free or captured?"

Sophia laughed and held up her hand. "Be still and I'll explain. We are free. As free as two such as we can be."

"A hint of ill fate," Thorfast said. "If I cannot leave this place of my own choice then I am not free."

"You were nearly dead. What more could I do?" She bit her lip and stared past the glow of the candle. "You had bled worse than I knew. And the flesh around the wound was hot and red. I had thought about leaving you. Do you know that?"

"It would have been your best choice," he said. "I would have left you."

"No," she said flatly. "I do not know you well, Thorfast the Silent. But I am certain you would not have left me. I have misjudged many people in my life. People I should not have been wrong about. But I am not wrong about you. Am I?"

He smiled weakly. "It is hard to abandon a beautiful woman in need."

She did not laugh, but brushed a lock of hair from her face. "Perhaps so. You are a killer and a heathen. But you know honor better than some Christians. You would not leave me nor would I leave you if there is still hope."

"And so you prayed to your god for his favor? He showed you a vision, then? Or else He delivered a holy messenger to you?" Thorfast, as weak and tired as he was, enjoyed teasing Sophia's faith. "However it came to be, we were taken to this barn. And we are not free, if my guess is right."

"We are freer than we were under the Arabs." She looked at him with hooded eyes. "We have obligations to those who aid us now. They are good people. God has chosen them to work His miracles for us. Check your wound. It is tightly stitched and no longer bleeds. You have been fed, though you do not remember. Bread and honey, a feast such as we do not deserve."

He sat up, feeling the stitches pull tight. But he swept aside the blanket and found the wound covered in clean cloth with only small brown spots marking where his wound had seeped before closing. He was not hungry, at least not as ravenous as he had been.

"It is true," he said. "I feel renewed. Perhaps I was wrong to jest about your god. But as you said, all this comes at a price."

"These are Greek fishermen," Sophia said. "They are not at peace with their Arab masters. Yet neither do they dare rebel. They have aided others shipwrecked like us before, both Arab and Roman. They are poor. Our Arab weapons can be traded for coin or goods. It has been enough to pay for our lodging and food, as well as the risk they have taken to hide us."

Thorfast closed his eyes. "Those weapons were to see us through to your people."

"We kept the daggers," she said, leaning toward him as if expecting praise. She sat back again when he sighed.

"Daggers against spears and swords are of no use," he said. "We are targets for whoever would attack us."

"What does it matter? Were you expecting to fight the Emir's armies yourself? Weapons just invite violence. We should be avoiding armed men. The goal is to reach the border with the Empire. Then we will rest and ready ourselves for the journey home."

"My home is far to the north," he said.

But as the words left his mouth, he realized that was no longer true. He had no home any more. The last of Yngvar's cousins, Brandr, might welcome him. But he and the others had left Norway under the premise they would return wealthy enough to buy forgiveness for their transgressions. He would be lucky to see the north again, never mind as a rich man.

Sophia shuffled closer to him, replacing the wool blanket over his bare chest.

"I meant my home. You owe me your life, now twice over. I have a task for you there. When it is done, you will be freed of any more obligation to me." Her voice lowered and trembled over her last sentence.

Thorfast frowned at her. She looked away, the weak yellow light fluttering across her shining hair. She seemed to drift away into thought. Cleaned and rested, she was a beautiful woman. No wonder the Arab captain wanted to keep her. She would fetch an incredible price in the slave markets or else make a rich gift to a powerful lord. As capable as she was, she would also make a fine wife.

"The sea is my home. The wind is my sole companion. That is all in the world left to me now. I have one goal in life after serving you, and that is to take revenge on Prince Kalim and Jamil the Moor. But when that is done, I would remain with you. Though I expect your husband would not welcome a man as charming, handsome, and strong as me. Think of how foolish I would make him feel."

Sophia laughed. She leaned close again, her small hand brushing against his arm.

"Making him feel a fool is the least of what I want from you."

"Ah, so not all is well at home?" Thorfast smiled, his heart bounding with hope. "It is time you explain what my task is. You have hinted much and said little. No matter what it is you expect of me, you must know I will do it or give my life in the attempt. I am a man without anything but his own blood and breath. And I would own neither if it were not for you. Tell me your story, Sophia."

Her eyes glittered in the low light. A warm smile spread across her face. She slipped her hand beneath the wool blanket to rest it over his.

"I don't want you to give your life," she said, her voice a whisper. "And I don't want you to be alone in this world."

Their eyes met and Thorfast turned his hand to grasp Sophia's. He tugged at her and slid over on his bed of hay. He raised the wool blanket and invited her beneath it. She rested beside him, then pulled close to his side. Her clothes were warm and soft as she tucked into the bole of his shoulder. She slid her arm across his chest.

"My father is an olive oil merchant," she said. "I grew up learning the trade from him, along with my two brothers. I had two sisters, as well, but they died as children. Anyway, it was unusual for a girl to learn these things, but my father favored me. He is the largest olive oil trader for a hundred miles around. So he could afford to indulge me. He imagined me working with traders from across the Empire and beyond. So I learned Frankish from a servant and studied Latin from a tutor. I had begun to learn Arabic but not the kind spoken here."

"A pity," Thorfast said. "Though I doubt words will be much use dealing with the Arabs now."

She sniffed. "Judging from how you imitated their words, perhaps it was just as well I did not waste time in that study. Anyway, my father secured his business by buying olive farms and contracting with other farmers. When I was nineteen years old, he gave me in marriage to the largest of the independent olive farmers. My husband's name is Quintus."

Thorfast repeated the name, but must have done poorly as Sophia snickered at his attempt.

"With me married to Quintus, I increased the reach of my father's business. Now he owned or had contracts with all the growers and pressers. And he owned all the distribution. His olive oil was even sold to the imperial household in Constantinople."

"Where does this story fall afoul?" Thorfast asked.

"For years after marriage, I was not able to give Quintus a child. Never mind the son he wanted. I cannot carry any child. That was four years of trying and Quintus is not a young man. His former wife and all his children died of pox. He alone was spared. So he was eager to start anew. When I gave him nothing, he married a second wife. Her name is Fausta."

"He did not divorce you?" Thorfast asked. "He is wealthy enough for two wives?"

"Quintus has a large estate," she said. "His union with my father only brought him more wealth. So he would never divorce me, at least as long as my father lived."

"And your father was not opposed?"

Sophia shook her head against his chest. She pulled tighter against him.

"My father blamed me. Quintus's seed was strong, he said. He had raised a whole family before me. So I was the problem. Father tried everything he knew to help me. A wise woman fed me potions that made me sick. He donated to the church and begged the priests to ask God to bless me. Nothing worked."

"And so this other woman, Fausta, she is the problem?"

"Yes. She is not a beautiful woman and is older than me. But she became pregnant soon after she married Quintus. She must have had the child by now." She paused, and Thorfast felt her body tense. "I hope she died in childbirth and took the baby with her."

"From that much hate in your voice," he said, "I take it this woman is not only your competition but also a threat. Maybe the cause of what led you to be resting at my side now?"

"Fausta is an ambitious woman and comes from an ambitious family. Her father and brothers are also traders. They have a fleet, but nothing like my father's. Marrying Quintus gave Fausta an opportunity to worm into the olive oil trade. Though my dear husband, Quintus, has a contract with my father, Fausta seems to think he could do better with her brothers.

"She planned to offer Quintus better rates and a greater share of the profits than he gets under my father. Fausta didn't think I could find out such things, being just a young and pretty brat, as she called me. But I did and I confronted Quintus on it. He said it was just a test and nothing to be feared. If Fausta's family could arrange a better deal, then he would simply renegotiate with my father. He promised he intended nothing more."

She sighed then remained quiet. Thorfast let her think and squeezed her hand.

"I believed him, like a fool. Fausta has twisted his thinking against me and my father. He is besotted with her and the heir she carries. I am nothing more than a game piece that tied him to my father's success. Well, I learned that Fausta's family intends to relieve my father of his business and move in for themselves."

"Like overthrowing a jarl," Thorfast said. "Kill his hirdmen, his family, and the jarl himself."

Sophia nodded. "Now that Quintus realized he could work through Fausta's family, he saw less of a need for my father. If his business was destroyed, his ships burned, and his heirs killed, then the olive sellers would be in swift need of a new merchant house. Of course, Quintus would lead them all to Fausta's family. And he would not be a mere seller as he was under my father. He would join Fausta's house as a merchant as well. His wealth would grow by bounds."

"But you learned all of this before it came to pass?" Thorfast asked.

"I was crafty enough to learn this through spies, but not crafty enough to use the knowledge to help anyone. Fausta had also discovered I knew her plan. So the night I intended to send a message to my father, I was captured from Quintus's home. They caught me in the courtyard. Thugs hired by Fausta, of course."

"Yet they did not kill you," he said. "It seems that Fausta should have just put her plans into action earlier and killed you first."

"They bound and blindfolded me," she said, her voice shaking. "I was raped by stinking men with rough hands and hairy bodies. They never let my blindfold off. I was held in a room, though I know not where. I too thought I would be killed. But I began to wonder if Quintus had a part in keeping me alive. Maybe he was also being manipulated, and once my family was gone, he too would die in a convenient accident."

"It fits the way people like Fausta think," Thorfast said. "It seems unlikely her family would want to share any wealth with your husband."

"They are not so powerful now," she said. "But they might be if their plans are carried out. They were to hire mercenaries to attack all my father's fleets. With renewed fighting between the Empire and the

Sicilian Emirate, there are fewer Roman ships to patrol the coasts. Pirates are everywhere. My father has his own guards, but they are typical mercenaries. Loyal until the coin runs out."

"How did you end up on the Arab slave ship?"

"I am not certain of Fausta's intentions for me. Maybe she was going to bring me back after her plan succeeded. For some reason, I was sold off to the Arabs. My blindfold was not removed until I was placed aboard their ship. We stopped in Licata to take on more slaves, which is where you joined us. The rest you know."

Thorfast nodded. "So we are going back to stop Fausta? It would seem she must have carried out her plans by now."

"I don't know what we are going back to," she said. "You are to protect me on the journey. If Fausta has not carried out her attacks, then you are my witness to what has happened to me. If she has destroyed my father—"

"Then I will take revenge for you."

"If she has destroyed my father and family, then there is much killing to do. It is then that you will need a sword."

Thorfast smiled and stroked her head.

"The gods have sent you the right man for this task. I will fill the ocean with the blood of your foes."

"Good," Sophia said. "Now we just have to escape this island."

11

Voices came from beyond the small barn that Thorfast had called home for the last week. The morning light fought through as yellow lines between the loose boards forming the walls. The door was closed but unbolted. Sophia had gone to fetch water from the well. He listened closer, unsure if the voices carried notes of panic. The sound did not sit right with him, but as he held his breath, he heard nothing more urgent.

He rubbed his face and pulled aside the blanket that had covered him through the night. Damp night air still brought a chill despite how hot the days were. He missed cold weather, but imagined winters here would be amazing. His stomach growled. Sophia would bring bread and meat scraps from the farmhouse.

These Greeks had been kind enough that Thorfast worried they held some other motive. For poor fishermen, they were a handsome family. The husband was lean and strong, with dark hair and eyes that were creased from smiling. The wife was stout but shapely and her singing voice was magical. Their two oldest sons resembled their father, and their three daughters did as well, even the infant. Thorfast had given up learning names that he could not pronounce. Sophia still insisted he did not say her name correctly, though he could not hear how he was wrong.

He picked straw from the stubble of his hair and brushed it from his shirt. The father had given him worn-out clothing, a gray shirt and brown pants both of threadbare cloth. He was not going to pass himself off as a lord, but he at least no longer seemed a castaway slave. If only his his beard and hair would lengthen, he would seem no more than a farmer.

Of all the gifts bestowed on him, he was most grateful for soft leather boots that rose to his ankles. Sophia had insisted this was too generous of a gift and wanted Thorfast to return them. But the wife had seen the condition of his feet and insisted. His eyes stung with tears to receive these shoes. He bowed low to the wife, who had blushed and giggled at his display.

The trade of his captured weapons for care and clothing were undoubtedly worth it. He sniffed the air of the barn, still smelling the goats that had once been penned here. Compared to the places he had been in recent months, this was a luxury. They had not changed the hay in a week, and it was beginning to rot. Yet he was feeling strong enough now that he could start to repay the fishermen for their generosity. He would clean out their barn, help with repairs to their home, work their fishing boat, and whatever else they needed. For he had never met better people.

They had redeemed the entire place called Sicily. Until this day, Thorfast had seriously considered how he could kill every person on this horrid island. Yet it was only the masters of Sicily that deserved death. The common people were like poor people every-where. They lived their desperate lives in hopes no one would bother them.

He heard another call in the distance. The husband and his sons should still be on the water. They usually did not return until late morning with their catch. Yet he thought the voices sounded like males shouting.

The stitches still remained in his flesh. They tugged as he rose to his feet. The wound no longer burned or ached, at least as long as he did not strain himself overlong. The flesh around it itched, which was a sign of healing. He might soon remove the gut thread that held it shut. Now that he stood, he listened closer. Nothing.

"You've grown soft, Thorfast," he said as he stretched. "No more lying about while everyone else works."

The door swung open, slamming against the wall. Sophia stood framed in the white brilliance of midmorning light. She was a silhouette holding a bucket of water against her thigh.

"Men are approaching," she said. "They are not Arabs, but I am not sure they are friendly. The family has gathered in the house."

"What are you doing with that water?" He pulled it from her, sloshing it over the threshold as he set it inside. "Have they sold the spears and swords yet?"

Sophia shook her head.

He grabbed her wrist and pulled her back into the yard. Grass fields sped away toward the shore, obscured by lines of palms and other trees. The shoulders of the hills rose to the west and curved to the north. From out of a forest that spread around the feet of the hill, a group of men ambled forward. They were spread wide, calling to each other across their line.

"Twelve," he said. "Or one more or less. Get to the house with the others. The men are still away?"

"They won't return until midday." Sophia looked toward the approaching line. "These are poor folk. What could they want here?"

Thorfast knew the answer. He had long been the raider and could see the value in everything around this farm. Sophia, being raised in a merchant's home, might only count wealth in coins.

The home was a square building with a roof of red tiles that sloped to one side for runoff. White plaster stained with brown streaks formed the walls. The wood door hung open and the wife peered out. Her large brown eyes were wide with fear. She cradled the infant girl in one arm, while another dark-haired daughter clung to her skirt.

"Tell them to give me a spear," he said as he led Sophia inside. "I will return it to them when the trouble is gone."

"One against twelve," Sophia said. "Are you mad?"

"Only one can fit through this door at a time. If they try to burn us out, then they must start a fire. I do not see any smoke from them. So we can set ourselves here."

Inside, the hearth glowed orange in the low light. It was a small, round construction with a black iron pot on a trestle. Smoke curled up to the roof and escaped from a hole in the ceiling. Rough furniture vied for space with casks, clayware, buckets, and sundry wares for maintaining a home. The wife grabbed a spear and handed it to him.

He weighed the smooth wood and saw the blade edges still white and sharp. The shouting from outside grew more distinct. It sounded as if they called a name.

"Is that the husband they ask for?" Thorfast asked. Sophia nodded. "Then are we in danger?"

The wife did not speak Frankish but she seemed to intuit his question and began to flow out pleas that Sophia rushed to translate.

"They are the resistance to the Emirate," Sophia said. "She doesn't know what they want, but it cannot be good."

"Resistance?" Thorfast said. "Then they should be welcomed."

Then he thought of the young, strong boys working with their fathers on the sea. He realized what these men wanted and why the wife was so fearful.

"I just asked her why the fear," Sophia said. "But she just wants us to send them away."

"Stand back," he said. He planted his spear and drew a breath. "You speak, but I will give you the words."

Twelve men picked their way across the final stretch of grass. From here, Thorfast appreciated the strategic positioning of the home. There was no approach that could not be observed except from the hills to the rear. Yet human threats would not come down from those stony peaks.

These men were dressed in a variety of styles. Some appeared to take after the Arabs. Others wore flowing pants in the Arab style but plain shirts and belts more common to the people to the north. They carried spears and swords. A few owned small, round shields of bronze that were battered and stained. These they carried on their arms.

The man in the lead represented them all. He was tall with broad shoulders and a waist that spoke to infrequent meals. Black rings surrounded his eyes such that it seemed like he had colored them so. A flash of gold dangled from his ears, hidden beneath greasy black hair stained with gray.

He smiled as he approached. A set of yellow teeth showed wide gaps between each one. His sword was curved and remained in its leather sheath.

Thorfast stood in the doorway, spear leveled in both hands. He remained forward enough to have range to work his spear but still be able to leap back into the doorframe. From behind, the wife spoke soothing words to her girls, who held a frightened silence.

"Stop where you are," he said in Frankish, pointing to the earth with his spear. "Who are you?"

He waited for Sophia's translation. She stood close enough that he might accidentally strike her with the spear butt. He pulled forward to create more distance.

The twelve men took it as a threat. They reached for swords or else set their spears in both hands. The dark-eyed man in the lead pulled up short.

He spoke with a voice rasping and dry. He looked to Thorfast for understanding. He sneered at the leader's confident smile.

"He says his name is Dimos," Sophia said. "And he wants to know who we are."

Thorfast ran his gaze along the tall man's length, then spit to show his disgust. "Tell him who we are is not his concern. That he comes with twelve armed men to this house is a threat I shall not overlook. If he wishes to know more, he can learn about me from whatever hell his gods have prepared for him."

"Shouldn't we try to bargain?" Sophia asked.

"Translate, woman!" Thorfast shouted over his shoulder but did not look away from the man called Dimos. "We are bargaining with him. This is how it is done."

Sophia sighed and spoke a few words. Dimos raised his brow.

"You did not say all that I said. Make the threat."

"I threatened him enough."

Heat came to Thorfast's cheeks. This Dimos and his ragged band smirked. Whatever Sophia translated had been dismissed. He narrowed his eyes and decided if she would not translate, then he would shout them down in a language he knew best. Whether they understood the words would not matter. He would leave them no doubt.

"You dog-fucking bastards had better turn around or I'll make a pile of your guts before this door that'll reach to Asgard! Test me and see!"

Dimos stepped back with both brows now raised. He laughed, maybe nervously, and looked to the men at his side.

One of them stepped forward, his sword lowered and his face bright with joy.

"A Norseman!" he said in Norse. "What are you doing here, brother?"

The sudden clarity of the language stunned Thorfast. He felt as if wool had been pulled from his ears. Yet he gave the Norseman no satisfaction. Regaining himself, he frowned.

"Brother? My brothers never came to me with drawn swords in hand."

The sudden exchange in a language no one else understood shifted everyone's attention to Thorfast and the Norseman. Dimos's brows remained arched in surprise. The rest of his men stepped back as if they had been struck. Sophia gasped.

"What is he saying?"

She gently touched his elbow, but he shook it away. Instead, he studied this Norseman.

He was stout, perhaps half a head taller than Alasdair had been. But he was well-proportioned and gave the appearance of a much taller man. His hair and beard were dusty brown and full. Intense green eyes stared from beneath angry brows. His chin pushed out too far, imparting a brutish cast to an otherwise handsome face.

"You have a strange accent," the Norseman said. "I am Ragnar the Dane."

Though the man smiled as he spoke, he seemed unable to shake his angry appearance. His simple, almost boyish, introduction eased Thorfast. Though he noted Dimos was shifting his eyes toward his men, likely waiting for a time to move closer. He could not allow these men to see any weakness in him.

"Go fall on your sword, Ragnar. You seek to distract me while your man-loving friends prepare to overwhelm me. I count more scars on my ass than you have on your whole body. I know how to fight and win against any odds."

"You have scars on your ass?" Ragnar asked, apparently impressed.

"You'll see them when you're bleeding out in the grass and I'm shitting on your head." Thorfast swept the point of his spear at Dimos. "Tell that bastard he'll die first. So if he loves himself he'd best stand down."

Ragnar spoke a few rough words to Dimos. His speech carried none of the elegance that Sophia's did. But Dimos understood enough to incline his head and give a dry-throated reply.

"He said I can speak for him," Ragnar said.

"He said the Norseman can speak on his behalf," Sophia translated. Thorfast rolled his eyes.

"Never mind the woman. I know what you are here for, and I will not allow it."

"We don't intend violence, brother," Ragnar said.

"Your sincerity is as real as tits on a tree. Don't take me for a fool."

Ragnar laughed and held up his hand. "You have not named yourself. Give me a name, and I will state what we want."

"I am Thorfast the Silent. And if you are a Dane, then you might know me as one of Yngvar Hakonsson's crew. We regularly killed your people for sport. Maybe I killed your mother. Or maybe she died fucking a frost giant. I bet she was loose enough to try."

Ragnar's smile vanished and his face reddened.

"You had best be silent, Thorfast. You have enjoyed insulting me enough. But your next curse will be your last, and I don't care how you die. There are twelve of us to you alone. Do you hold the magical spear Ridill in your hands? Will you cut out Fafnir's heart with it? No, it is a man's weapon. One easily broken and shoved back into its wielder's teeth."

Thorfast grinned. "That's it. Now we are talking to each other. No more of this Arab and Greek foolishness. So, I've named myself. Now tell me that you have come to take one or both of the boys from this family to fill your ranks. Isn't that true?"

"It is," Ragnar said. His cheeks remained ruddy but he softened his voice and the tension in his sword arm eased.

"Well, that is what I cannot allow," Thorast said. "So we have reached the end point of our discussion. It was nice meeting you, even if you are a Dane. Now trot along."

Ragnar offered a quick translation to Dimos, who began shaking his head before it was finished. His bone-dry voice dictated stern words in reply.

"The oldest son was promised to Dimos," Sophia translated from behind. "And he's come to collect."

The wife inside the house began to sob and added her own shouted protests. Dimos stepped closer and called back into the house. A flurry of Greek shouting erupted with Thorfast and Sophia in the middle. He held his spear level and Sophia tried to explain.

"She says the promise was forced on them at sword-point. But Dimos says it was the price for his help. They let the son alone for a year. I guess they had a bargain."

"This is a mess," Thorfast said. "Who do you believe?"

"Both of them," she said.

Throughout the exchange, everyone kept silent. Dimos's men swabbed sweat from their brows or waved off flies. They seemed unworried for the outcome, and looked into the distance. Two men watched the approach from the shore.

"There's no escaping this," Thorfast said. "We are trapped here and the husband and his sons are trapped out there."

He looked back at Sophia. Her lips were pressed together.

"I will die if I fight," he said. "I hoped they would scare off at the threat of violence and find easier prey. But they are desperate."

The shouting continued in volleys until Dimos shook his head violently and raised his hands as if calling for silence.

"Brother," Ragnar said. "You either step aside or hold that spear tight. You will be in Valhalla soon."

"They're coming in," Sophia said. She pressed her hands to Thorfast's back as if he needed to be propped up.

"The boy and the others are not here," he said in Norse to Ragnar. "They are still at sea. You should know this is too early for fishermen to be home."

Ragnar translated and Dimos spit something back.

"Brother, Dimos wishes to be out of the sun and have a drink while he waits. You are not master of this house. So stand aside and let the woman show us hospitality."

While Sophia translated the same words, Thorfast considered his choices. He owed this Greek family at least as much as Sophia, perhaps even more. While they had taken payment for their kindness, it was no hardship to him. Looking at Dimos's dark-ringed eyes, he knew the man was nothing better than a bandit. He smirked with the knowledge that he had all the power.

Once again, Thorfast was backed into a corner with no way to escape. An ironic grin tugged at his mouth. This must be why Yngvar drew up all the battle plans, he thought. I can do nothing better than corner myself then hope to talk my way free.

"I will not stand aside," Thorfast said. "Tell your master that he has no need to tarry here. I will give him something better. I will join in place of the boy."

Ragnar's face brightened. "Is that true? Another Norseman to share a mug with? To sing songs I understand. It's as good as going home again."

"You make it seem we will be lovers," Thorfast said. "Be glad if I even speak to you. Now tell your leader."

Dimos had paused at their exchange. His face brightened as Ragnar translated for him.

Sophia screamed. "Join them?"

"What would you have me do?" he called back over his shoulder, keeping his spear facing Dimos.

"What about me? You owe me your life!"

"And I owe these Greeks my clothes, my boots, the stitches in my wound, and the bread and beer in my stomach. Losing their eldest son would be too bitter a blow for them. Besides, aren't these rebels fighting Prince Kalim? I would enjoy that."

"Enjoy?" Sophia's voice shrieked, stopping all other speech around them. "Life is not yours to enjoy. It is owed to others. To me! These Greeks couldn't have given you all of that if I had not led you away from the beach. Think of what happened to your friend. You'd be as dead as he is were it not for me."

"Brother?" Ragnar's voice was almost embarrassed. "Your woman protests. But Dimos would be glad to have you in trade. He thinks it's a pity to kill you otherwise. You are bold and we admire that."

"No more Norse!" Sophia grabbed his arm and swung him around. His heart leapt, for he expected Ragnar and Dimos plus half a dozen others to pile atop him and grab his spear.

Instead, he faced Sophia's smoldering eyes. If her natural expression was one of anger, now it was of unbridled hatred.

"You are going to leave me here?" She grabbed his shirt and drew him close. Her voice dropped to low growl. "You think you are helping these people? Where will I go? I will remain here, a stranger in need of food and shelter. Soon I will become a burden to them, and then they will cast me out. Then what? Capture by the Arabs again. You cannot leave me to this fate. Let them take the boy if that was their bargain. We cannot stand against this many. You tried. It is all any could ask."

He heard snickering from behind.

"Brother, your woman is welcomed with us. But Dimos said she will have to earn her place."

Thorfast held Sophia's eyes a moment, then turned back. Dimos had his arms folded and his smirk as wide as his thin face allowed. The others grinned at him as well. Ragnar extended his hand as if welcoming them into their ranks.

"It is your best choice," he said. "We live a simple life, but we lack for nothing. And from one Norseman to another, you need friends in this land. These fishermen won't protect you when the Arabs come for their taxes. They'll hand you over for a reward. Believe me. There are no friends in this land for our people."

"The woman is my wife," he said. "If Dimos thinks earning a keep means spreading her legs for you lot, we might as well sort out the living and dead right now."

Ragnar did not even translate for the others.

"Understood, Brother. She is your woman alone. None will touch her. You have my word upon it."

Thorfast lowered his spear and nodded.

And with that nod, joined his fate to these scraggly bandits.

12

The fisherman's home faded into blue haze as Thorfast trudged in line with his new companions. Dark clouds had gathered and the blue sky now threatened rain. Anything to relieve the heat and chase away flies. He would be willing to stand all day in a downpour to be rid of both.

Dimos led his band in a song. The tune was sad and slow, and poorly sung. The bandits had their spears shouldered and their few shields slung over their backs. Swords were set into sheaths that swung from their hips.

Thorfast had not been relieved of his spear, and the fisherman's wife could not meet his eyes to ask for it back. So he parked it on his shoulder. His palm was sweaty against its smooth haft. Grass sighed with the gusting wind that ran through the stubble of Thorfast's hair. He glanced a final time at the fisherman's home and the rocky mountains behind them.

"At least they appreciated it," Thorfast said in Frankish. "Did you see the oldest girl? She kissed my hand."

He wished Sophia would say something. Curse him, curse Dimos or Ragnar, curse the Greeks. Anything but the silence. The moment she had realized they could not escape Dimos, she fell into gloomy silence. She hadn't even said a word to the wife or her children before leaving.

She continued to ignore everyone, staring at the horizon as if she could hear nothing at all. Yet she did not leave his side, stopping short of taking his arm as they walked.

"She's a hard woman," Ragnar said. "A beauty, too. Can't say I understand what she's doing married to you. You must enjoy it, eh?"

Thorfast blinked at him, then squinted into the glare of the distance. Dimos and his band of warbling singers were leading them across a grassy plain toward a woods.

"I mean, women with fiery tempers make for a good roll when their mood is up," Ragnar explained. "I bet that's why you lost all your hair. Fell right out while she was riding you."

His laugh was like chopping wood.

"We were prisoners of Prince Kalim," Thorfast said. "We've escaped. But we want to return him all the courtesy he showed us. I'll trim his beard closer than he trimmed mine. I may even keep his skull to make a drinking mug of it."

"A fine idea," Ragnar said. "Can't say I love the Arabs. But in truth, these Greeks aren't much better either. Your woman is Greek?"

"Says she's Roman."

Ragnar shrugged. "Foreigners are all the same. All of them are wrapped up in God and priests. You'd have an easier life with the Greeks if you became a Christian."

"Did you?"

"I pray with my brothers and it seems to help. If I ever go back to sea, though, I'd look to Thor for my blessings."

"You are a shrewd man," Thorfast said. "I will give your suggestion more thought."

He would never kneel to the Christian god even if it meant a better life with these bandits. Besides, he did not intend to remain long with Dimos.

Their singing ended as they entered the woods. They followed hidden paths that Thorfast would not have noticed on his own. Palm trees had ringed the outside of this wood, but as they proceeded deeper, these gave way to what seemed more like regular trees to him.

Though none of them were trees of the northlands. Stumbling along at the center of the column of Dimos's gang, his idle his mind wondered at the properties of the trees. Was the wood suitable for ship-building or weapon-making? One day, he thought, he might need to know. This island was an utter mystery to him, and even the trees could not be depended upon to be what he expected.

The forest smelled of earth and rotting vegetation. The sweet scent that had pervaded the coast had fallen away. The dappled light blazed emerald on the undergrowth. Shade did not relieve the sticky heat. Yet where flies had tormented him along the coast, here in the woods they were replaced with gnats. They stuck to his sweat and made him wish for a bath.

Sophia took his arm for stability as she followed. Her silence remained unbroken. Yet somehow he felt she was reconciling herself to his choice. He was not certain how he knew this, other than he sensed if he tried to force her to speak she might not stab him with he dagger she hid under her skirt. He feared to test this impression and so left her in silence.

Dimos's camp was the disaster he expected it to be. Yellow tents that had probably once been white were pitched in a clearing. An extinguished campfire ringed with logs for benches sat in the middle. A lean-to had been constructed against a gray boulder that leaned like a drunk man away from the camp. Beneath it, sacks, casks, and wood chests were piled.

"Like I said, we live a simple life," Ragnar explained.

"Rats lead simple lives," Thorfast said. "I expected as much."

Ragnar laughed. "You must have a story to tell, brother. We will sit by the campfire tonight and share stories. You will have news of the north, I expect."

Dimos spread his arms wide, welcoming Thorfast. He bowed to Sophia in mock respect. He pointed out tents and made grand gestures as if pointing to some imaginary vista. Neither Sophia nor Ragnar translated. The rattling language of the Greeks bored him. So he swept his spear to his shoulder and wandered off to investigate the tents.

Dimos shouted at him, but Thorfast ignored it. He used his spear tip to prod aside a tent flap. Another shouted in protest.

He smiled. These fools had to understand he owed them no fear. He was their equal at least, and likely their better if put to the test. It would not do to appear like a weakling. The surest way to get the fight underway would be to start claiming another man's property for his own.

"This tent will do for me," he shouted back to Ragnar. He ducked inside. It was dingy, smelling of sweat and body stink.

A red-faced man with eyes like a pig's stuck his head inside. He blustered and shouted, spittle flying from his mouth. Thorfast turned, carelessly letting the blade of his spear sweep before the babbling man.

"Was this your tent, friend? Well, where I am from it is simple hospitality to offer your home to a traveler in need."

He backed the man out of the tent at the end of the spear. In the campground the bandits were shouting at each other or at Dimos. The offended man, whom Thorfast decided he would forever call Pig Eyes, stared at the spear tip his with his mouth open. Once he recovered, he drew his own sword.

"What are you doing?" Sophia shouted at him.

"Just setting some rules and getting us a place to sleep." He smiled at her, then looked at Pig Eyes' drawn sword. "A drawn blade? Ragnar, tell this man he misunderstands me. I can't help that my spear has no sheath."

Ragnar's expression was trapped between laughter and shock. He stumbled through some sort of translation to Dimos, whose dark-ringed eyes had narrowed.

Pig Eyes gave a halfhearted jab with his sword and cursed again.

"Stop this!" Sophia shouted. "You're getting us in trouble."

"I'm saving us trouble later on," Thorfast said. "We'll be tested sooner or later. Best we get it done on our terms rather than theirs. We might get a tent out of this as well."

"I don't care about a tent!"

"You will when it rains."

"Thorfast!"

Dimos shouted the name with greater clarity than expected. He folded his arms and formed a sardonic smile. All the other shouting stopped while his husky, dry voice filled the clearing. At last, he paused to let Ragnar translate.

"He does not appreciate you causing trouble so soon. But he understands you are challenging for your place among his men. So to satisfy you and get the new order settled, you will fight for your place."

"I agree," Thorfast said, nodding to Dimos.

This needed no translation. Dimos waved men back to create a space for the fight. He then gestured for Thorfast to stand at the center.

Sophia snapped her head back and forth between Dimos and Thorfast. Her frown creased her face with deep shadow.

"Your wound is still stitched," she said. "All they have to do is strike it and you'll fall."

"No one knows I'm hurt. Besides, you haven't seen a Northman fight. This won't take long."

Dimos pointed to Pig Eyes, a man with a lumpy scar like a worm on his cheek, and finally Ragnar. The rest of the men cheered these choices, raising their fists or clapping.

The three men gave their weapons to others. Thorfast handed his spear to Sophia. Her face had turned as white as her hair.

The three men drew up to a semicircle before Thorfast, with Ragnar at the center.

"Looks like we're going to trade a few blows, brother," he said, smirking. "I'll remember what you said about my mother."

"Yes, I remember your mother now," Thorfast said. "Fucking her was like banging a stick in a barrel."

Ragnar's face flushed red and he struck hard.

Thorfast had expected it. He stepped to the side. The dodge took him before Pig Eyes, who also lurched for him. But Thorfast had his measure. He twisted aside, feeling the painful tug of the stitches in his flesh. Yet he grabbed Pig Eyes by both sides of his pant waist.

He threw Pig Eyes forward onto Ragnar, so the two crashed together in a pile.

The onlookers cried out, laughing or cursing depending upon

how they had placed their bets. The scar-faced man staggered around, having jumped to the wrong position. He glared at Thorfast and threw an arcing punch at his head.

Thorfast ducked beneath it, then landed his fist in the man's gut. He then drove into him with his shoulder, catching him beneath his arm and lifting him off the ground.

He grabbed the attacker's crotch and squeezed as if he were trying to crush walnuts. The man screamed and thrashed. Thorfast twisted and yanked as hard as he could. Then dropped the man as a worthless, screaming wreck that curled up over his crotch.

He whirled in time to meet Pig Eyes. The punch connected solidly with his jaw and his head snapped back. Pain flared across his face and he saw white flashes. But he set his feet so he would not stagger.

Pig Eyes laughed with his victory and took a second swing. But Thorfast had skipped aside, knowing Ragnar would be upright by now.

His so-called brother was only on hands and knees. So Thorfast leapt up to him and swept his foot into Ragnar's face. Spit and curses flew from Ragnar's mouth as he flopped over.

The audience wailed again. He glimpsed Sophia pointing behind him.

He leapt forward as Pig Eyes tried to jump onto his back. Pig Eyes grunted as he crashed to the ground. Thorfast stumbled into Sophia, who screamed in surprise.

"I'll take this," he said, grabbing his spear and regaining his balance.

Ragnar lay flat on his side, dazed. Pig Eyes crawled to his feet. The crowd called foul at Thorfast's weapon. But before anyone could grab it from him, he leapt back into the fight.

Pig Eyes looked up in time for the spear butt to slam into his forehead. He snatched at the spear, but Thorfast pulled it overhead. Then brought it down again with a crack across Pig Eyes' crown. His head pressed into his shoulders and he collapsed to his hands and knees.

He beat Pig Eyes with the spear haft as if he were driving a stake into the earth. After a half-dozen quick blows, he was flattened and motionless in the dirt. The scarred man was still mourning the destruction of his crotch, curled so tight that he could be rolled away.

The rest of Dimos's men were shouting in rage or roaring with laughter. Some exchanged coins already. Dimos continued to observe with narrowed eyes and a dark frown. He shifted his weight to one leg and tightened his folded arms across his chest.

Thorfast turned to face Ragnar, who had now staggered to his feet. Blood flowed from his mouth to drizzle over his shirt.

"You got a spear," he said through his split lips.

"And you had two friends to help you, and you've not touched me yet," he said. "I suppose I don't need this after all."

He slid toward Sophia, keeping Ragnar in front of him. She took the extended spear from him, her face bright with surprise. Enjoying the sport, he offered her a wink.

"We got to finish this, brother," Ragnar said. He hunched over then set legs and arms wide as if preparing to wrestle him.

"I will," Thorfast said. "But stand up straight so I can hit your face properly."

"Afraid I'll twist your head off?" Ragnar's smile revealed red-stained teeth.

"It's just distracting. With you bent so low like that it reminds me of your mother sucking my prick. You look so much like her."

"I'll kill you!"

He lunged with blind rage and Thorfast let him connect. Ragnar threw his arms around him and attempted to drive him to the ground. Thorfast fell back with the force and set his knee against Ragnar's gut.

When he collapsed atop Thorfast, all the air was driven from his lungs. Thorfast quickly shoved him off and reversed positions. He scrabbled onto Ragnar's back and grabbed his right arm. This he bent back behind the Norseman. It reminded him of breaking the legs of the dog that had savaged Hamar. The fury of the memory drove him harder.

"I yield!" Ragnar screamed. "You're breaking my arm!"

Thorfast paused, drawing his memory back. He straddled

Ragnar's defeated body still. He released the Norseman's arm, then leaned by his ear.

"Ragnar, I don't know your mother. A bit of advice. Don't take insults to her so seriously. It's your undoing, man."

"I can't help it," Ragnar said into the dirt.

The bandits cheered him, forgetting the defeat of their companions. He had given them a good show. Sophia glared at him like a mother upset with her child for messing her hearth. Dimos had shifted neither his stance nor his demeanor.

"I win," he said, jumping up to his feet. "So I claim Pig Eyes' tent. The Norseman will serve me. And the one whose stones I crushed, well, he's going to be useless for a long time."

His demands remained untranslated, as Ragnar was still collecting himself from the ground and Sophia remained wrapped in anger. Yet Dimos seemed to understand. He simply bent his mouth in acknowledgement.

He received appreciative back-slaps from some and halfhearted curses from others. In return he offered smiles and words of thanks. No matter he intended to betray these men at the first opportunity, for now he had to remain on good terms.

Their boisterous laughter echoed through the woods as they broke into their cliques. One threw a small bucket of water over Pig Eyes to rouse him from his stupor. His friends laughed as he jolted awake, shaking water from his face and his small eyes blinking. The scar-faced man was hauled away between two men. Of the three, he had likely suffered the worst injury. Thorfast knew he had made an enemy of him.

"I am thinking God was not so kind to send you to me," Sophia said, shoving the spear back into his hands. "You are stupid and violent and have no thoughts for tomorrow."

"I am the man you need," he said, looking past her to Ragnar as he clambered to his feet. "Remember your wish to stain the sea red with the blood of your foes? That's my trade, woman."

He set her aside as Ragnar waddled toward him. She sniffed at his touch, but did hold close. Dimos had gone to his tent, but he paused to glare back at them.

"Brother, I'm not going to serve you."

"Yes you will. Or I'll splatter your brains from one end of this island to the other. Though I don't think you have enough to cover it."

Ragnar laughed and rubbed his face, which had swollen where Thorfast kicked it.

"My mother always said I was stupid. My father, too. But I showed them, didn't I?"

"Well, you learned Greek. So that's a step better than me. But your family is not interesting to me." Thorfast slipped his arm over Ragnar's shoulder. "Tell me something. An hour ago I was ready for you all to kill me. Now we're all slapping backs and old friends. Am I going to get a dagger in the back tonight?"

Ragnar thought about it. "Not from me. Not from anyone, really. We need fighting men, and you've shown you can fight. None of us have any place left in the world except here. So it's a good thing when we add a good man to our number."

Thorfast laughed. "Fine words after I insulted your mother and kicked you in the face. I suppose I will believe you. One Norseman to another, yes?"

"Of course," Ragnar said.

He seemed as genuine as a man could be. Yet Thorfast did not count himself a shrewd judge of men's true natures. He would have to sleep lightly and keep Sophia at his side.

"Well," Ragnar said, his expression suddenly troubled. "I would warn you about your wife. She reveals much of her body. I've twice seen up to her calf in this short time we've traveled together. We need her to cook, sew, and tend our illnesses. But we're just men. Some have lovers in villages. But most do not."

"I understand," he said. He turned to Sophia, who had folded her arms beneath her breasts. He shook his head, and looked beyond her to where Dimos peaked out at her from his tent.

"I understand," he said under his breath.

13

———

A week of rain had turned Sicily into a bog. Cool mud sucked at Thorfast's feet as he trudged beneath a gray sky. Misty rain still speckled his face as he marched across a rocky field in a line with Dimos's men. Despite the rain, his flesh still pricked with the humidity. Gnats swam through his sweat. He had never faced an enemy mightier than the gnat. Defiant and impervious to violence, they had crushed Thorfast's will. They now regularly danced in victorious circles across his skin. He offered only token efforts to remove them. Truly, they had mastered him.

Sophia held his arm as they marched. She had shown herself to be as hardy as any of the men. The week of rain had not dampened her spirit, nor had it done anything to soften her anger at Thorfast. He had tried to explain his intent to remain with Dimos until they could break away on their own. But he received only curt nods and the one question, "Are you finished," for his efforts.

So now he journeyed across the Sicilian countryside with an angry woman pretending to be his wife and twelve ragged men who fancied themselves some sort of resistance fighters for an independent Sicily. Thorfast knew them for opportunistic bandits that mostly attacked Arab targets. Though the rain had prevented any act of rebellion grander than opportunistic thefts from wretched hovels where the sad-eyed Arabs offered no resistance.

A cluster of white houses showed in the hazy distance. A dog barked there and echoed off the mountains on their opposite flank. Sicily was a green land of mountains and grass, it seemed to Thorfast. Too many different people mingled here, speaking different languages and creating distrust of either side. The Arabs ruled and every other race served.

Thus far, he could not understand why anyone wanted to live here. But then he felt the same for his own people who lived in the ice-bound north where the sun either never set or never rose depending on the season. Those were lands for madmen. Like this land.

"If I didn't know this land to be an island," Thorfast said to Ragnar, who marched ahead of him, "I would think this field stretched to the top of the world."

"The meeting place is in those hills," he said, pointing to the range of haze-shrouded foothills that popped above rows of dark thin trees.

"And these men will have real food? I cannot stomach rice and vegetables any longer. Rice is a terrible thing."

"You get used to it," Ragnar said. "But they should have provisions for us, including meat. They usually do."

Dimos turned back, giving him and Thorfast a dark look.

"He doesn't like it when we speak Norse," Ragnar said.

"Of course not. He assumes we're plotting against him."

Thorfast smiled at Dimos, whose dark-ringed eyes narrowed at him as if in warning. He noted how Dimos's gaze lingered on Sophia before he turned back. She might have noticed as well, for though keeping a stony silence she tightened her arm around his as they picked across sucking mud and rocks.

"Well, you're more popular than he is and you can't even speak to these men," Ragnar said. He rested his hand on his sword hilt as he walked. It was a good Norse sword and Thorfast envied it.

"I can't help but to be better than most men," Thorfast said. "Should I be blamed for it?"

Ragnar laughed. "But you'll never be known for humility."

"I'm humble enough to the man that lays me out and puts a sword to my neck. But that's not going to be any of you lot."

"So your story," Ragnar said. "Is it all true? You broke free of your chains, killed your captors with them, then stole their rowboat to come ashore? No one followed you?"

"Who would dare follow me after I burst iron bands with my own strength?" Thorfast touched his chest in feigned surprise. "I had been patient in Prince Kalim's cells. Only because I knew I could never fight my way to his throne room and give him the death he so deserves. He feared my strength, so kept me weak and sick on some potion forced on me. But once I had my own will back, I could have sunk that Arab slave trader with a single blow from my fist. Instead, I strangled the captain with my chains and dared the rest to prevent me from taking their rowboat. Cowards let me go. Then I found Sophia and we were married on the spot. Women cannot resist me, you should know."

"But this seems strange," Ragnar said. "What was she doing on the beach?"

"Waiting for me, you ass!"

Ragnar scratched his head. Thorfast hoped he scratched vigorously enough to loosen the mud in his brains. The man was as dumb as his mother had said he was. Yet he was likable enough, and a fellow Norsemen.

He turned back with a sly grin. "You tell strange stories, brother. I wish my story was as exciting. But I followed my jarl south to get rich, got killed to a man attacking a town too big for our strength, and so here I am. Picked up by Dimos's men when I fled. But you have had a far greater adventure. There must be more to it than you've told."

"Enough about me," he said. "What about Dimos? You say he used to be a Byzantine soldier."

"That's what he claims," Ragnar said. He kept pace with the line of men following Dimos, but their conversation had caused them to fall behind. He quickened his pace, the mud making squelching noises as he closed the gap. Thorfast and Sophia did not speed up.

"And these men we go to meet are real Byzantine soldiers? Won't there be trouble?"

"All will be well, brother. Dimos has taken us to them many times before. They leave messages for each other in villages along our paths. So they know when to connect. Like today."

He stared at the back of Dimos's strangely proportioned body. From his wide shoulders, Thorfast guessed he might have once been an archer. He did not like Thorfast, but seemed to appreciate his potential. Thorfast could not decide on Dimos. In the end it would not matter. He only followed the man because he had not figured out how to break away. The time wandering about and avoiding Arab authorities had taught him much about survival here. For that at least he was grateful to Dimos.

The ground grew firmer the closer they approached the hills. Thorfast was happy to no longer struggle against mud. His new boots seemed a decade old now. He could not guess what his bare feet would have been like otherwise. He checked Sophia's feet, finding them encased with mud. But she did not complain.

Dimos led them along hidden paths that threaded through the trees and up into the hills. Thorfast could not determine how Dimos knew where to go. Perhaps it was just long years of practice. He heard the dog barking again in the distance. It did not sit right with him, for the village was now a white smear in the distance. Another dog must be near to another settlement he could not see. Sicily was densely settled. It was a sign of the great age of this place that families had lived here since the beginning of the world and so spread into every corner of the land.

The meeting place was a reasonably flat stretch halfway up the hillside. Dark-leafed trees and bushes dotted the area. The shoulder of the slope obscured every approach except the eastern one they had just climbed. Dimos began to shout orders, men dropped their packs and began to set up camp.

Despite having won his fight with Pig Eyes and the others, Thorfast was unable to claim the tent. None allowed it and Ragnar had warned him off of it, telling him men shared tents as needed. Since ownership meant carrying the tent, Thorfast had surrendered it. He wanted to stay as mobile as possible and not have a bulky pack on his shoulder. Perhaps surrendering the tent after having won it had also angered Sophia. She had little to say to him since.

No fires could be set both due to the misty rain and the secrecy of their meeting. Thorfast aided Ragnar in erecting a tent with another man. He hoped to get shelter this night and it seemed being helpful was the right way to secure it.

While helping Ragnar drive in the center pole, he had turned his back to Sophia. She had released his arm and left without a word. She might believe he had betrayed his promise to her, but she would realize her error in time. What other purpose did he have in life now with all his kin and friends dead? He certainly did not want to become like Ragnar, wandering around with Dimos until death arrived.

Sophia shouted.

Ragnar looked up, his eyes widened, then he looked to Thorfast.

The light crack of a slap echoed over the wide clearing. Thorfast's stomach tightened and his face grew hot. He turned toward Sophia.

She stood apart from Dimos, who held his hand to his cheek. Sophia glared at him, and Thorfast noted her left hand was feeling for the dagger hidden on her opposite hip. She had better not reveal that now, he thought.

"Dimos!" he shouted. "Have you insulted my wife?"

He straightened up and wiped his hands on his pants. His spear had been set against a low rock. He was keenly aware of it but resisted the urge to escalate the trouble. Now was not the time, not with the Byzantines arriving today.

"He tried to grab me," Sophia said, backing away. "He wanted me to stay in his tent tonight."

Dimos set his jaw and folded his arms. Thorfast met the challenge and stood before him with hands on his hips. He met Dimos's dark eyes and determined he would not flinch. Every other man had gone silent and still, frozen over whatever work they were in the midst of. Thorfast was aware of them as fuzzy shapes in the corners of his sight. He drilled his gaze into Dimos.

He turned aside with a dry sniff, then raised up his hands. He rattled off excuses in Greek. Sophia protested back, wagging her finger at him.

"Have a care, woman," he said from the corner of his mouth. "We're not in your father's house anymore, if you haven't noticed."

That wisdom caught her short and she withdrew her hand to her chest. Still frowning, she translated for Dimos.

"He said I misunderstood him and that he just wanted my help with mending a hole in his tent. He says I heard something else."

"That's what he said, brother." Ragnar joined him, the only other of Dimos's men bold enough to move.

Thorfast matched Dimos's scowl. He spoke in Norse, not trusting Sophia to get his words right.

"Well, I'll let it go. But you're warned. Never lay your hand on my wife again, even in innocence, or I'll cut it off and feed it to you."

"Brother, I don't think I'll translate that exactly. He knows you're angered."

"Gods! I must learn these languages for myself. Am I so bold that my words cannot be spoken as I've said them?"

Thorfast grabbed Sophia and pulled her aside, more to ensure everyone realized she belonged to him. Surprisingly, she did not resist but stumbled after him. Once he drew away from the others, he glared back at them. They faded back to their work, and Dimos crossed to where his tent had been set. He did not carry it himself, but had one of his men bear it for him.

"He just grabbed you in front of everyone?" He turned to Sophia, who continued to frown past him at the others.

"Why did you join us to these fools?" She folded her arms, still not looking at him. "You could have stepped aside and let them take that boy. The parents had made an agreement."

"And their charity would've remained after I surrendered their son? Think on it. They would see it as betrayal of their kindness. They would seek to lay blame for their loss, and we would take it. If they didn't set us back on our own then they might've fetched Arabs to take us away. No matter how I decided, we were not going to remain safe. So I chose this lot. They at least have weapons and share a common enemy."

Sophia shifted her eyes to him. She glared hard, but soon her expression eased and she sighed.

"You are right," she said. "I suppose I also want someone to blame for all this. I've placed it with you. Yet really it's all my fault. I acted so naively when I learned of Fausta's plot against my father. Had I at least organized protection for myself first, then I would not be standing here now."

"But I would've died without you," Thorfast said. He took her hand again, this as a lover would. "And the world would suffer so much for my loss."

Her expression caught between confusion and laughter. She tugged her hand free and smiled. "You are strangely lighthearted considering our situation."

"I am," he agreed, turning back to check on Ragnar. He had returned to pitching their tent with his companion. "I've learned that we are meeting here today with real Byz, er, Roman soldiers."

Sophia's eyes went wide. "Romans? Are we closer to the border than we know?"

"We must be." Thorfast shrugged. He scanned the glare of the horizon. The thin drizzle had faded, leaving behind the scent of rain and a sheet of haze to obscure the distance. "Of course, I wouldn't know where the border really lies. But from what I gathered from Ragnar, Dimos works with these Romans on a regular basis. They resupply him. I would assume your Roman friends support bands like Dimos to harass their enemies."

"The enemy of my enemy," Sophia said. Despite her nodding gravely at her own words, Thorfast did not truly understand.

"Something like that. Romans use bandits to kick the Arabs in the balls once in a while. It's a good trick. Not the way my people go about wars, but this isn't my place to say. What I will say, though, is that Roman soldiers can help us return to your family."

Sophia clasped her hands together and answered breathlessly. "Yes! Dear God, I will get home at last."

"I wouldn't jump that far just yet," he said. "We need to see what they are about. Besides, they've come here with their own duties to fulfill. They're not going to sweep you home because you showed them your shapely calves."

"What are you talking about? I would never lower myself like that."

Thorfast pursed his lips.

"Don't be too fast to decide against doing so. Men sometimes need encouragement. Anyway, let's just you and I stick close. Once the Romans are here I will get you before their leader to explain our situation. We'll have to do it out of Dimos's sight. After all, he'll be losing two prizes if we march off with the Romans. He'll try to prevent that from happening."

They returned to help create the camp. By late afternoon they were sitting on stones or cloaks folded out over the wet grass. Sophia and Thorfast kept themselves alone, with Ragnar butting in.

He would be harder to lose, Thorfast thought. Perhaps Ragnar would be willing to come. At least he was a Norsemen, if only a Dane. He would be good company around a campfire and in a battle.

They sat in a half-circle at the edge of camp. Seven weather-stained tents bobbed with the low wind behind them. With nothing to do but wait and with no one sharing a language common to all, the day passed in halting conversations.

The Romans arrived at twilight without announcement. Dimos had posted a single sentry, and rather than warn the camp of the Romans he had simply returned with them.

They did not match the descriptions Sophia had reeled out all afternoon while anticipating them. Nor did they look like the Byzantines Thorfast had faced at Pozzallo. They were supposed to be stout men in heavy leather armor clad with iron plates. Their shields were to be body-length rectangular works of iron and painted in brilliant colors. Their spears were to gleam and the plumes of their helmet were to dance in the wind.

The Romans that did appear were little better than vagabonds in tattered green cloaks. They climbed over the rise with Dimos's sentry in the lead. Thorfast counted about fifteen men. They gathered together at the edge of the camp, as if waiting to pass through an invisible door.

Dimos came forward, arms outstretched. Muted greetings were exchanged between some of Dimos's band and counterparts in the Roman group. Others stayed back like Thorfast and Sophia.

"That's Sergius Barbas," Ragnar said, pointing to the squat but solid man who greeted Dimos. The name drew Sophia's attention, and she leaned across Thorfast's shoulder to get a better view.

"They look no better than us," he said. "I'm a bit let down."

"Don't be," Ragnar said. "Under their cloaks are leather armor set with iron studs. Their swords might be short but they're keen and they wield them like heroes. Each one of them can disappear from sight if there's a tree or bush within a spear's length of them. You will be impressed, brother."

As Dimos's newest members, they received no attention. Sergius and Dimos spoke in hushed voices. The Roman commander pointed out a number of his men. These came forward with heavy sacks they set beside Dimos's feet.

"Gold," Ragnar said. "And other supplies. Oil for our weapons, flints, salt. Everything we need."

"A kingly life indeed," Thorfast said dryly.

The Romans began to make their own camp and Dimos met with Sergius in his tent.

"You need to get me to that Sergius fellow," Sophia said once he had slipped inside the tent.

"You're the only woman here," Thorfast said, stretching. "He'll find you soon enough and ask to see you. Dimos will get mad about it, but I'll be in a sudden good mood and let you have some time with him."

She stared after the tent, squinting. "I hope he is an honorable man. He's Roman, at least."

"I'm not sure honorable men exist," Thorfast said. "But remember what I said about showing him some leg. Don't be surprised if he wants to see quite a bit more before he's convinced to escort you anywhere. And also don't be surprised if he fails to do anything more than claim you for himself."

Sophia touched the base of her neck and raised her brows.

"But you'll protect me? You're my husband, after all."

Thorfast laughed. "The lie soon becomes the truth, eh? I will protect you. I've sworn myself to it. And if the three whore-sisters have weaved the thread of death into my fate, then I spit on their loom and go defiantly. I am a great warrior, but not one to set back fifteen professional soldiers of the Roman army on my own."

She stared at the tent in silence, her hand still resting on her neck.

The other Romans mingled in conversation with Dimos's men. Thorfast and Sophia remained apart with Ragnar for company. They sat on their cool, hard rocks and waited in silence. Soon the Romans were craning their necks toward her.

"Your woman is going to get attention," Ragnar said. "Like us, these men spend their time hiding from the Arabs and moving place to place. Not sure what they'll think of a woman in their camp."

The sun burned below the horizon and the sky flared orange and yellow. No fires were struck. Whatever meal would be taken tonight would again be cold and salted meat. Sophia took Thorfast's arm as if she feared a sudden wind might whisk her away.

Then Dimos's tent flap opened and the shadowy shape of Sergius appeared framed against its yellowed cloth. He looked right at them.

"Sophia Palama," he called out from across the camp.

She squeezed Thorfast's arm tighter and looked to him.

"These Romans are our best chance," he said. He raised her head by her chin and smiled. "I will be near. If he forces you or hurts you, call out to me. I will kill him where he stands. I swear it."

"I have to get home to my father," she said in a shaky whisper. "I have to prevent Fausta from destroying everything my family has achieved."

"You will. Now don't keep our rescuer waiting."

Sergius waited with arms akimbo, his stocky body an inscrutable shadow. Dimos stood beside him, though Thorfast could read the outline of a smirk in the dying light of the sun.

Sophia dipped her head and raised her skirt as she started toward the Roman commander.

"It must be hard, brother. I fear your wife will have to entertain him this night."

Thorfast instead glared at Dimos.

"She will be fine," he said. "But I fear tonight will turn bloody."

14

Thorfast lay in the grass as close to Sergius's tent as he dared. For once he was glad his pale hair had been shaved down to stubble, though now it was a thick white mat atop his head. Still, it was easier to hide than swaying locks that betrayed him in low light like a white flag streaming from his head. He heard a cough from the tent and instinctively flattened out. The scent of damp earth pressed into his nose as he held still.

The half-moon was hidden behind thick clouds. He had timed his movements to its intermittent appearances. Sweat still matted his face despite it being near midnight. He blinked it away as he stared at the tent.

No more sound or light came from it, no matter how he strained to detect anything. The entire camp remained equally dark and silent.

Ragnar had learned they were linking up for more than just resupply. They were going to make a joint strike at an Arab supply train heading toward the border.

"I hear there's going to be a battle," Ragnar had said while clapping his hands together. Like a true Norse sea wolf, he was hungry for any battle even if it was not his own. "The Romans want to draw off some of the Arabs and to hurt their supply. Looks like we'll be in the thick of it soon, brother."

So they had all gone to their tents at sunset with the orders to rest well for the upcoming days. Sophia had disappeared into Sergius's tent with one tentative look back to Thorfast. He felt a strange sensation when she ducked beneath tent flap. It was made of cleaner cloth. It was military and precise. But it was only tall enough for a grown man to sit. Knowing that Sophia would lie with Sergius in this tent made his breath come faster and his stomach tighten.

He had taken up a tent with Ragnar and left a space for Sophia on the assumption she would return during the night. Ragnar had offered a sympathetic nod and pat on the shoulder, but nothing more. But when the crickets were chirping and the wind rustling the grass and rippling along the tents in the depth of night, Thorfast remained waiting. He snuck away while Ragnar snored.

Surely she would need him, he thought. She was probably gagged and unable to call out. If he could get close enough, he might hear her struggle and her muffled call for help. Maybe she had been given over to Dimos as a gift. That bastard. Sophia is no slave to be traded like property.

He rested in the grass, spear held close to his side. The single sentry posted at the only logical approach had nodded off, resting his back against a rock and curling over his knees.

When he failed to detect anything more than a cough from Sergius's tent, he crawled forward. When he drew close enough to jab his spear through the rear of Sergius's tent, he stopped.

No sound came from it.

But sound came from beyond it.

Thorfast pressed down wishing he could meld into the ground. He heard the distinct swish of footsteps across the grass. The sound came in a flurry, then halted, only to resume again.

And it drew closer.

His hand tightened over the spear. On his belly, he was at a complete disadvantage. Still he pulled the shaft closer and hoped his plain, earth-toned clothes would mask him in the darkness.

Yet the figure swished past him. He glimpsed the man, bent at the waist to cut his profile and head tucked in as if walking into a storm. He moved through the shadows thrown by the clouds. But now that he had cleared the line of tents, he stood and strode with more haste than caution. He slipped through a pool of silver moonlight.

Dimos.

"You little bastard," Thorfast whispered to himself. "You're up to no good."

Thorfast scrabbled around in the grass to watch Dimos flee up the slope. He was headed away from camp. Thorfast knew nothing of the land but could not guess why Dimos would go where others claimed no one could travel. He carried something heavy and unstable in his arms. He seemed about to drop it, then paused to gather it back up.

He might be going to relieve himself away from camp, Thorfast thought. He acted with suspicion, but Thorfast knew he was inclined to judge him harshly. So he decided not to alert anyone yet, but to follow and learn his motives before doing more.

He crawled forward feeling like a lizard in the grass. Every time he prepared to stand, Dimos looked back as if he knew someone followed. The warm night air blew across Thorfast as he crawled, catching his shirt and billowing up his back. On knees and elbows he chased Dimos until he finally disappeared over a rise.

Groaning with relief, he clambered to his feet then collected his spear. In imitation of his prey, he too ducked down and tucked his head in as he strode to catch up. When he reached the rise where Dimos had vanished, he fell flat again. He inched up until he was even with the edge. Remembering that his hair, though short, could still blaze under the moonlight, he pulled his shirt overhead as a makeshift hood. Then he peered over.

The ground fell away into a rocky slope that was all black darkness. Thorfast's breath caught when he did not see Dimos. Maybe he was waiting in ambush. He pulled his spear close, but saw nothing.

Yet he heard rocks and dirt sliding away. He looked toward the noise, and at the bottom of the slope he found Dimos again. He emerged from the shadow into a pool of light. The half moon shined through a hole in the clouds and poured a veil of light over the rough stones of another ledge. Dimos halted there, his broad shoulders painted white in the moonlight.

He drew up into a crouch and flopped his burden down. He then turned toward the ridge and stared. No longer was he fearful, but seemed like a hawk on a perch lazily surveying the land for its prey. He seemed to look right at Thorfast.

Knowing sudden movement would betray him, Thorfast held still. He trusted to distance and darkness and prayed Dimos had poor sight. He remained crouched and staring, as if wings would unfold then send him swooping to snatch Thorfast away.

But Dimos was no hawk and his sight did not penetrate the darkness. He instead turned to the ridge and peered down. He picked up a stone and tossed it over the side, then waited.

In the space of a few breaths, Dimos leaned over on hands and knees and called down. He gave a tentative wave to someone below. His voice did not carry beyond deep, mumbled tones. Yet Thorfast understood he had signaled to someone.

Now Dimos stood and stepped back from the ridge. He searched around until he found whatever he sought, then turned to his burden. He pulled out a length of rope. Shaking and holding it up, he revealed a rope ladder outlined in moonlight.

Thorfast scowled at Dimos as he tied off each side of the rope ladder to something hidden in the darkness. He thought to run back to camp with a warning, but he needed to see what climbed up that ladder. If it was merely a forbidden lover, he thought, his spying on Dimos would bring him great shame.

Dimos had secured then dropped the rope ladder over the ledge. After a brief wait, he crouched down and extended his arm. Thorfast saw he did not meet with a lover.

An Arab dressed in his traditional robes and head cover took Dimos's outstretched hand. Clouds wandered before the moon and cut the light in half. The scene turned shades of gray. Yet there was no mistaking the dull-colored robes and the black head covers. The Arab wore a short sword and carried a curving dagger in his belt.

Directly behind him, another Arab reached up from the rope ladder. Dimos pulled him over and gestured him to join the other.

He turned back to await another Arab.

Thorfast scrabbled back from sight. His heart thundered in his chest.

They had been betrayed. For whatever reason, Dimos must have sold his own men and Sergius's to the Arabs. It had to have been a plan long in the making.

He was aiding them in a night attack. The moonlight was perfect for it, and the terrain was suited for a massacre.

Gods, Thorfast thought. The terrain. There is one way out of camp and the Arabs are striking from a place no one would expect. They are going to herd us onto the main force that will ambush us on the way out. We're trapped.

He blinked into the darkness. If this had been a long-planned trap, designed to rid the Arabs of harassing enemies before their main attack at the Byzantine border, then the Arabs would strike in force. He did a quick count in his mind, figuring thirty for his own side. This would mean the Arabs, armed with Dimos's reports, would bring at least double the numbers to ensure a smooth victory.

He stood and ran at a crouch for a short distance, then once sure he was out of anyone's sight he sprinted back toward the camp.

A dark shape lurched out at him as he reached the camp perimeter. He nearly shouted in surprise as the form grabbed for his spear.

"Where have you been, brother?" Ragnar whispered. His warm hand clamped down on Thorfast's arm to prevent an accidental strike.

"Dimos is bringing Arabs over the ledge," he said. He did not lower his voice now, as the camp needed to be alerted. "I left him with three already mounted. I've no guess how many more will come. But there will be enough to send us fleeing and the rest of the Arabs will be waiting in ambush."

"What?" Ragnar shook his head. "Dimos?"

"Go see for yourself," Thorfast hooked his thumb back toward the ridge. "But don't be seen."

"I don't believe you," Ragnar said, frowning. "I will go see for myself. This had better not be a trick."

"It is a trick," Thorfast said, wresting his arm from Ragnar's grip.

"But it's Dimos's. He's tired of this life, and so he has betrayed us to the Arabs in trade for a new life with them. I'm certain. Go watch and warn us of their approach. I'll rouse Sergius."

Ragnar frowned, but sped off toward Dimos. Thorfast hurried to Sergius's tent. He tore it open, expecting to find him entwined with Sophia. The danger was too near for him to confront Sergius now. He would deal with the Roman later, if they survived.

But when he ripped open the flap and ducked his head within, he found both Sophia and Sergius asleep under a light red blanket. They touched their backs together like familiar lovers sharing a peaceful night. He stared at them. Somehow it felt worse than if Sophia was being held against her will.

"Get up!" he shouted, louder than he needed. He wanted to see the both of them jump.

Sophia shot up, the blanket falling away to reveal she had not even disrobed for sleep. She blinked against the low light following Thorfast inside the tent.

Sergius also shot upright, revealing he had not removed his clothes either. Though whatever dreams might have occupied him were now gone. He gave Thorfast a hard look and spoke harsh, incomprehensible words.

"Sophia, tell him Arabs are coming. We have a short time to act before we are overrun."

Sophia rubbed her eyes with the backs of her wrists.

"Gods, woman! Sorry to have ruined your beautiful night of rest. Tell him!! Hurry!"

He backed out of the tent and looked to where Dimos had gone. It was dark and quiet. Had he not seen the Arabs climbing over the ridge, he would doubt that way offered any threat. He turned to where the sleeping sentry hunched against his rock. He should awaken him as well, but Sergius needed to understand first.

Now both he and Sophia emerged from the tent. Shadows filled the angry lines of his face in the low light. Despite having just awakened, he carried his sword and was already buckling the strap across his chest.

"He says that you better—"

"Have a good reason," Thorfast interrupted waving his hand before his face. "I do. Translate this for me."

He reeled off all he had seen and all of what he guessed, omitting his spying on Sergius's tent, which no one needed to know. Sophia rapidly translated into Greek.

Sergius stared hard at him while he spoke, shadowed creases deepening across his brow. During this time, the other Romans had awakened to the voices. These soldiers had crawled out of their tents to listen. Now, they ducked back inside to fetch their weapons.

When he was finished, Ragnar sprinted out of the dark. Thorfast gave a grim smile, knowing he would bring confirmation. He was breathless, and leaned on his knees as he spoke. "You were right. A dozen or more Arabs are already up there and still more are coming."

"Tell him that," he said, pointing to Sergius. "Ragnar and I'll get the others prepared."

Thorfast ran among the tents shared by Dimos's men. He tore open flaps and shouted the occupants awake. None of them understood what he shouted, but the urgency was clear enough. They scrambled into the night, shirtless men rubbing their eyes and protesting. He hushed them to silence.

Sergius organized his men with less commotion. He also held Sophia close to his side.

"Ragnar, explain things to them," he said. "I will arrange a plan with the Roman."

Sophia saw him coming and pulled free of Sergius, who let her go with no more than a glance. She ran the short distance to him.

"Stay with me," he said. "Keep your dagger ready, and we will escape."

"Are we surrounded?" Her eyes were wide and bright in the dark. She pressed against him, grabbing his arm. "I cannot go back to the Arabs. I have to get home. Please, you have to keep your word to me."

"I will," he said, gently removing her grip on him. "But we have little time to prepare. I need you to translate for me with the Roman. Come."

Sergius had his men lined up, each one now in their leather

armor and tattered robes. Their weapons were prepared, but kept sheathed. He greeted Thorfast and spoke his commands.

"He says you should take your men to confront Dimos while he takes his to clear the path off the hill. Then we should flee into the countryside to diffuse their attack."

Both waited on Sophia's translation to finish, but Thorfast was already frowning before she did. Sergius inhaled to give more orders, but Thorfast cut in first.

"Do not ask Dimos's men to confront him. Others could be in on his plans. Send me and the men down first. You and your men raise a din here. We will make it seem as if we are fleeing the attack. They will spring their trap, and you will follow on behind."

As Sophia translated, Sergius began shaking his head. Thorfast remained undeterred.

"They will have numbers over us, but their flaw was in splitting their force. We deny their flanking force a target, at least for a while, and make them useless. If we spilt our own force we will surely be destroyed. So we move as one group and punch a hole in their lines before. We will break free and force them to give chase in the dark. Once we lose them then we can disperse, but with order so we can find ourselves again at a place you choose."

Sergius's frown faded and he nodded agreement. He snapped a few words to him, then began explaining to the others. Dimos's men too had huddled closer, led by Ragnar. They mumbled timidly as Sergius detailed the plan.

"He liked your plan," Sophia said. Thorfast laughed.

"That's clear. Now we just need to hope the Arabs have not been watching our camp or they will know we are alerted. Success rests entirely on surprise."

She nodded, then pulled the dagger from beneath her dress. It flashed in the night.

"I'm ready."

"So are the others," he said. Then he turned to Ragnar. "We all know our parts. Look like we're fleeing and expect an attack from all sides as we run down that slope. Let's show these dogs how Norsemen fight."

Ragnar clapped his hands together. "We will kill a score each."

With no time to spare, Thorfast led Dimos's men to the edge of camp. He signaled that Sergius should begin their mock attack.

The Romans shouted and began to clang swords together. After a few passes, one sounded a horn.

"Let's run," Thorfast said as he readied his spear. Sophia stood to his left and made the sign of the cross. Then they both started to run down the slope lit only with murky light.

The crew let up a cry and followed.

Halfway down the slope, Arabs shouted as they sprang from the darkness.

15

The Arabs struck like pale phantoms out of a murky nightmare. Their billowing robes flowed over their bodies, heightening their ghostlike visage. They shrieked and raised curving blades overhead. Thorfast wore a grim smile as he ran. Even though he had anticipated the attack, the sudden appearance of enemies before and beside him sent a chill into his guts.

Moonlight spilled onto the slope as if the gods had pulled aside the clouds to better view the battle. The spotty grass turned deep blue in the light. Black shadows filled the ridges and rocks that flanked the path. More enemies were revealed in the splash of light.

A half-dozen Arabs ran directly at Thorfast as he was in the lead of his men. Out of the corners of his vision, other Arabs swooped in to press the sides of his column. Their war cries pounded against his eardrums.

The wisdom of his plan suddenly broke apart at the sight of these enemies. With only Sophia to his left and Ragnar on his right and no shields between them, he felt naked. Arab blades would slice his flesh to the bone and they would leap his corpse to attack the next victim.

But then a direct attack was never his plan.

"Fall back!" he shouted in Norse, meaning only Ragnar understood.

He barred Sophia with his arm, then pulled her back. Ragnar skidded to a halt, and started to fall back as commanded.

The rest of Dimos's men did not need the encouragement. They were already screaming and scrabbling away from the Arabs' assault.

Thorfast had no time to plan with them. So he had set his own plans according to what he expected of Dimos's men. They were opportunists and he doubted they ever fought an enemy stronger than themselves. He expected them to flee and so they did. They ran back toward Sergius seeking protection from the better-trained soldiers.

The Arabs, however, had not expected a swift retreat. Truly ambushed men would be stunned before reacting. In that gap, their initiative would be lost and they would be run down. But Dimos's men all knew the Arabs awaited and so turned heel the instant they had struck.

The Arabs' attack was like a hand snatching at a fly. It lashed out with suddenness and force, but its target had already slipped away leaving them empty-handed.

"Why are we running?" Ragnar shouted as he fled alongside Thorfast.

"To get them lined up before us," he said. "Look now."

As expected, the Arabs had sprung a gauntlet on them which when closed left behind a fist. They were now gathered at the bottom of the slope, reorganizing their attack. By quick count, Thorfast guessed thirty enemies were lined before them. It was a rough match to their own force.

"And now Sergius joins," he said. He smiled at Ragnar and nodded up the slope.

The Roman led his men in their full battle gear. Their swords and spears gleamed with the moonlight. Their hoods were drawn, casting their faces into shadow so each seemed a specter of battle ready to swoop down on their foes.

"And we have high ground," Thorfast said. "So let us begin killing!"

Sophia screamed and fell back.

Thorfast whirled to discover the Arabs had not wasted their moment. They were already bounding up the slope, and the first enemy to arrive held his sword in both hands at his side.

"We have to hold until Sergius gets here," Thorfast shouted to Ragnar.

"A shield wall, brother!" Ragnar shuffled closer. "None shall pass our blades."

The first Arab stabbed at Thorfast. But his spear easily prodded the Arab aside. He dipped the blade into the shoulder and found it cut the material with ease, drawing blood like blue ink in the moonlight.

Sophia shrieked again and backed up. Thorfast interposed himself between her and the injured Arab. His strike had been deflected, but he was only marginally wounded. His snarl was bright against the shadows of his beard.

But Thorfast wove his spear with precision. Though longsword and shield were his preferred weapons, like all Norsemen he had learned since his youth to fight with the spear. If he kept the Arab to the front, he would remain disadvantaged and eventually lose the struggle.

Yet Thorfast could not indulge in teasing away his enemy's defense. A dozen of his companions were already reaching their position.

His spear slammed past the Arab's sword and through the base of his neck. The blade caught on bone and Thorfast yanked it free before the falling body could bend the blade.

"Brother, Sergius has joined!" Ragnar stood over an Arab who looked as if he had curled up to nap. Yet Ragnar's longsword shined with dark blood.

The Roman led his men in a furious charge that slammed home into the Arabs rushing forward. Their swords rang and their battle cries echoed in the collision. The rest of Dimos's men, encouraged or else dragged along by the Romans, also joined the battle. With surprise lost, it was now a man to man battle.

Sophia screamed again and pushed Thorfast forward. He caught himself on his right foot in time to greet two Arabs rushing for him.

Without the comforting weight of a shield on his left arm, he had nothing to block. Instead, he fixed his spear lengthwise and caught both blades at once. He kicked the lead Arab in the side of the knee. The column of his leg collapsed with a crack and the Arab toppled.

He tipped is spear to dump the other Arab using his own force against him. The blade stuttered over the shaft, leaving behind white scores in the wood. But he was now on his hands and facing the ground. Thorfast impaled him through the kidney, withdrew, then whirled to face the next attacker.

The Arab with the broken knee had grabbed Sophia by her ankle. She fell beside him, and he clawed up with a dagger drawn.

She stabbed him through the arm, neither screaming nor struggling. The fearful woman had vanished and now a grimmer, more determined woman fought in her place.

The Arab released his grip and screamed. Sophia backed out of his reach, then kicked him in the face with her heel.

Thorfast could not determine the flow of battle yet. Both sides remained locked. Dimos's men and the Romans knew they had to fight their way through the Arab line. That realization lent desperate fury to their attack. But the clash had only just begun and only a handful of men lay in the grass.

He grabbed Sophia by her arm and hauled her up.

"Good work," he said. "But you're not going to hold up in this fight. I've got to get you away."

She began to speak, but he dragged her off the edge of the main battle where they fought. She stumbled after him as he found a spot at the edge of the path.

"It was good enough to hide the Arabs," he said, pointing at a patch of rocks and bushes. "Hide there. If I fall, then you should flee. Otherwise, watch me and follow. I will stay at the edge of the battle line."

"But we can both flee now," she said, looking down the slope into the shadowed night. "There's no one to stop us."

"I can't run from battle, woman!" He pushed her to the bushes. "They need me."

Without looking back, he bounded the short distance to rejoin the fight. He leapt the corpses of his first enemies. The press of men filled the slope from edge to edge. The Arab line buckled. Being lower on the slope meant the ground worked against them. They were easily shoved back. If one tripped then he would die.

"I thought you fled, coward!" Ragnar fought at the edge of battle, his sword buried in an Arab's gut. His face was splattered red.

"Leave me an enemy, brother. My spear is still fresh."

He leapt into the line next to Ragnar. Long had it been since he had fought a straight battle. Though the Romans were foreign warriors, they fought with organization familiar enough to him. They maintained a line and protected each other. It was not his way of fighting but he adapted.

The horrors of combat rippled over him and his lancing blade. The foulness of spilled bowels assailed his nose. The ear-splitting chime of iron on iron rang in his head. Sweat stung his eyes and his hands numbed to the battering of enemy weapons. Copper rolled along his tongue, blood from either himself or a foe. In the battle-craze he could not tell where the gore on his face had come from.

As in all battles he had ever fought, it seemed the enemy before him would never relent. Then, in the next strike, the enemy was gone. The Arabs retreated. One still attacking Thorfast struck low with his sword to create space, cursed in his strange language, then ran.

"It's a ruse," Thorfast shouted to Ragnar. His companion, however, knelt in the grass and held his leg. He did not seem to hear, bent over his wound as he was.

"Don't chase!" Thorfast shouted. But even had he shouted in their own language, Dimos's men were already speeding after the fleeing enemy.

The Arabs, he knew, were repositioning themselves to better ground. They had not lost the battle yet. Perhaps only a dozen Arab corpses lay on the ground. He looked back up the slope.

The group of Arabs that had planned to infiltrate the camp were now stalking them. Forgotten by all in the battle frenzy, they crouched low with drawn swords and dark robes fluttering in the blood-misted wind. They had just crested the rise as shadows against a brilliant moon.

"Sergius!" Thorfast leapt past Ragnar and found the Roman commander. His face was thick with blood and sweat. He had just finished an Arab that clung with both hands to the hem of his cloak. Hearing his name shouted, he snapped around to Thorfast.

"Are you so stupid?" He pointed with his blood-caked spear up the slope. "You knew they would come."

Sergius blinked then scowled. He kicked the dead Arab at his feet.

Thorfast read the expression as anger, hopefully at his own foolishness. But he could not blame the Roman too harshly, for in the lust of battle he had also forgotten the overall plan. That was something he had relied on Yngvar to do. His dearest friend had been a master at dreaming up a plan on the moment and holding it all in his head, even as he adapted it to new challenges. Thorfast had been content to fight alongside him and wait for direction. He regretted not learning more from Yngvar when he still lived.

Dimos's men sped away, either to chase the Arabs or else to flee for their lives. Sergius's men, however, kept their discipline. But now there were no more than ten of them.

"Here's the plan," Thorfast said, grabbing Sergius by his cloak. "Flee into the hill, onto the difficult paths. Let them chase. Some stay behind to delay, but give me five men. We will hit these Arabs from behind, kill their leader. That should end this battle, then we can flee."

His words bounced off Sergius, but he tried to pantomime his thoughts. The Arabs were halfway down the slope now. Some of their profiles vanished into the darkness of the earth. Perhaps they were just about to spring their attack.

Sergius nodded then began to shout to his men.

Thorfast turned and grabbed Ragnar off the ground. He held his leg with both hands, and hissed through his teeth as he was hauled to his feet.

"Out here you're a dead man," he said. "Get to the side. Come on, don't be a baby. I've seen men fighting with javelins through their balls. You can do this."

He tripped and stumbled to where Sophia hid between rocks and bushes. She popped up at his approach, her pale hair brilliant in the moonlight. She raised her pale arm and pointed behind.

He expected a sword to the neck as he wrestled Ragnar to the edge of the path. But instead he turned to see Sergius and his men fleeing into the dark just as the Arabs sprang their attack with shouts and horns.

Down the slope, he heard the other Arabs return their calls.

Ragnar slumped beside Sophia. His thigh glistened with brilliant scarlet. His hands were slick with blood.

"I'm going to die," he said.

"Sophia, tie his wounds and protect him."

"Protect him?" Her timid demeanor washed away with indignation. "Who will protect me?"

"God will," he said. He looked around but found none of Sergius's men had joined him. They had all taken to the invisible paths of the hill, probably to never be seen again. "And I hope he will protect me, too. I've got one last task before we flee."

"What task?" She grabbed his arm and pulled him close. "We must flee or else be captured. I have not come this far to fail."

He shook her arm free and glared at her. "Stay low and quiet. You will be fine here. What I go to do is for your benefit. Believe me."

Sophia held her arm to her side and backed away like a child shrinking from a raised switch. He realized he must seem a beast to her, red-faced and covered in blood. Yet he had no time to soothe her fear. She would appreciate him soon enough.

"My leg," Ragnar hissed through his teeth. "This really hurts."

"See about his leg," Thorfast said. "I will return soon and then we flee."

He left Sophia crouching down in the small ditch covered with bushes. He picked a short path through the rocks along the path, watching his left for enemies. The Arabs had not been foolish enough to pursue Sergius and his men into the darkness where the landscape would work against them. Instead they now rushed down the slope toward the dying cries of Dimos's men. They would be all killed, trapped between two enemies.

Once confident he had slipped past the last of the Arabs, he gained the path and charged up toward camp. He ran into its perimeter, finding most of the tents cut down by the Arabs that had passed through. But he was unconcerned with shabby tents. He sought a man here.

Dimos ducked out of what had been his tent. He cast a quick glance over his wide shoulders. The whites of his dark-ringed eyes were clear against the shadow of his face. Moonlight broke the scene into sharp divisions of blue light and perfect dark.

Thorfast ducked as if dodging a rock thrown at his head, but Dimos did not linger on him. Instead, he rushed to what had been Sergius's tent and slipped inside.

"That's right," Thorfast whispered. "Collect all the gold in one bag for me, you weasel. Make this easy. I have little time."

He raced across the destroyed camp, bloody hands tight on the smooth wood of his spear. If he timed this right, Dimos would emerge from the low tent onto the tip of his spear.

But Dimos burst out of the tent with his curved sword drawn. He must have heard Thorfast's feet thumping across the ground.

Loath to waste his momentum, Thorfast continued in hopes to overwhelm Dimos. He bounded three steps and lunged.

Dimos skipped aside and Thorfast crashed into the tent. He fell forward and brought it down over himself like pulling into bedcovers.

The scent of old leather and dirt filled his nose as he rolled through the ruins of the tent. The derisive laugh from behind spurred his recovery. He rolled aside. Dimos's sword chopped down, catching his left shoulder and slicing away a thin patch of flesh. The pain burned and blood bubbled up.

Yet he had avoided death, and laughed rather than cry out.

He levered himself upright with his spear while Dimos recovered from his rage-filled blow. In the next breath, the two of them squared off. Bloody spear tip faced a clean, gleaming sword blade. Across the weapons both men glared at each other.

By Dimos's feet sat two lumpy sacks. Doubtless the blood-gold he had been paid to betray his men and whatever else he had looted from the camp. Thorfast smiled, knowing it would be as good as an anchor stone to keep Dimos in place. He had given all for this treasure and would never surrender it.

"You got everything you wanted, except my woman," Thorfast said. "And I'm sure you had some mad plan to get her back from the Arabs."

Dimos narrowed his eyes and curled the corner of his mouth. He answered in his dry, breathless voice. The foreign words held no meaning but the challenge he offered was evident in the emphasis he gave his sword. He dared Thorfast closer.

"You really think you can best me?" He glanced to his bleeding shoulder. "You traded your life to give me this cut. I'll remember your foolishness every time I look at the scar."

Dimos barked another challenge.

Thorfast laughed. The gold at the bandit leader's feet radiated unseen power over him. He seemed ready to snatch at the bags and run, but knew he could not while Thorfast kept near.

"I'm not going to let you delay for help," he said. He pointed his spear at the gold. "That's what I really want. If you run, I'll let you go. Just leave it here."

They did not speak the same language though both understood the choice. Dimos's dark-ringed eyes flared with hatred. He lowered his sword and backed away. Thorfast waited, weapon ready. When Dimos hesitated, he brushed him back with his spear.

"Run," he said. "I'm not picking up the gold until you're gone."

Dimos stared longingly at his lost treasure. He made a poor act of sighing with resignation and turned as if to walk off. Thorfast wanted to hurry to the inevitable reversal, so he held his spear in one hand and made as if to bend over the gold.

As expected, Dimos whirled with sword raised. It would have been a good plan had Thorfast not expected it. Even so, Dimos might have had a better chance if Thorfast was armed with a sword. But he held a spear.

He skipped back as Dimos charged. He had gripped his spear ready for a cast, and so let it fly.

It sank into Dimos's chest. He collapsed to his knees then fell forward onto it, driving it out his back until the shaft snapped. He screamed, voice wet and hoarse. His blood rushed out over the sacks of gold as he died.

Thorfast kicked him over. "How poetic to die atop the gold you betrayed your men for, but stop bleeding on my treasure."

Dimos's eyes fluttered as life drained away. Thorfast picked out the two sacks from the fresh gore and set them aside. As he did, Dimos exhaled his last breath.

He retrieved Dimos's sword. The blade was honed white. He smirked at the corpse at his feet.

"What a coward. This hasn't even been used. But it will be now."

Grunting, he chopped off Dimos's head with three sharp blows. He pried it from the stump of the neck and let blood and fluid drain while he searched for a bag. Among the ruins, he found one as well as packs of rations and bladders of water. He gathered it all, then placed Dimos's head in the bag he had found.

Loaded with skins and packs strapped across his body and gold underarm, he returned to the edge of the camp. With Ragnar injured, he was unsure whether he and Sophia could bear everything away. Yet he would have no chance to return for any of this.

His lighthearted spirit put a spring to his step. This had been a horrid defeat for Sergius and the others. For Thorfast, it had simply set him back to the start. In fact, he was better off than when he first met Sophia. The gods had favored him.

As he reached the start of the sloping path, that joy fell away. He discovered Arabs swarming back up it toward the camp.

He was standing directly before them.

"And the gods laugh all the harder," he said.

16

Thorfast did not run at the approaching Arabs. The moonlight painted the slope silver and blue and rendered the Arabs as robed ghosts floating along the ground. Though he stood in plain view, they were expecting Dimos here. One shadow must seem like any other to them. So Thorfast had a moment to consider his next step.

The Arabs were loud, full of merriment and noisome boasts typical of victorious warriors. They moved through the humid night air with speed but not haste. They savored their victory. Thorfast was pleased to allow it to them.

But they interposed themselves between Sophia and himself.

He could not run, not while burdened with two sacks of gold, packs of supplies, and Dimos's severed head in a bag. None of these were anything he would willingly surrender. All had a purpose to their survival.

Yet there would be no survival if he remained trapped atop this craggy hill.

He turned back toward the camp as if he were Dimos awaiting the return of his conspirators. He had hoped the Arabs would have lingered at the base of the slope. Now he was forced to abandon what he had risked his life to obtain. The packs sloughed to the ground. He kept a skin of water, the smaller sack of gold, and the sword. He debated the worth of Dimos's head now. It might have fetched a bounty from Sergius had be been able to find him again.

He dumped it out beside the gold. It thumped softly to the ground and rolled back up to face him. His dead eyes were wide and staring.

"You got the gold after all," Thorfast said. "Tricky little bastard, you."

With his burdens lightened, he ran for the high ridge where the rope ladder had been set. The gold jangled in the sack as if laughing at him for choosing it over rations. He could buy food he needed now. So he clutched the sack tighter to his side to silence it. As he reached the ledge where the rope ladder was set, he heard the whooping of the Arabs behind him.

He gave one last look toward the camp. How he would find Sophia and Ragnar again was beyond him. The thought of abandoning them soured his spirits. But he consoled himself knowing the gods had made the choice for him. He knew nothing of these hills or how to get back to his friends besides following the path. He might be able to find them if he could follow the slope up from the base, which for now remained impossible. Retreat was his only other option.

So he set his foot on the rope ladder, testing its strength. Then he scrabbled down a sheer cliff that felt as high as a mountain peak. No wonder everyone believed no enemy could approach from this side of the hill. The rock was cool and hard as he bumped his knees against it during the descent. At last, he came to its end and leapt into softer grass.

He had come to a gentle slope that flowed out to a stretch of field that would eventually lead to more hills. The ground was trampled flat by the dozen or more Arabs that had gathered here to scale up with Dimos's help. A quick search revealed a stand of dark trees.

Though the enemy was near, they were also high up on a cliff and would be wasting their time to search for a lone man. They would find Dimos and his gold, and assume he had been murdered by one of his own. They would probably laugh as they reclaimed their bribe and threw his body from the very cliff he had helped them climb. The Arabs would also have their own wounded to occupy them.

He pushed into the trees and scooped out a nest among the bushes. No matter how desperate the situation, sleep was always available in the hours after battle. In the warm shadows, blanketed in the scents of earth and leaves, he fell asleep with his hand on his drawn sword.

The next morning, sun slashed between the branches to form a lattice of light across his face. He awakened to bird song and the gentle whispering of leaves ensconcing him. Wakefulness brought stiffness and soreness to his every joint. Exertions of battle were never felt until the next day. It was the revenge of the slain upon the living. His shoulder wound, nothing more than a burn from the last night, was a roaring flame this morning. The stitches of his hip wound felt as tight as a cat's jaws clamped to his skin.

He groaned and carefully raised to his side. His hideout had been set no more than a hundred paces from the base of the cliff. He looked to it now, not finding the rope ladder he expected to still dangle there. This chased away the vestiges of sleep. His eyes now widened and searched for signs of the Arabs. Had they descended during the night? Were they on top of him now?

But if the ladder was gone, then it had to have been drawn up. A rope ladder of that length was a valuable thing, and not something to cut down and cast off. So the Arabs had claimed it, content to let whoever had slipped them remain to be caught another day.

Thorfast breathed a sigh, realizing he was unimportant to the Arabs. They had come to destroy enemy harassers in their territory, apparently ones that had been long evading capture. To that end, they had succeeded.

He pushed up, ducking against heavy branches of these strange trees. They were tall and thin, with dark leaves that brushed against his face. The bushes surrounding him were filled with red berries, but he did not trust these to eat. He could scarcely forage in his homeland of Frankia. How much worse would he fare here? So he patted the sack of gold. Someone would sell him what he needed.

He stepped out into the light, but held to the edge of the trees. He returned his sword to the sheath. Rust was already forming on its edges, or perhaps Dimos had not cared for his blade. No matter, the sword needed scouring and oil to remain useful. Again, gold could buy him these.

The only barrier to buying what he needed was language.

Sophia and Ragnar were on the top of that giant, rocky hill. He owed it to return for them, at least for Sophia. Ragnar was in the hands of the gods now. So he sipped from his skin of water, held his hand against the rumbling of his stomach, then set off to relocate the slope back up the hill.

Though only early morning, the sun was already lashing the land with heat. Flies had found him and he let these dance across his exposed skin. He followed the contours of the hill until he came to the slope base.

As expected, the Arabs had carried away all the dead, friend or foe. Their own would need proper burials and their enemies would be carted to wherever their corpses would warn other rebels of the price for resistance.

He picked his way up the slope. But in the light everything seemed different. He did not know where he had left Sophia and Ragnar. He had not come this way when he separated from them. So he called their names as loudly as he dared, but earned no reply. He pulled aside every likely bush and revealed nothing.

At last he found a familiar spot. Blood had dripped across a rock and the bushes and grass were flattened here. The blood was dried and did not seem like a spray from a fresh cut. It had been drizzled like from an open wound. Nothing else revealed who was here.

But he determined if this had been Sophia and Ragnar's place, then they had gone deeper into the less hospitable parts of the hill. They had left a trail, and Ragnar's blood let him follow a short distance. Looking back up to the peak, he realized the Arabs were still there. Dark smoke from their campfires rose into the air.

The trail was difficult among the rocks, but as long as he made a careful study, he found the telltale blood drops to show the way. He was heading back down the mountain through narrow paths that allowed only a single man to pass at once.

Soon he returned to the foot of the hill where the blood trail led off into heavy bushes. Someone had rested here, much as he had. The ground was flattened out and branches and brush had been cut to form a hiding place. But now it was empty.

He touched his hand to one hollowed-out bed of leaves and drew away sticky blood. Scanning around, he could not determine where they had gone. Then he heard a dog barking. He had heard it the day before and suspected a village was nearby.

Perhaps they were friendly to the Byzantines? Even if they were not, the remains of Sergius's force would be enough to overtake any farmers in the area. Sophia was not strong enough to have had carried Ragnar this far on her own. One of Sergius's Romans had fetched them down from their hiding place. Perhaps they had led them to this village.

He followed the distant echo of the barking dog, taking no effort to disguise himself. A lone man was neither threat nor reward to the Arabs, unless perhaps they thought him to be Sergius. A man like him would be a worthy bounty. The dog's incessant barking meant the animal felt threatened, probably from the strangers that had descended on its home. So Thorfast confidently passed into a shaded path through a line of more tall, narrow trees.

The land carried the barking much farther than he expected. For he walked near half an hour before emerging from the maze of trees to the loudest barking of the dog. He stood before a large, low home made of cream stucco and brown roof tiles. White smoke rolled along the tiles until catching the draft up to the blue morning sky. A wood fence surrounded a yard beside it, and the dog was tied to it by an iron chain. It sat on its haunches, gray and brown fur blending it into the grassy yard.

Two men with tattered robes stood outside the door, leaning on spears. The dog barked at them.

Thorfast raised his hand and waved. These were Sergius's men. He quickened his pace as a smile came unbidden to his face. As he drew closer, the men nodded to him but the dog leapt with a snarl. Its chain yanked it back, and the poor dog twisted and strained against it.

"Sergius?" he asked as he joined the men guarding the front door. It was the only word he could share in common with these men. Their faces were dirty and rusty stains speckled their cloaks. They furrowed their brows at the name, then laughed when Thorfast repeated himself.

"You two boy-lovers would last not a single day in the north," he said with a false smile. "Let me inside to food and drink or you won't be laughing much longer."

He enjoyed the threat as a vent for his frustration. The two guards opened the doors and gestured him inside. Out of habit, he thought to set aside his weapon before entering. But not in these lands. Besides, hadn't Sergius slept with Sophia? These Romans might not be friendly under the light of a new day. He slipped past both guards with one hand by his sword hilt and the other holding his gold.

Inside was dark and smoky. A half-dozen men stretched out on the pounded earth floor. A small, half-circle hearth blazed with fire on the far end. The heat, already miserable, was worsened for it. Two women bent over a black iron pot there. One was swarthy skinned and plump, wearing a single robe of plain beige cloth pinned at the shoulder. The other was more delicate and her brilliant hair shined in the low light.

"We thought you were captured or worse, brother."

He turned left toward the familiar Norse voice. Ragnar sat among the men, his pant leg cut open to his hip. A bloody white bandage wrapped his thigh. Yet his handsome face shined with happiness.

"Had I been better rested I'd have killed all those Arabs myself." He flipped his hand in dismissal. "How fortunate for them."

"So you fled?"

"If you mean I traveled opposite the Arabs' approach, yes. I used Dimos's ladder to climb down the cliff."

"Don't speak that name, brother." A scowl replaced Ragnar's smile.

"There'll be no need to. I took many prizes up in that camp. Best of all was Dimos's head. I swear to you by all the gods, he is dead."

Ragnar stared hard at him, then nodded.

"He saved me once, only to trade my life for what?"

"Gold," Thorfast said, then patted the pouch he carried. "I shall pay you a share of it."

"I'd stand and kiss you, brother, if my leg would support me."

"Speaking of kisses." Thorfast turned toward Sophia, who had just stood back from the hearth to notice him. Her naturally severe expression unfolded to joy.

The hall was wide and furnishings and belongings of the owners had been shoved to the sides. Yet it was not so wide that he and Sophia could rush together in a happy reunion. Moreover, one wall was lined with smirking Romans who rested under their weather-beaten robes. He might trip over their legs in his rush. Sparing himself the horrific indignity of stumbling, he waited for Sophia to approach.

He swallowed hard. He only realized at this moment how much he had suppressed his worry for her fate.

"You seem to have fared well," he said, looking her over. Blood had dried on her skirt, melding into the faded brown fabric. "I hope that is Ragnar's blood and not yours."

She nodded, smiling, and touched his cut shoulder. "Can you go nowhere without taking a wound?"

"I ran into our friend, Dimos. But you should see him. In fact, I was going to bring his head so that you could. It was too much to carry. I brought us gold instead."

"I'd rather see gold," she said. Her smile had not faded and her eyes had not shifted from his. She massaged his wounded shoulder, which only heightened the pain. Yet he did not want her to stop. He wanted more of it, and more of her.

"I'd rather see your—"

The door opened again and Sergius rushed inside with another of his men. His stern gaze swept the room, then he began shouting commands.

Sophia withdrew her hand from Thorfast and touched her chest.

"The Arabs are moving," she translated. "They will follow here. We must go now."

The Romans groaned but threw aside their cloaks and gathered their weapons. Of the original men Sergius had brought, only nine remained. The swarthy woman in the robe rushed forward, chattering in panicked tones to anyone who would listen.

"She's worried what the Arabs will do to her when they discover their enemy hid here," Thorfast said. "Some things need no translation."

Sophia nodded. "This conflict brings nothing but suffering to the people caught between both sides. If the Arabs would just realize they have no claim on Roman lands, think how much better the people would be."

"The land belongs to those strong enough to hold it," Thorfast said. "I don't love the Arabs. But they are strong now. So they rule. Seems the Byz—Romans—bring grief to this land."

Why he had chosen to ruin this moment with Sophia escaped him. Whatever happiness she held at his arrival vanished with his brilliant Norse thinking. She stepped back with a frown.

"This is Roman ground, you savage. It was won by the blood of our ancestors and we will see it returned. By God, why would I think you could understand? You are a heathen from the north. You worship the bloodied blade. You trample the weak. You thieve from the Church."

"Well, I only meant to say—ah, Sergius! Yes, I have survived."

He was never so glad to have anyone interrupt him as he was for Sergius. The Roman leader clapped him on his uninjured shoulder and looked him over approvingly.

"He says you are looking fine for one he thought dead." Sophia's translation was sulky and she did not look at him as she spoke.

"I killed Dimos," he said. "I'd have delivered you his head. But I swear I left it separated from his body."

He barked a laugh at Sophia's translation. The others, hearing this as well, gave muted cheers as they collected their gear. Sergius then explained their situation, which Sophia translated.

"All of Dimos's men were killed or captured but for Ragnar. Sergius needs to return to his base to resupply and report on what happened here. They will also see us to the border, but we must go with them. It's to the north, not at all where I wanted to go."

Thorfast nodded. To him, it did not matter how long it took to get to the border or to fulfill Sophia's revenge on her enemies. He was drifting through this world, biding time until he could find a way to extract vengeance on Prince Kalim and the treacherous Moor, Jamil.

Sergius patted his shoulder once again and was about to turn away when he looked to the sack of gold still cradled in Thorfast's arm. His eyes went wide with delight. He pointed at it and gasped a few words.

Sophia gave him a wry smile.

"He's glad you found his gold. He worried it had all been lost."

Thorfast felt his arm tighten around it.

He was not letting it go.

17

"Do not argue with him over the gold," Sophia warned.

"We need this if we're to reach your home," Thorfast said. The gold weighed heavier in his arms now. He became aware of the sword hanging at his side by its threadbare baldric. Nine other Romans tightened the straps of their own weapons as they prepared to flee the approaching Arabs. The plump, dark-skinned woman who hosted them held onto one of the men and pleaded with him in Greek.

Sergius smiled and held out his hand.

Thorfast set the bag into the commander's palm. But he did not release it.

"Tell him my reward for returning his gold is that he must deliver us to wherever you really want to go."

"I cannot presume—"

"Tell him."

His curt exchange raised Sergius's brows. He did not close his hand around the sack of gold but listened to Sophia's translation. When she finished, he looked back to Thorfast. His expression flattened and his brows fell. He snatched the gold back and raised it high.

The other Romans cheered the sight of their lost treasure.

"You owe me your lives," Thorfast said in Frankish, hoping Sophia would translate. "I should be awarded all that gold, but I merely ask this single favor. Do you Romans have no honor?"

None of what he said was translated, but his anger silenced the celebration. Sergius squared up to the challenge. Sophia whispered a few words in Greek. He nodded, but tossed the heavy sack of gold to one of his men. It clinked as the Roman caught it. Sergius gave a short answer then returned to preparing with the others. The moment of tension dissipated.

"He had better have agreed," Thorfast said.

"Or you will best ten men with a dull sword and a blindfold over your eyes?" Sophia crossed her arms and shifted her weight to one leg.

"This sword is actually quite sharp. I could take them five at a time. Two strokes and they will all be fanning the devil's ass in hell."

"Well, then I've certainly found the right champion to aid me."

"And what was Sergius's answer? Will I need that blindfold?"

"He will escort us to where I wish to go. Though there are many Arabs in our path."

Thorfast bent his mouth in satisfaction. "You have quite a way with Sergius. Seems he regrets to let you go."

Sophia unfolded her arms and gave a wry smile. "You wonder about our lying together? He is just a lonely man, Thorfast. He has not seen his wife or family for two years while he serves the empire. He just wanted the company of a proper Roman woman for a night. He is a good Christian, and would not commit the sin of infidelity."

"Whatever that word means," Thorfast said, waving away the entire topic. "So we're going to wherever you've instructed him to deliver us?"

"He will take us to the fort at Pozzallo. My cousin has been named commander there after the previous commander was relieved for letting the Arabs climb the walls and losing ships. I don't know more details."

"Neither do I," Thorfast said, his heart suddenly racing. Of course, he and his fellow Wolves had raided Pozzallo as mercenaries. Yngvar and Alasdair had actually entered the fort and wreaked destruction. Now he was returning to seek refuge. The gods must be drunk with laughter at this.

Despite the urgency of the encroaching Arabs, Sergius and his men were not panicked. They murmured to each other as they filed outside to await their next order. Sergius gathered the frightened woman to one side, then pulled two gold coins from his sack and pressed them into her hands. This silenced her but her face remained creased with worry.

"Brother, looks like they're leaving me," Ragnar said, watching the last of the Romans exit into the morning light. He struggled to gain his feet, but his injured leg defied him.

"The right thing is to abandon you," Thorfast said. "You're a burden to everyone. So you should be brave and volunteer to remain behind."

Ragnar's face turned white and he dropped his head back against the wood wall. They stared at each other, then Thorfast reached out a hand.

"But I am prone to make mistakes. I cannot carry you, but can lend you my shoulder."

"I thought you really meant to leave me," Ragnar said, laughing.

"I did. But I'm sure Sophia would never let me live it down. So thank her Christian nonsense. You know as well as I, the strong live and the weak die. It's our way."

"I've said the same before." Ragnar grabbed Thorfast's hand. His palm was clammy. "But it is different when you're the weak one."

They both laughed, and Thorfast hooked Ragnar's arm over his shoulder. Outside, Sergius gave him a glance and quipped something.

"They won't delay for me," Ragnar said.

"Tell him I won't delay for him either."

Without another word, the entire group followed Sergius's direction toward a distant stand of dark trees. The dog tied to the fence strained to the length of his chain, barking them off the property.

The Romans showed Thorfast how little he knew of woodcraft or living off the land. They not only evaded the Arabs that trailed them but also any other living thing, man or animal. Even when they travelled grassy plains under the blinding sun they held to folds and dips that perfectly concealed them. These men made Alasdair, whom Thorfast had considered something of a ghost, seem as nimble as a stiff-legged old man. Sergius's scouts ranged ahead. They returned with reports and often with a hare or squirrel caught in the bargain. Otherwise, each night Sergius dispatched two men who returned with goods either stolen or traded from locals that Thorfast never realized were nearby.

They took a circuitous route that added days onto the journey. Sophia never complained. Though he and Ragnar mumbled their irritation as they limped along behind the others. One of Sergius's men fashioned a crutch for Ragnar after two days of letting him struggle. This relieved Thorfast for hours at a time, only having to help Ragnar onto hills or over rough ground.

The fiction of Sophia's marriage to him eroded with each passing day. She spent more time in friendly conversation with Sergius than he liked. Though they had lost all their tents to the Arabs, this still did not prevent Sergius from inviting Sophia to lay with him at night while everyone else bedded down under bushes or trees.

"That's your woman," Ragnar said every night as if he were discovering the fact for the first time. Thorfast said he planned to divorce her once he got home, which satisfied Ragnar until the next night where he would make the same observation.

The evening of the eighth day they completed a trek up steep hills and made camp. Sicily was all rocky green hills and groves, as far as Thorfast knew. The eerie similarity of this high hill to where they had been ambushed kept him awake all night. He was sluggish and slow to follow when they broke camp with the dawn.

So when he and Ragnar caught up to the others that had stopped to crouch behind a ridge, he had to blink his eyes to be certain he was not dreaming.

Hundreds of Arabs had gathered in a massive camp that filled the basin between him and the next range of mountains.

"A war camp," Thorfast said to Sophia, who rested beside Sergius.

"He says this is just one part of it. His men have been collecting rumors that the Arabs have gone into Roman territory to raze the countryside."

"To draw them out of their fort and into battle," Thorfast said. "And these bastards are hiding here to trap them when they do."

"He says there is a clear pass through those mountains that will lead to Pozzallo." Sophia shook her head. "But to reach it we must thread this Arab camp."

"There's no way around it?" Yet even as Thorfast asked, he could find no way that would not leave them exposed to the Arabs. "Maybe if we traveled by night, we could slip around the edges."

Sergius answered as if he understood what Thorfast had said. He pointed out spots along the Arab camp and at the foothills of the hazy mountains. A black fly landed on his outstretched hand and tapped in a circle before flying off.

"They watch all points," Sophia said. "And they guard the pass. If they were to be discovered it would be by Roman scouts coming from that direction. We could head north and try to find a way around. But that would lead us to where the Romans and Arabs must clash. South would lead us to the coast where we would be exposed and probably captured."

Thorfast's fists tightened and his teeth ground. If there were another obstacle the gods would throw in his path, he could not guess what it could be. He narrowed his eyes at the scores of red-striped tents and the dark figures that moved between them. He caught the flash of iron, heard the soft and distant neighs of horses, smelled the smoke from a dozen campfires. He did not imagine these foes. Prince Kalim's army lay between him and safety.

"If Yngvar was alive, he would know what to do." He spoke in Norse to himself as he withdrew from the ridge. Ragnar, who leaned behind him, hobbled aside on his crutch to let him pass.

"You have mentioned that name before. Who is he?"

"He was my best friend and my leader. I told you he and I raided Denmark's coast. You must know him."

"I've been long from home, brother. There was too much of this wide world to see for me to remain in such a small land. But I've paid for that, haven't I? Anyway, what would he do if he were still alive?"

Thorfast thought on this while Sophia stared after him. The Romans also peeled back from the ridge with their shoulders bent and heads down.

"Yngvar would do something no one expected. Something I would call foolish but then do anyway because it would succeed. He always said the gods favor a daring plan and piss on a timid one. I say no one knows what the gods favor, for all plans fall to shit once they become involved."

"Well said, brother. But those plans worked for your friend. So what would be the most foolish thing to do?"

"I'm glad only you and I can understand this talk, for it would set everyone else rolling on the ground with laughter." Thorfast rubbed the back of his neck and shook his head. "Those mad plans of Yngvar's only succeeded because he had his Wolves and a loyal crew. They are all dead now. But for me. And I was the most useless of all."

He returned to Sophia's side, where she knelt against a rock and looked out across the Arab camp. She followed black birds that swooped above it.

"If we could but fly as they do. We have come so far, and are so close. But God has set me one more challenge. He knows I mean to sin most deeply. This is His hand protecting me from my own evil. For if I reach home, I fear what I will find will only lead me to damnation. God is merciful."

Having learned to curb his speech after sharing his opinions on the Roman and Arab war, he simply nodded. He doubted Sophia's god even noticed her.

"And if you can't reach home?"

"Sergius has offered to take me as far north as Catania. Or I could go to Syracuse. From both cities I could eventually get home. But by the time I reached those places and found us passage on a ship, Fausta would have already worked her evil."

She sighed and turned from the sight of the war camp. She slid down the rocks to sit in the patchy grass.

"I would think," Thorfast said cautiously, still standing over her, "that Fausta has already done whatever she planned to do. Much time has passed since you were discovered."

143

He expected her to explode in anger. Instead she turned aside and bit the knuckle of her first finger. Tears brimmed in her eyes. He sat beside her, glancing at Sergius who also looked on. To his credit, he inclined his head then rejoined his men who squatted in quiet conversation away from them.

"I just thought if I could reach Pozzallo, my cousin would help me. He could order a ship to take me back with all haste. I know I am rushing toward ruin. But is it wrong? The man I am married to—I hesitate to call him a husband—and the woman he wed to replace me plan to destroy my family for their own profit. As you said, they've likely already carried out their evil."

She cupped both hands over her face. The calls of the free-flying birds and the low murmur of conversation among the Romans filled the pause. Thorfast waited, staring at his battered, mud-crusted boots. At last, her hands slipped down to reveal her face flushed red.

"I've known from the first that I would not get home soon enough to help. But I had to try with all my strength to return swiftly. What kind of daughter would I be had I not? It was a vain hope. I'm sorry to have pushed you. There is a chance Fausta has either met delay or else reconsidered her plans. No matter. I want revenge. Even if she has confessed all her sins and thrown herself on the mercy of God's altar, I want revenge for what she did to me. Am I wrong?"

"Revenge is right," Thorfast said. "It is all that keeps me alive. For I will not die until I have slain Prince Kalim and all those who sold us to our deaths. Or else I will die reaching for their throats. My gods demand I do nothing less."

"The true God asks us to forgive our enemies. But I am not so perfect. Fausta and even Quintus, if they have done what I know they have planned, must die. They must. Yet, all these Arabs ..."

She pressed her hand over her mouth to stifle her sob, then turned her head aside. Thorfast closed his eyes and sighed.

"You keep speaking as if this is your task alone. It is mine as well. I am sworn to it. And I know what to do. Yngvar has whispered the plan to me from Valhalla. A favor to his oldest friend. It is madness, but because it is madness it will succeed."

144

Sophia dropped her hand from her mouth and looked at him. Tears stained her cheeks but her eyes glimmered with hope.

"I am not sure if God or Satan has sent you to me, but I don't care."

She wrapped her arms around his neck and pulled him close. Her breath was hot on his cheek as she squeezed.

Conscious of the others looking on, he gently set her back.

"You might not appreciate me so much after hearing the plan. To start, it is for just us two. Failure means our deaths at best, perhaps torture at worst. But success means we have lost no time here."

She took both of his hands in hers. Her hands trembled in his. She gave him a twisted smile.

"Show me the path to sin and damnation."

Thorfast laughed. "At least if my plan fails, you will not have sinned by your god's laws. We will surely die."

He held her close as he outlined a plan he believed both reckless and mad. A plan to entertain the gods.

18

Thorfast adjusted Sophia's blue head cover so that it hid her face in shadow. She chased his hand away, then stuffed her platinum hair back into the folds so nothing more showed. "Do I look convincing?"

She held her arms wide to display the blue and white Arab robe she wore over a padded gambeson. A curved dagger held to her side by a rope belt. Her old clothes were in a beige cloth pack now sitting at her feet, which were still clad in her own leather shoes and not the sandals of the Arabs.

"Loosen the belt, or else your waist will give you away," Thorfast said.

"Any looser and the dagger will fall off." Yet she loosened the belt as asked.

They hid amid trees at the base of the hill. Sergius, Ragnar, and the rest of the men huddled behind them. Sunset cast them into deep shadow thrown from the hill. The Arab camp lay several hundred paces ahead. It now seemed impossibly large. Each tent stood as imposing as a jarl's mead hall, or so Thorfast thought. Arab warriors and laborers hurried through the maze of the camp. Now the echoes of their harsh language were clear across warm evening air. Thorfast could smell the rank scents from waste pits dug at the edges of camp.

He wicked sweat from his brow, not all due to the humidity. He stared at the length of the camp.

"Brother, this is surely madness," Ragnar said, adjusting his weight on the crutch for his injured leg. "It's like sailing into a fog in unknown seas."

"Here I thought I was a skald," Thorfast said, still watching the fluttering shapes of Arabs about their final tasks of the day. "Your fine words do describe the peril, though. We're as likely to wreck before we reach the far side as we are to succeed."

"I'd say you will be wrecked," Ragnar hobbled closer. "I regret encouraging you to this foolishness."

"Do I pass for an Arab?" Thorfast, like Sophia who now fiddled with her belt along with Sergius's help, spread his arms wide.

"As long as no one looks too closely and no one sees the blood stains on the hem of your robe."

Sergius's men had overtaken two sentries earlier in the day when they had just taken over a shift from other sentries. The thought was no one would expect their return for several hours. So far no alarm had been raised. Yet the guards had resisted. One had been stabbed to death and the other captured. The captive remained in Sergius's camp for interrogation. Both had been stripped and all their possessions transferred to Thorfast and Sophia.

"If we pause long enough for anyone to notice blood drops on my hem, then we are already undone. We must flow straight through camp to the pass, then count on our wits from there."

Ragnar shook his head. "I wish I could follow, but Fate has decided for me. My leg."

Thorfast nodded and clapped Ragnar's shoulder. "You're a good man. A bit sensitive about your mother, though. I pray Fate will put us together once more. I will return to kill Prince Kalim and burn his palace to ash. You should join me for it."

"You have daring plans," Ragnar said, smiling. "We shall see if I live so long. Sergius will hire me if I can survive the journey to his base. I fear they're going to leave me behind with my leg like this."

Mention of the Roman commander drew his attention. For he now joined them in the shadow, guiding Sophia by her shoulders. He sized up Thorfast, appreciating his disguise. He adjusted the curving sword at Thorfast's hip, setting it to his satisfaction. He also reset the leather band on the head cover. At last he stepped back with a grim nod.

He released Sophia to him and spoke in long, tired sentences that no one translated. It seemed he might have prayed for their success. Sophia had bowed her head. Even Ragnar did as well. Thorfast waited, feeling the pulse in his temples against the newly adjusted headband. The damned thing was like wearing a helmet all day. Why would anyone adopt such a custom?

At last Sophia translated the Roman's last words.

"He says he regrets our choice, but appreciates our daring. He and his men cannot do more for us, for they must go north and warn of what they have seen here. We will warn the fort at Pozzallo, God willing."

Sergius gave another nod and spoke more words that made Sophia blush. Yet all the while he stared hard at Thorfast.

"He's warning me to protect you," he said.

"Something like that," she said.

"You can always change your mind, brother," Ragnar said. "He's offering a last chance to go with us."

"We were never going to remain together," Thorfast said. "Thank him for me, and tell him I will protect Sophia."

"Protect her?" Ragnar said. "He says you're not her real husband and you'd better not lead her to sin. Or else God will curse you."

Thorfast laughed. "One more curse is nothing. Let all the gods shit on me and laugh. I will defy every one."

Sergius did not share the laughter. He pulled out the sack of gold he had taken from Thorfast. He dug out ten gold coins and held these in his palm. Thorfast was glad for the generosity. Ten coins would not buy them an army, but it might buy them enough to get Sophia home.

Then he thrust the coins into his own purse. He tossed the weighty sack to Sophia, who barely caught it. The coins clinked in her hands.

She staggered under its unexpected weight. Once she recovered, she offered it back to Sergius with a stream of apologetic sounding words.

"Don't be stupid," Thorfast said, collecting her outstretched arms to himself. "We need the gold more."

"But they have nothing and this is too much for us."

"You've no idea what revenge costs, do you?" He pulled her to his side and inclined his head to Sergius. "Even if your cousin provides us a ship, gold will make men row faster. We will need every one of these coins, and probably more still."

She looked helplessly at the sack. After a long moment, she handed it to Thorfast. Then she drew up to Sergius and raised to her toes, planting a brief kiss on his cheek.

"Well, onward to the greatest adventure of your life," Thorfast said. "We've gold, weapons, and friends to watch us go. Your god has blessed you. No time to waste."

Thorfast wished he could linger under the shadows of those trees. This was the final bound to Pozzallo, where he would board a ship to take him from Sicily. Leaving this place felt like leaving Yngvar and all the others. It made no sense, and he had not yet succeeded in threading the Arab camp. But the feeling was there, a pebble in his heart that had been gathering debris so that it was now a painful lump. He was truly leaving his friends forever.

Sophia held close to him as they strode into the blue shadows on the grass.

"Don't stand so close to me," he said. "We're not lovers. We're sentries returning from duty."

"Of course," Sophia said. She shuffled aside, perhaps too far. Yet it was better than too near. She glanced behind.

"And don't look behind. We don't want to give away Sergius if Arabs are watching. In the camp, we don't want to seem like we're fleeing from someone."

"Of course," Sophia said. Her voice was rigid with fear.

"We've got some time before the original owners of these robes are missed," he said. "Keep your head down, look relaxed, and don't stop for anything. I will get you through this."

"But what about the guards at the pass? What if there are a dozen Arabs watching it?"

"I am fed and rested. So I can probably kill all of them with a sneeze. Do not worry for it."

She snorted a laugh, but fell silent as they approached the edge of the camp. A bare-backed man in voluminous gray striped pants was bent over a box and digging through it.

"We walk right past him as if we know where we're going," Thorfast said under his breath.

"You don't know where we're going?" Sophia's voice was rough with fear.

Thorfast strode right past the shirtless man. From the corner of his eye, he noted the man pause to glance at him then return to digging in the box. Sophia hustled behind him.

They were inside the Arab camp.

"Don't rush," he whispered.

"Of course."

"Don't answer me. Just follow."

The high tents formed alleys that either gathered shadow or channeled the final rays of light from the west. The sky was purple and the clouds thick and gray. Orange campfires and torches popped up all around them. The murmur of Arab voices they had heard from afar were now clear bursts of banter, laughter, shouts, and curses. Humidity turned typical camp scents of sweat, horse, and smoke to an oppressive mix that slathered Thorfast's face like paste. He disliked crowded camps, having spent most of his life aboard a ship where wind and rain swept odors to sea. He feared he would choke in these confines.

People of all skin colors crisscrossed the camp. Most numerous were the swarthy Arabs in their blue and gray robes. But also lighter-skinned folk in Arab dress accompanied them. Olive-skinned locals toiled as slaves or as laborers, hustling behind their masters and carrying all manner of burdens. Outside one tent stood a guard with burly arms crossed over a broad chest. He was dressed only in plain brown pants and had skin like charcoal that glistened with sweat. He was no Arab, but one of the legendary blue men Thorfast had heard of. He could spare no time to study this rare person. Instead, he chose a path where no one walked.

"Don't stare or you'll draw attention," Sophia hissed as they passed into a shadowed alley between tents.

"I've never seen so many different people at once."

She clucked her tongue at him, but both fell silent as a soft crash came from within one of the tents they passed.

Despite the rush of activity surrounding him, Thorfast found his way into the midst of the camp without drawing interest from anyone. Taking his own advice, he kept his head lowered and hands relaxed at his side. Sophia's proximity was not an issue in the crowded camp. Everyone navigating it had to bunch up.

Clanging of iron rang out to the left. He knew it would be from one of the small forges constructed to care for the weapons and gear of the army. Even at rest, swords would be bent, spears broken, shield boards loosened. The forges would also be protected at the center of camp. A quick scan to the left showed that the tents thinned out in that direction, and most traffic headed into wide tracks leading toward the noise. A place would be cleared at the camp's center for men to practice their sword work while waiting for their orders.

"We're halfway," he whispered to Sophia at his right. "I can see the start of the foothills over the tents ahead. Keep your hand close to your dagger."

"I thought you said to act relaxed?"

Without missing a step, he chose what seemed a path to the opposite edge of camp. Three Arab warriors, all dark with white scars dressing their muscled arms, passed them. None even glanced at him, even though his shoulder nearly clipped one of the warriors. Had the gods made him invisible?

They slipped confidently to the edge, passing among people more interested in finding their beds for the night than finding infiltrations. Had Thorfast been here to attempt something more daring than passing through, he might have encountered more resistance. But the Arabs seemed confident in their position. After all, they were in their own territory and protected by mountains to either side and a friendly sea to another. No enemy would assault them here.

The edge of the camp was ungaurded, at least the section they had found. The pass up into the mountains was wide and dark ahead of them. The sentries posted there would be hidden, watching the east for their Byzantine counterparts. None would be watching behind.

"We've made it," Thorfast said.

He glanced around. The sun had sped behind the steep hills of the west and the camp was now in darkness. Orange lights flickered as shadowed figures passed before them. He noted movement in the near distance, Arabs exiting from a tent. But these men were in no hurry and congregated together in idle conversation.

"We must hurry," Sophia whispered. "We can't just stand here or people will wonder what we're doing."

Then he heard it.

At first it was Arabs shouting in the distance which had not registered to Thorfast's mind. But what followed clanged against his head like a hammer to a helmet.

A deep, resonant shout. A bellow of fury. A stormy gust from Valhalla.

"Bjorn?"

"What?" Sophia grabbed his sleeve. It was a feminine gesture guaranteed to draw attention. But Thorfast's attention strained at the distance.

More shouts and more bellowing followed. It was bellowing from the throat of one man.

One man whom Thorfast had fought beside in scores of battles. One shout he knew split enemies with fear as an ax splits firewood. A withering fury possessed only by the great berserkers of the northlands. The war cry of his childhood friend.

"I saw him drown."

Had he? He had seen Bjorn sucked into the explosion of water flooding through the hull breach in the slave ship. Thorfast considered if he had survived, then could not have Bjorn?

"What are you doing?" Sophia asked, now pressing up against him. "Look at me!"

Her desperate shout bounced off his eardrums. Thorfast felt her soft gambeson pressed against him.

His hands went cold. He shoved her back.

"What are you doing?"

"That's my question to you? You're like a stone statue."

"Do you hear that shouting?"

Rather than Sophia answering, the Arabs gathered outside the tent nearby called out. Thorfast snapped back from straining to hear what he thought was Bjorn's roar.

"Dear God," Sophia said, touching her hand to her chest. "We've been found."

The Arabs called out again, one raising his hand as if demanding an answer. Five of them began to approach. Each of them carried swords.

Thorfast relaxed and appeared to wait, turning his back to them. He used the moment to guide Sophia on the plan.

"We're going to run. There is one way into the mountains. So our choice of direction is made for us. Fortunately, night has fallen and the clouds are working for us."

"They're getting closer, Thorfast."

"I can hear them," he said with a smile. "Their shouting after us will alert the sentries along the pass. We'll have to fight through."

"Thorfast, they're moving faster." She pulled at his sleeve again.

"I will make an opening in them," he said. "I don't know how many we will face. But I will cut you a path."

"They're almost here!"

He thrust the sack of gold into her hands. "Keep running and let me fight. Get to Pozzallo. Buy a mercenary and take your revenge."

She stared at the sack, her mouth agape.

The Arabs behind them were shouting, impatient and angry at being ignored. They had still not recognized him and Sophia as enemies. At worst, they might consider them deserters. No matter. The crunch of their sandals against the gritty dirt was nearly to Thorfast's back.

He took Sophia's arm. "Run now."

The rough ground grabbed the soles of Thorfast's feet as he broke

153

into a run. Sophia stumbled after him, but kept her footing. The Arabs shouted, but did not raise an alarm.

The ground ahead was slipping into darkness. The sun was down but light still scattered across the land in faint rays. The path ahead was like giant stairs or natural rock leading into the foothills that led to the mountain pass. While light skimmed atop the great boulders and waving bushes, soon all light would vanish. He picked the clearest path he could as he rushed.

Halfway up the slope he dared a glance over his shoulder. He held Sophia by her arm. Her cheeks were flushed and puffed out. Behind her the Arabs scrambled after them. His slight lead had widened over them. Yet one stumble and they would overtake him.

"Don't stop!" Sophia shouted.

He pulled her forward again, lurching and darting from stone to slope to stone again. The way up fought against them, but it would offer the same challenge to their pursuers.

Another glance behind and shadows had flowed over the camp and the foothills. The sun pulled beneath its blanket of earth to hide from the impending bloodshed.

His legs ached as he stretched across dips and gaps. The Arabs below continued to shout, but their chase had relented.

"They've stopped," Sophia said. She began to laugh.

"But we will not." He tugged her forward into darkness.

The Arabs hurled insults and anger into the dark. But they had ceased chasing. While Sophia celebrated escape, Thorfast understood the Arabs had left them for the sentries ahead.

"Be silent," he said, pulling her arm for emphasis. "We're not away yet."

They crept together along the stair-like climb into the pass. In darkness, Thorfast could hardly see more than a dozen paces ahead.

But then a yellow light flared ahead.

Then another.

Mounting tall, flat boulders, a dozen Arabs appeared. They were dressed in gray robes to match the rocks. Two held torches aloft that cast golden brilliance into two wide globes. Thorfast, caught in the circle of light, looked not to the Arabs' faces, but to the strung bows in their hands.

One of the sentries frowned then barked impatient commands in his native language.

"What do we do?" Sophia whispered.

Thorfast moved before her. A dark path lay between the two boulders where the Arabs stood. It was a natural choke point for all traffic along the pass. Even if they could flee between the boulders, they would be shot in the back on the other side.

Sophia tugged at his arm.

"Looks like I will take their first volley and you will flee over my corpse."

19

The Arabs stared down at Thorfast. The wavering globes of yellow light from the two torches defined the hard, callous lines of their faces. All dressed in gray, they seemed outcroppings of the giant boulders they stood upon. Sweat leaked down Thorfast's face, which was hot both from his exertion and his fear.

Their pursuers still shouted after them. Yet their voices were feeble over the distance. Still, the Arabs standing over them with strung bows looked out toward the shouting.

Their leader came to the edge of the boulder and glared down at Thorfast. His face was now cast into shadow, but the hate still radiated from the black of his head cover.

"I didn't save you for you to die now," Sophia said, the fear in her voice replaced with ire.

The leader again shouted his command, gesturing at Thorfast's sword.

His first instinct was to fight. Against twelve bowmen lined up over his head, he had no chance at all. He would be feathered with arrows before his sword left its sheath.

"They think we're deserters," he said to Sophia. "They probably want to take us back for punishment."

"I knew this idea was foolish," she said.

"It might have succeeded if there were fewer archers here."

The leader roared at their whispered conversation, and a few of the archers laughed. He crouched down and pointed at them, a stream of foreign curses spewing over their heads.

"We're not done yet," Sophia said.

She raised the sack of gold she still held, displaying it to the leader. The sharp light of the torches delineated the coins held within.

The Arab bolted up as if he had been shown his mother's severed head.

"Well, he's an honorable fucker," Thorfast said. "But it's a good idea. Distract them with it. We might yet escape this."

The leader raged. Spit flew from his mouth, glittering in the yellow light. He held his head between both hands as if it might pop off his body. Sophia still held the sack aloft, though her arms trembled with the weight.

The other Arabs gathered to examine the source of their leader's agony. Those on the opposite boulder clustered at the edge for the same purpose. More than one mumbled something that sounded appreciative.

This stopped the leader ranting at the proffered bribe and drew his invective toward his own men. While he chided those who seemed inclined to bribery, the others directed Thorfast and Sophia toward the far edge of the boulder. A natural path led to the top where he could join them.

"Let's get up and have a talk with our new friends," Thorfast said.

"You're feeling good about this?" Sophia lowered the bag, letting it slump against her thighs.

"This way I might die with a sword in hand and their blood on my face. Much better than taking an arrow through the eye and dropping dead." He led her to where the Arab indicated. "And this way you might also escape. Run when I create the distraction. They won't follow you, at least not in force."

"You can't leave me alone," she said. She held close behind him as he found the step up. "You swore an oath not to die before you got me home."

"You're close enough now. Your cousin is just over this mountain." He stepped up from one rock to the next, finally to reach a point where he could haul himself onto the ledge of the boulder.

"I'm not leaving you," she said.

Her protests ceased as Thorfast pulled up to the ledge. He faced the leader and five other Arabs. This was not a boulder as he expected but an outcrop of the rocky walls. Adding himself and Sophia to this space created the crowded condition he had hoped for. Also, he had split the Arab numbers in half, stranding six on the opposite boulder.

The leader had now composed himself. He stepped to within a hand's breadth of Thorfast and whispered what must be deadly threats. Up close he smelled of sweat and alcohol. He was darker than all the others, with a nose that hooked over a hateful mouth. His eyes were hidden in shadow as his torch bearer circled behind him, standing at the edge of the outcropping.

Thorfast smiled.

Sophia opened the sack to reveal the gold. The five Arabs strained to see over their leader's shoulder to the sparkling fortune within. It must have been more wealth than any of them had ever known, for they all gasped. Even the indignant leader. The Arabs across the gap called out in irritation, probably demanding to know how much gold was on offer.

Thorfast casually examined the opposite side of the ledge. From this end a rock led off the high ledge down to a lane of boulders and bushes that must be the screens for the sentries watching the pass.

If he and Sophia could gain that screened area, the archers would have no shots between the boulders and darkness. They would have to pursue. But not all would. Greed would keep some behind.

"Let's run," Thorfast said, smiling at Sophia. She looked at him, as confused at his words as the Arabs.

He punched the bottom of the opened sack of gold in Sophia's hands. Glittering coins sprayed into the Arab leader's face. They clinked on the rock around his feet as he flayed back like poison had been thrown in his face.

Without pause, Thorfast shoved the torch-bearing Arab off the boulder. He plunged over the ledge, taking the light with him.

Sophia screamed. Thorfast snatched away the sack and snapped the open end at the remaining Arabs. The faint light from the opposite gap lit the coins with orange glints. They plinked and clacked over rock and the Arabs leapt back with their leader.

He had grabbed Sophia's wrist with his free hand. Now he dragged her forward to the where he hoped to find cover.

She stumbled with a curse.

The sudden shift of weight yanked him back before he even jumped off the rock. The Arabs stumbled around and another slipped of the ledge. With only a single torch to light the darkness, they were barely within its circle. They batted at their faces and bodies, afraid they had somehow been injured.

"Get up," Thorfast growled as he dragged Sophia forward and pointed. "Follow that path through the rocks. Do not stop or look back."

She clambered to her feet in time with the shouts of all the Arabs on both boulders. Yet those within the light had their companions blocking their line of sight to Thorfast. Those on the boulder with him were too close to shoot. Instead, they fumbled to draw swords.

It was enough of a delay that he and Sophia both gained the lane of stones and brush that had formed the Arab screen. Sophia went before, still holding the deflated sack.

"I can't see where I'm going!"

"You don't need to. Go straight up the path."

He shoved her ahead so that he could have the space to fight. He drew the heavy, unfamiliar sword at his hip.

"I will give you the space to escape. Go. I'm right behind."

"I won't—"

He shoved her again, but could no longer spare her any more attention. The Arab leader pounced down from the boulder above. The meager torchlight sparked across the edge of his drawn sword.

Thorfast met the strike with his own sword, holding it in two hands. He was bigger and stronger than the Arab, or at least so he thought. For what the Arab lacked in size he made up for in strength.

Their blades ground together, yellow sparks lighting the furious lines of the Arab's face. The scrape and hiss of iron on iron rebounded from the surrounding rocks. He drove Thorfast back onto one, laughing as he raised his blade for a beheading strike.

Thorfast kicked out with his booted foot, slamming into the Arab's knee. He screamed and buckled as the joint popped. His blade clanged against stone by Thorfast's left ear. The force of it rippled over the pale stubble of his hair.

If he was not the Arab's match in strength, he was the better in speed. In a blink, he drove his blade into the leader's neck. Even off-balance and leaning against a rock, he had defeated his foe. He cursed the unwieldy sword that felt as if it wanted to drop from his grip. Yet he sloughed off the dying Arab and turned to run.

He collided with Sophia. She bounced from him, her pale face still shining in the night. She held a heavy rock overhead.

"I told you to run!"

She did not answer, but flung the rock past him. He heard a thump and grunt.

The other Arabs were clambering down from their boulder perch. Sophia's cast had struck the lead man and bowled him back against his companions.

Bows thrummed then wood clattered and snapped around them. One arrowhead struck a brilliant spark as it skimmed a stone.

"Run!" He pulled her into the darkness ahead, lit only by the reflected light of the torch and the first stars of night above.

The Arabs had little hope of hitting them, but only risked a few arrows on the poor chance of success.

Their decision to shoot was an error Thorfast had counted upon. They would follow their instincts and use weapons in hand. In the time they wasted to switch weapons he would pull far enough from them to remove them as a threat.

Yet the others pursuing had not been as greedy for gold as he had hoped. They called after him, throaty foreign curses echoing through the narrow pass. But he and Sophia were carried by fear while mere duty drove their pursuers. They both sped over rocks, leapt bushes, and dove back onto the main path with speed that left the Arabs far behind. That he did this all in a robe astonished Thorfast.

"They're closing," Sophia said, glancing over her shoulder. Her platinum hair streamed like a banner, marking them to their enemies as long as any light remained.

He did not slow his pace, but also looked behind. Dark shapes raced up the slope, picking through and jumping over the rough patches of the pass.

Were these other Arabs he had not seen? They hardly made noise and were much closer than he expected to find those who had pursued him. The torchlight by the boulder pass below bobbed and wobbled, but was not nearing in pursuit. Perhaps they were gathering the coins he had scattered, and other Arabs had come to pursue.

"How many can they stick in this pass?" His voice cracked with exertion. But he redoubled the pace. He stumbled forward. Sophia crashed to her knees with a scream. The pass was narrowing to another choke point. Ahead he saw a gap suitable for perhaps a single pony to thread.

"Get through that and keep going," he shouted after her. "I will hold them long enough for your escape."

Fear had finally claimed Sophia's wits. She did not acknowledge him or shorten her stride. She would likely run until she hit the eastern sea. Confident she would flee, he skidded to a halt.

The shallow slope gave him a slight advantage over his enemies. The narrow rock walls of the pass protected him from becoming surrounded. He might be flanked on one side. But by that time, he would have cut a swath through his foemen.

"If I die, I die a hero! Welcome me to your hall, All-Father!" he shouted down at the approaching mass of shadowed warriors. Less boldly, he spoke to himself, "And if I'm captured, I'll cry like a fucking baby. Gods, let me die a hero."

The Arabs were all lurching shadows that called out in shrill, lusty battle chants. Their weapons glinted in their eager hands as they picked a course up the slope.

He readied his sword, wishing it was not this ill-balanced, curving thing. What fool swordsmith had convinced the Arabs this was a shape made for battle? This was a sword you gave to an enemy in hopes he would cut his own leg off trying to wield it. But he had nothing more.

The whites of the enemies' eyes shined in the dark. Their wicked smiles flashed. They had tired themselves as he had, but they had the delight of slaughter awaiting them at the end of their efforts.

And he had the glory of battle and death for his.

"Come and die, dogs! I will taste your blood before I join my sword-brothers in the feast hall!"

He pointed his blade at the lead enemy.

The Arab sprawled back with a shout, landing atop the others following him.

Thorfast stared.

The gods had just struck an enemy dead before him.

Four more of the leading Arabs collapsed, creating a wall of writhing and screaming bodies. Those behind stumbled over the first, their swords slamming into rocky dirt rather than Thorfast.

How was he seeing this in such clarity? Had the gods also granted him the eyes of an owl that he might see in the dark?

Realization spread over him. The entire area was filled with wavering yellow light. His shadow reached out before him, dancing with the fire at his back.

Nor had those Arabs all simply fallen dead. Only now penetrating his fear-clad mind came the delayed sounds of thrumming bows and arrows slicing the air.

He turned behind.

Atop the second choke point and along the walls, a half-dozen torches had flared to life. The small area before the gap had become as daylight. By each globe of light stood a gray-cloaked archer, every one calmly setting another arrow to their strings as if only at target practice.

It was target practice.

Returning to the Arabs, Thorfast discovered they had fallen over their companions in their lust to reach him. Yet now dark-feathered shafts were streaking down into their prone bodies.

Those still standing fled back down the pass. Their haughty screams had been supplanted with terrified wailing.

They left behind more than a half-dozen bodies of their companions. When one raised his arm as if calling out to his god, another arrow screamed out of the dark and pierced his side. The hand fell and did not rise again.

"We are saved," Sophia called out from the gap in the rocks.

"So I see." His voice could not have been audible. He stared in surprise and a flush of embarrassment at the dead bodies lined before him. To think, he believed the gods had noticed him.

Men called down in the smooth language of the Greeks. He continued to stare after the bodies, but waved acknowledgement. Sophia called him again, and he broke with the spot he had resolved to die upon. Fate was strange, but perhaps he should have expected the Romans to hold such a strategic position.

He followed her into the darkness, where she waited with her sharp face beaming joy. Her hair was limp with sweat yet she could not have appeared more radiant. She had at last found her people.

Three tall men in gray cloaks and dark leather jerkins surrounded her. They were typical of the folk of in this land with dark hair and haunted eyes. Their olive complexion blended them into the shadows they wore as tightly as their cloaks. One of them smiled and spoke. Sophia answered.

"They have been waiting for a spy to return from the Arab camp," she said. "They thought you might be their spy and me a freed prisoner."

"It's not far from the truth," Thorfast said.

The Romans had carried their torches down from the walls of the pass. They examined the foes they had slain, retrieving what loot they found on their bodies. Thorfast smiled. Warriors were the same everywhere.

The lead Roman was a head shorter than anyone else. Yet from his bearing he was unmistakable as a man of authority. He pulled back his hood revealing a round head, gave a name Thorfast could not grasp, then proceeded to speak at length. He gestured toward the Arabs, at the sky, at the stone walls, at his feet, at Sophia. Thorfast wondered what else the man thought he could not see with his own eyes. Yet Sophia listened with a rapt expression and translated nothing.

When the leader finished, he snapped his fingers at those picking over the corpses. The others had already gathered their packs. Perhaps fifteen Romans plugged this gap in the pass, all armed with stout bows and short swords. Thorfast looked longingly on those blades and again regretted the heavy iron dangling at his hip.

"They're taking us back to Pozzallo," Sophia said, wrapping her arms around his. "We will be sent directly to my cousin!"

"They're not waiting for their spy?"

She shook her head. "He must be dead. In any case, their mission is finished now that Arabs have found them."

Thorfast grumbled. Perhaps there was more to this story than they had explained to Sophia. The Arabs had likely known of their enemy counterparts. But whatever the reason, Thorfast was glad to at last escape the Arabs. He loved no Byzantine or Roman or whatever they called themselves. To him they were another potential enemy. Yet Sophia at least had a place in their world. For once he might not wonder where to find food.

The Romans turned their torches on the path ahead, leaving the corpses where they had fallen. They had surrendered their choke point and if they returned, Thorfast guessed it would be occupied with Arab defenders. Or else the day of battle was near and they had no more use for the pass. Neither side could launch an attack through that narrow way, not while both sides were aware of its existence.

So they followed the Romans up into the mountains and the night, threading a pass that led to some fate Thorfast could only hope would be better than what he left behind.

But he had visited death to Pozzallo not long ago. And if his own gods did not delight in the irony, then the Christian god of the Romans might come down from His cross and strike Thorfast for his insolence.

Once they had achieved the height of the pass, he caught sight of the fortress at Pozzallo in the distance below. As they proceeded along the pass, the orange lights dotting its walls and tower seemed to assume the shape of a giant cross.

Thorfast alone paused at the sight, his hands cold.

20

The room at the top of the fortress's central building was lit with a gently flickering hearth fire. Brass lamps provided extra lighting around the room that smelled of leather and oil. Thorfast appreciated the clever construction of the command room. He had experience raising nothing more complex than halls and barns of wood. To build stone to such heights and add wood planks for floors was a feat of construction he could scarcely understand. How did they build so high without everything falling down?

Sophia waited beside him. Both were still dressed as Arabs, though now their hems were frayed and the robes faded with brown dust. She rubbed her hands together and twisted her torso like a fish dangling from a line.

"Why are you worried? Isn't he your cousin?"

"I have not seen him in ten years," she said. "We were not close."

Thorfast nodded. For some reason, he felt calmer knowing Sophia was nervous. This made no sense to him, but he recognized it as a necessary way of things. If one of them were worried then the other needed to remain clear.

"But he is family," Thorfast said. He scanned around the room. A table with a large skin map held with stones dominated the space. A clay jug and a half-dozen brown glazed mugs surrounded it. A knife stuck out of the wood like a guard watching over the map next to it.

"On my mother's side," she said. "We will be fine. At least I hope we will."

"If he intended us harm, then we would not be left alone in his hall, would we? We'd be bound in chains and tossed in a pit."

"But they took all our weapons."

"Of course. Family or not, no one brings weapons into a hall without the leave of the hall's master. This is true everywhere."

Yet Thorfast could not help but remember the cross he had seen the night before. Though they had been received at the gates as friends, and given a comfortable pallet to share for the night, he still wondered at this man they called Commander Staurakius. Simply speaking the name caused Thorfast to spit all over himself. It could not be a good sign if a man's name alone brings grief to the speaker.

His feet begged relief as he stood awaiting the arrival of the commander. Outside the iron-bound double doors he heard footsteps receding. The guard at the door had left, it seemed. This was as strange to Thorfast as the trust he was shown by being left alone in this hall. Perhaps there was nothing of value here worth a care.

Then he heard two soft female voices.

The words plucked the bones of his spine with ice.

"They came in the night. A woman and man."

"The woman is the commander's cousin."

"Really? Valerie said she was quite beautiful but needed a bath."

The two tittered then suddenly went quiet.

They had been speaking Norse.

Thorfast rushed to the doors and reached for one of the handles. It swept open. He recoiled as if flames had lashed out at him.

A bold man with a strong jaw and thick beard entered. He wore a white robe held at his shoulder with a gold pin. He flinched back when he discovered Thorfast nearly brushing against him.

"My cousin," Sophia said, under her breath. Then she spoke up, proclaiming her cousin's name along with other words Thorfast did not understand.

The man framed in the single door stood back and focused

beyond Thorfast. His wary, eagle-like bearing melted when he saw Sophia. He threw his arms wide and Thorfast felt relief flood through his body like hot mead.

Then he remembered the Norse voices. He stepped out into the area beyond the door. He found nothing but dark corridors leading off to either side and the stairs down before him. A guard barely had his head over the top of the stairs, and gave him a lazy glance before continuing down. The Norse women, girls more likely from their voices, had vanished.

"Thorfast?" Sophia called him a like a mother does her misbehaving son. He reacted as much, retreating back into the room with heat on his face.

"You must greet my cousin properly. Come, present yourself and I will translate."

During their lengthy wait he had amused himself thinking of different ways he could chide his host for the delay while masking it all with Norse. But now he dared speak nothing but honest and polite words.

He bowed low to Commander Staurakius. "I am in your debt, lord. I am Thorfast the Silent of Frankia. Your cousin has honored me with her bravery and wit on this long journey to your hall. Now I see such worthiness is in your family's blood."

Sophia paused and blushed with a smile, a detail that Commander Staurakius noted with a brief smile of his own. But she dutifully translated for Thorfast, or at least whatever she told him seemed greatly pleasing. For the commander folded his strong, hairy arms and nodded appreciatively.

The commander then focused his attention on Sophia. He invited them to take seats on low stools that had been pushed beneath the table. Thorfast sat beside Sophia as the commander spoke. Though he tried to seem attentive, he had found himself excluded from conversation due to his language.

As the two cousins prattled on, Thorfast's mind wandered back to the Norse voices. When he had ventured this far south with Yngvar, he believed he might be one of the few Norsemen ever to do so. But now he was beginning to feel as if he were the last man to the mead hall. Still, if he ever did return to the north again, he would have an amazing story to fill the long winter nights.

To be cold again! This heat of this island called Sicily must blow off from Muspelheim itself, a world where fire giants bathe in molten rock. The gently crackling hearth fire added to the thick heat. He fanned himself with an open palm, which drew both cousins to smile at his suffering.

He waited for them to finish their talk. His mind wandered back to the bellowing he heard in the Arab camp. Had that truly been Bjorn? Could he not have heard something similar to his friend's voice and then let his own hopes take over? That was perhaps the most likely reason. He frowned in thought, realizing he had heard what he wanted. He was just like those men he had tricked in the hills back at Licata. They had heard Arabic commands to abandon their pursuit simply because they had desired to hear it. They did not realize they had simply heard nonsense. Thorfast had made a similar mistake.

Bjorn and all the others were dead. He had seen them all flung into the sea by a torrent of water. The gods had spared no one but himself and Hamar, who they later fed to Arab swords.

He was alone in this world.

At last the commander had direct questions for Thorfast.

"He hopes you can detail everything you saw in the camp," Sophia translated.

"I did not have time to see much, but I will tell what I know."

Yet as he began to recount his memories, he realized he had absorbed much more than he realized. His years of raiding and battling had trained him to be alert, even without conscious effort. He estimated their numbers based on the count of tents he had passed. The clanging of blacksmiths at their forges had revealed perhaps three or four supported the force. Based upon that, he could guess over a hundred warriors in addition to their camp laborers.

Sophia relayed all of this as he spoke. Staurakius's raptor-like face did not resemble Sophia's until Thorfast noted the stern and thoughtful expression spreading with each additional detail he learned. He asked about the spy.

"I heard a deep bellowing, like a man being tormented. Could that have been him?"

The commander shrugged his answer.

"He did not know the spy well enough to say," Sophia said.

"Did you hear it?"

Sophia began to translate then paused, realizing he had asked her. Her brow raised.

"I was so terrified all I could hear was my own heart beating in my ears.'"

Thorfast turned back to the commander. "I heard Norse women speaking just before you entered. Who are they?"

Sophia gave him a suspicious look, but translated for him. Staurakius chuckled.

"They were his servants. Two girls that have been with him many years. He did not realize you are a Norseman. He thought you a Frank."

"Let him know I am a Frank. It's better that way."

She again regarded him with confusion. He wanted to avoid any potential for connection to the raid of Pozzallo only months before. He would not afford the gods another chance for mischief at his cost.

The two cousins continued at length, but the commander at last stood and called beyond the doors.

Thorfast recognized the Norse name, Valgerd. The girl who answered was a golden-haired beauty. She swept Thorfast's thoughts home again. In the north she might be regarded a comely woman, but not one that would set men clashing for her favor. But here in this world of foreigners, she was that cooling gust of northern wind he had longed to feel.

She bowed to Staurakius and listened to his orders. She offered Thorfast a faint smile and spoke Frankish to him.

"You have news of my home?"

He sat straighter with the shock. Something about this smacked of the gods' caprice. Rather than answer, he nodded stiffly. Valgerd responded with a tinkling giggle that was not unpleasant to hear.

Sophia stood and put her hand on his shoulder as if assuming ownership.

"My cousin has offered us a bath and a change of clothes. Will you show us to the baths?"

Valgerd again bowed, and without a word gestured they follow her.

The rest of the morning was spent cleaning, shaving, and combing. Lice had feasted on his head long enough, and with a slave's aid he had picked most from his scalp before noon. He was offered a new shirt of gray linen and light pants with a leather belt. He cleaned his boots and washed his feet. In the officer's barracks he had a bath in hot water poured into a wood basin large enough to seat a whole man. This was something he had never experienced and wholly enjoyed. If he could take one thing back north with him, it would be this kind of soaking bath. The wound on his hip had healed, and after servants noticed the stitches, he was sent to a healer who removed them.

He was reborn in the course of a day. Once his hair and beard grew back, he would be restored to his former self.

Sophia's transformation had taken place separately from his. When they were united again in the commander's feasting hall, he could scarcely recognize her. Her brilliant hair shined now that it had been combed and dressed in braids. Her ragged costume was replaced with a fine dress of blue and white. Her pale skin now shined with health and vigor. A thin chain held a delicate golden cross over her chest.

The Norse girl, Valgerd, accompanied her as if she were a servant to the queen of Sicily. In fact, Sophia seemed so to him.

"I am bitterly jealous of your husband," Thorfast said. "And I curse myself for a blind fool. I've traveled beside legendary beauty and not once admired it."

"I believe you chastised me for showing my calf," she said, blushing. "And you did admire me overmuch, if you will recall."

He smiled. "So I did. Much has happened since and I regret losing sight of what was before me the whole time."

Sophia's flush deepened and she turned aside. Valgerd, though she stood beside them, held a faint smile as she gazed off at some point in the hall. He had to remember that now whatever he said would be understood by others.

"And you look like a noble," she said, sweeping her hand the length of his body. "You stand taller now."

"You have a poor idea of what makes a noble. But I will not deny I feel much like I did before I ever came to this accursed place."

Valgerd glanced knowingly at him. Had Sophia told her of him? He imagined a whole day of women gossiping together. Of course they would have discussed him. But would any of that detail threaten him?

"I am eager to sample the food," he said.

Sophia nodded. "This is a military hold, but my cousin will eat well. Be glad we are invited to his table. Later, he will speak with me alone."

Thorfast inclined his head. He now watched more Roman soldiers entering the hall. Like warriors everywhere, they carried themselves with pride and strength. Each man took the measure of the one beside him and determined his place in the ranks of heroes. At least that was the way Thorfast knew. These Romans seemed to obey rank more than anything else. For none of the common soldiers were with them. There was no equality here.

Once Staurakius arrived, the feasting began. Thorfast ate as well as he had at Prince Kalim's table. The food textures were strange and the flavors stranger still. But after being a slave and then a forager, he was glad for hot and seasoned meats and vegetables no matter how foreign. The wine was bitter on the tongue, but he drank as much as was offered. He stopped only when warmth had spread from his cheeks and nose to his hands and feet. He dared not become drunk.

His language kept him isolated from all but Sophia. The girl Valgerd had left them at the start of the feast. Sophia sat beside her cousin, leaving Thorfast at the end of the table to smile and toast men who could not share their bragging with him.

By the end of the night, Sophia explained that she would meet with Staurakius privately. Valgerd reappeared to lead him away to his lodging. The other soldiers tottered away from their tables with red cheeks and inebriated laughter.

"You will be posted outside Lady Palama's room, since you are her bodyguard." She led him through a narrow hall lit only by the stubby candle she carried ahead of them. "Though you will want to rest. There is a bed for you in the room next to hers."

"I heard this fortress was raided recently," he said. "How safe are we here from the Arabs?"

"It wasn't Arabs, but Norsemen working for them," she said without turning back. "Their true targets were the ships at bay outside the walls. We are safe."

"What if the Norsemen return?" His curiosity had the best of his discretion. Yngvar and Alasdair had brought ruin to their walls as he had to their ships. He wanted to hear of their exploits, even if only from a slave girl.

"Norsemen in these lands are mercenaries," Valgerd said, now coming to wooden stairs to the second floor. "They have probably sold their swords elsewhere by now."

"Of course," Thorfast said. "It seems Prince Kalim has a fine plan to take this fortress. First he cut off defense from the water, now he leads your warriors into the field. He's cutting down the giant one stroke at a time."

Valgerd continued up the stairs, shrugging. "Fate is everything. I cannot be called to God until the day he has chosen for me. I do not worry for it."

"That is good Norse sense laid over Christian foolishness," he said. She led right of the stairs to where a small room with an opened door stood. "You should pray to the old gods and they will hear you. The Christian god is deaf."

She turned at the opened door and smiled. "Your gods are dead, Thorfast the Silent. In time you will see it is true. Ragnarok has come and gone, and the world did not notice. Now, this is where your lady will rest. I've taken all day to prepare it for her. You should sleep now, while she is occupied. This storage room will be your space."

The room designated for Sophia was small and dark. The place Valgerd directed him to was smaller still. He poked his head inside and smelled oil in the bare room.

"It's as narrow as a grave," he said. "I am to sleep here?"

"It must be better than where you have been?" Valgerd bowed to him. "I leave you here and wish you pleasant dreams."

He settled in for sleep, but found no dreams would come. Instead, his bladder led him to rise once more. Time meant nothing in this bland darkness. He had learned in the depths of Prince Kalim's prisons that he could not trust his own judgement of time. He often felt a week had passed when only a day had. An hour could become a month if one tried to reckon every moment of it. So he did not know if Sophia would return yet.

In his own hall, he would relieve himself in a corner. But these Romans seemed a fussy lot with their baths and bowls for cleaning themselves. He expected they might protest his pissing in a corner, as natural as it might be.

The hall outside was dark, but a light shined at the far end. It was a guttering, dying light that drew a thin golden line from the commander's map room.

If someone was inside, he might ask where he could empty his bladder. He was confident he could ask that through gestures.

His footsteps creaked against the wooden floorboards.

A small, crouching figure stepped into the hall. Valgerd followed behind, holding her short candle aloft.

Thorfast's limbs weakened with shock. His bladder dribbled urine into his clean pants.

He stretched out his hand and found his voice could only form a hoarse whisper.

"Alasdair?"

21

He stared at the apparitions of Alasdair and Valgerd. The hallway was lit only with a thin slice of golden light thrown from the burned-down candle that Valgerd held.

The floorboards beneath him creaked again, drawing both Alasdair's and Valgerd's attention.

She snuffed the candle before Alasdair—if it was truly him—could even meet his eyes. Footsteps scratched over the wood floor then faded.

He was in a world of black, frozen with shock and confusion. Alasdair was dead. What would he be doing here and why would Valgerd be with him?

The wetness in his pants from his weakened bladder drew him back. It was like cold water thrown over him. He called out Alasdair's name.

He bounded across the floorboards, but was blind. His face collided with the open door, staggering him. He cursed and slapped at it. The doors were heavy with iron bands and striking them hurt his knuckles. His face throbbed from the surprise impact.

The stairs were before the doors, he remembered. He turned toward these and saw a light at the bottom. But it did not recede, and instead grew brighter as the bearer approached.

"Alasdair?" he called down. "Is it you?"

Two women emerged with the pool of light filling the bottom of the stairs.

Sophia and Valgerd stared up at him.

He stepped back, pointing.

"I just saw you leaving the commander's map room." He realized his voice quaked and he sounded mad. Yet he could not change. "You were with Alasdair."

Valgerd and Sophia stared at each other, then both climbed the stairs without reply.

He waited, glaring at Valgerd as she approached. He looked to her candle. It was not like the stub he had just seen. It was a fresh candle with barely a drizzle of tallow running down its side. The pungent scent filled the hall when she and Sophia met him.

"You both fled when you saw me. What were you doing in the map room?" Thorfast pointed behind. But the door was closed rather than open. He hadn't struck it hard enough to close it. Or had he?

Again Valgerd and Sophia gave each other confused looks.

"You have been dreaming," Valgerd said. "I've been with Lady Palama since I left you."

"That is a lie," he said. "I know what I saw."

Then he looked to Sophia as if she could confirm all he had witnessed.

But her eyes were puffy and red, and her cheeks bright with fresh tears. Her slender hands clutched a white cloth close to her chest.

"What happened?" He put his hand to her shoulder and pulled her closer. "What did your cousin say?"

She shook her head as if she had forgotten speech altogether.

"Lady Palama has had news of home," Valgerd said. "Forget what you have seen while walking in a dream. Your lady needs you tonight."

He blinked at Valgerd. Her clear, cold eyes were set hard against him, as if daring him to persist in his accusations. Sophia stared at the floor, fresh tears leaking onto her cheeks.

"I, um, perhaps you are right. I must have walked in a dream. I have to piss, and so I awoke. My dead friends have been in my thoughts this day, especially after being ..."

After having questioned Valgerd about the raid, he thought better of hinting at his involvement in it. Yet being in this place did bring his thoughts to Yngvar and Alasdair. Why had he dreamed of Alasdair and not Yngvar, who had been his friend since childhood? Dreams were strange things better not considered too deeply.

"I still have to piss."

Valgerd showed him into the map room, where he was given a ceramic pot to drain his bladder. The relief brought shivers to him. When finished he felt confident that he had a restless dream, no matter how vivid it had been.

Sophia needed him now. No time to chase after the dead.

She had entered her room. Valgerd had left her candle to light the room but had disappeared. The room contained a small bed heaped with furs and blankets. The sight of those alone drew sweat to Thorfast's brow. The globe of light from the candle encompassed the entire space. Sophia sat at the edge of the bed staring at the gold cross she twisted between her fingers.

He knelt beside her. The blue cloth of her skirt spilled to the wood floor by his knees. She seemed as fragile as a twig in winter. Her pale hair, though skillfully braided, wilted. The driven woman who had saved him from death and braved the dangers of the Arab lands was gone. A broken and conflicted woman sat in her place.

"Your father has died?"

She nodded and wiped a tear with the back of her wrist.

They sat together. The fort was smothered in silence so deep that Thorfast imagined he could hear the ant exploring the floorboards by his knees. He studied its aimless wandering while he allowed Sophia her space. At last she sighed and let her hands fall to her lap, rustling against the stiff cloth of her new dress.

"The entire town was razed. Not just my father's estate. My cousin just received word two days ago, but the ashes of that disaster are already cold. It happened right after I was captured."

"I am sorry." The words were thick and awkward, but he could find nothing better to say. She gave a feeble smile.

"I knew it would be so. Fausta has what she wants now. The town, my father's ships, his wares, everything was either stolen or destroyed."

"Who actually attacked your estate?"

She stared at him, her eyes reflecting points of yellow light.

"Pirates and Norse mercenaries."

Thorfast sat back. He had long been a raider, destroying Danish holdings along their coast and terrorizing their people. He never regretted that life, nor thought himself evil for it. Those who lived along the coasts knew the risks. But to see Sophia so distraught, he wondered if he had left other Danish women in such a state. He shifted to sit flat, putting his back against Sophia's bed to avoid her accusing stare.

"Pirates and Norse mercenaries," he repeated. "Those are about the same."

"I do not blame them," Sophia said, perhaps too quickly to be sincere. "They were hired by Fausta's family, and no doubt aided in their attack by the same. My father has always had to defend against pirates. But he never expected to defend against what must have been an invading army."

"Is there some law to appeal to? A whole town was destroyed. Some lord must be angered at his loss."

"Fausta and her family would not have dared this had they not already bought their own innocence first. They gambled much, but won the toss. No one will challenge them. It falls to me to see Fausta die for her crime."

"And your husband?"

"Quintus?"

He twisted back to look at her. Her eyes searched something unseen, a frown tightening her sharp features.

"I must see what his hand was in all of this. He is just a means for Fausta's family to grab my father's business. Perhaps he too will meet an ill fate. If the child Fausta carried is a son, then I would expect Quintus's life can be counted in months."

"I don't understand your Roman ways," Thorfast said. "But I

178

understand revenge well enough. When Fausta is dead and her family with her, what will you do? Life lived for revenge alone is not worth much. There must be something after vengeance or else there is nothing to celebrate."

"What is life like in the north?"

He faced her, kneeling once again by her side. Tears shined on her cheeks but she smiled.

"There is plague and pox. Hunger and cold. Ice that never melts. And every place a jarl raises a hall there is war and strife."

"And yet you long to return there."

"I do," he said, his mind offering visions of misty fjords. "For there is glory and honor there. Law is simple and fair. The people, even the poorest, have voices in their jarl's hall. The land is rugged and proud. And the old gods still walk with us."

"You seem to dissuade me."

"No, I would rejoice with you at my side. Men would kneel before you and fawn. You would be at the side of a great hero and share in that glory. I would make you a queen of the north."

She smiled, then patted the furs on her bed.

"That is more interesting to me. Now come here. I cannot be alone this night. For tomorrow we are leaving so that I may commit my sins and damn myself to hell. What do I worry for the sin of adultery when I scheme murder?"

He climbed into the bed with her. After she snuffed the candle, Thorfast forgot all his dreams of dead friends and worries for the future. All that mattered was the warm, smooth skin beneath his hands and the hot breath on his shoulder.

The next morning they awakened together beneath the animal furs to the thumping of footfalls across floorboards beyond the door. Thin light slipped around it to gently illuminate the room.

Thorfast raised his head and listened. Sophia's naked body remained pressed to his. She grabbed him tightly as she yawned.

"They go to fight the Arabs today," she said. "It must be dawn."

"You're rather calm about it," he said. "You saw that camp over the mountains. If they attack while we are here ..."

Rather than create a terrifying image of defeat, he let Sophia imagine the result of an attack.

"They cannot cross the mountain pass quickly enough," she said. "My cousin knows they are a flanking force. He will not be tricked."

"And still he marches to battle?"

"Those are his orders. He must not disobey."

Thorfast rubbed his face against the remnants of sleep. He felt odd sitting so comfortably in a warm bed while men raced around outside in preparation for war. Though it was not his battle, he felt he should join them.

"Are we to await him here? If he is defeated, this fort will have little protection."

Sophia slipped out of bed. Despite a night of love making, she modestly covered her body with a fur as she gathered her clothes.

"We leave this morning. There is a trading ship and escort traveling the strait. My cousin has arranged passage for us with them. We will go to his sister's home. Her husband is a wealthy man and will provide us lodging while we plan our next step."

Thorfast began to dress as well.

"You've a large family. Will they join you in revenge?"

She shook her head as she pulled on her dress. "They are family on my mother's side. I'm sure if I pressed them, they might feel obligated to do something. But my mother died many years ago. They will not risk their own wealth on worthless feuding. Allowing us a place to live is about all the aid we might expect."

"But you could prove to them how dangerous Fausta's family is. Look what they did to you."

"My family is not close," she muttered. Her voice shaded into anger. "I am alone in this world. My husband has taken another wife and I have no children of my own. I am worthless to anyone."

"You are worth something to me." He pulled his belt tight over his pants, then found his boots against the wall. "I just think we will need help to—"

"Revenge is for me alone!"

Her shout bounced around the dark room. Her fists were balled tight and her face red with anger.

"Well, you guide my sword. I will clear the way to Fausta's throat. Keep your daggers sharp."

"I will," she said. "I will wear one under my skirt at the waistband. It is the blade that will pierce her heart."

"A painful and bloody death," he said. At last he was dressed. The simple act of wearing clean, whole clothes felt amazing after wearing rags for so long.

A perfunctory knock rattled the door and then it opened. Brilliant lamplight filled the room. Valgerd had arrived with a man wearing a chain shirt over his knee-length robe. He cradled a sword and pouch in his arms.

"Lady Palama." Valgerd's simple greeting was filled with sly accusation. She smiled at Thorfast as she entered.

Sophia blushed, then straightened her skirt. She glanced at Thorfast, but he did not know what it meant. He gave Valgerd a hearty greeting.

"Good morning! You bring us food, I hope."

"There is no time for it," she said. "But I trust you had enough sleep to give you strength for the day ahead."

"Well, I didn't dream of you again."

Both Valgerd and Sophia lowered their heads in embarrassment. But he gave a gusty laugh. Why not? He had not felt so joyous in many months.

The soldier's chain clinked and the floorboards creaked as he waited at the door. His dark eyes flattened at Thorfast's laugh. Stepping inside, he offered his burden with a frown. He spoke in Greek, which Sophia did not translate. But Valgerd translated to Frankish for both of their benefits.

"Commander Staurakius regrets he cannot attend you personally. He prepares the men to march to battle. He sends his wishes for a safe journey and hopes for good news soon."

"Please tell my cousin we are grateful for all he has done."

Valgerd inclined her head. "Your ship will be ready to sail with first light. You have little time to prepare."

"We have little to carry," Sophia said.

"The commander sends you these gifts. He regrets he cannot offer more."

She spoke to the mailed soldier, who presented Sophia a pouch that bulged with coins. While Thorfast had expected her to protest the generosity, she accepted the weighty pouch in cupped hands.

The soldier turned to him, spoke in Greek, then offered a sheathed sword.

"The commander believes you must be properly armed if you are to defend his cousin," Valgerd said. "He noted how awkwardly you wore an Arab sword. This one may be more agreeable to you."

He accepted the heavy sword from the soldier, who summarily dumped it into his outstretched hands as if glad to be rid of it. Thorfast had eyes for nothing but the weapon he accepted. He set his hand on the cool, wire-wrapped grip and tugged the blade. It slid easily from its leather sheath to expose a shining blade with a fresh edge.

He gasped at it. "This is a Frankish longsword, and unused. It is a precious weapon."

The soldier sloughed a belted pouch off his shoulder, then handed it to Thorfast. Inside was a bladder of oil, fresh rags, and a whetstone.

"The commander is a generous lord!" Thorfast beamed smiles to all. He shouldered the pouch, then began to adjust the baldric of the sword so it hung correctly at his left hip.

"Come," Valgerd said. "We must hurry to your ship."

They threaded wood hallways lit with oil lamps that left thin smoke but no odor. Servants and soldiers flitted about their business. Some greeted the mailed soldier that led all of them out of the fort at a march.

The courtyard of the fortress was filled with grumbling soldiers. Their rectangular shields were long and battered and slung across their backs so their formations appeared like iron turtles. Their leaders swaggered among them, cursing and chastising. They assembled before a small gate facing north away from the shore.

The sky was full of dull light. Despite the early hour, the heat of the day was already mounting. Thorfast sympathized with warriors going to battle wearing mail and robes amid such heat. How could anyone fight under such conditions, he wondered.

He was glad to be weaving through their ranks toward the main gate on the shore side. The damage Yngvar and Alasdair had done to the walls was no longer evident. The tower they had scaled stood in silence as if embarrassed at how it had been defeated by two determined men. He held back a laugh thinking of that night. Once more, he was slipping out of Pozzallo—though now as an honored guest.

At last they came to the gates. The heavy doors were bound in iron bars and one hung open. Two guards stood beside it where the heavy wood bolts had been lifted off brackets and set aside. An iron grate had been raised high enough to allow them to pass beneath.

The guards stared at them as they passed under the grate. Thorfast saw the envy in their eyes.

A rutted, well-trod path led down to the dock where Thorfast had burned ships only months ago. Two ships were docked there now, one a fat-bellied, triple-masted trading ship and the other a sleek fighting ship with two masts. The triangular sails were being readied and sailors scurried over the decks to prepare for cast-off. The sea sparkled behind them.

"I thought I'd never see open water again," Thorfast said. He drew the salty air through his nose and sighed appreciatively.

"We cannot accompany you to the dock," Valgerd said. "My escort has to rejoin his unit."

Sophia embraced Valgerd, and they spoke quietly and in Greek. Valgerd held both of Sophia's hands and nodded gravely. Throughout she glanced at Thorfast.

He turned aside with a smirk. Sophia must be begging her to keep from the commander that they had slept together. After all, she was still a married woman.

So they bid their farewells. The soldier stalked off, duty completed. Valgerd waited on the other side of the gates. The grate rattled and squealed as it lowered. It thumped to the ground.

Thorfast waved to her a final time. The heavy doors began to creak shut, grinding over the dirt.

His eyes wandered over Valgerd's shoulder to the masses of

soldiers forming up ranks. At the rear of all the soldiers facing north, a body of light skirmishers was assembling.

His legs buckled and his stomach lurched.

Beyond Valgerd's shoulder, with no doubt in his mind, he saw them.

Yngvar and Alasdair.

22

Thorfast threw himself against the cold, rough iron gate. The heavy wood door swung shut behind it. Never had a closing door thundered as loud as this. His glimpse of Yngvar and Alasdair had been swept aside. He pulled against the grate, gritty rust digging into his palms. But the fort of Pozzallo had shuttered itself against him. The wall stretched into the faint light of the morning. He wished he could vault it.

"Yngvar! Alasdair!" He pulled on the grate, not even rattling the heavy bars.

"What are you doing?" Sophia grabbed him by the shoulder. When he whirled to face her, she leapt back.

"They are inside," he said. "I saw them. Just as the door closed. I saw them as clear as I see you."

Sophia touched the small gold cross over her chest. She shook her head, eyes wide and mouth agape.

"We have to open this gate again. I can show you." He cupped his hands to his mouth and shouted up the wall. "Open the gate! We have to get back inside. Hurry!"

"Thorfast." Sophia spoke quietly, fingertips brushing the back of his arm. He recoiled from her. This time she did not balk at his violence. "Your friends are dead. You keep seeing and hearing them, but they did not survive. Only we two lived."

"So I believed," he said, still squinting up at the wall. Nothing appeared but a thick cloud that floated alone in the pale blue sky. "Yet I know what I have seen. The gods are testing us. I must get back inside."

"Our ship is ready to leave," Sophia said, her voice hardening. He ignored her irritation and considered if he could scale these walls. Alasdair made it seem so easy. Yet now the task was impossible.

"Wait! They are leaving by the north gate. I will meet them there as they leave."

He started to turn, but Sophia grabbed his arm. When he tried to pull away, she dug her fingers deeper into his flesh.

"Stop this madness," she said. Her fingernails bit into his skin. "The ship will not wait long for us."

"Your cousin has paid them. They will wait."

"They are traders. And they are fleeing this place. They will not wait."

"Then go to them."

Sophia stared, brows raised in astonishment. Tears brimmed in her eyes and her mouth trembled.

"There will be other ships," he said, trying to calm his voice. Yet his legs itched to run.

"You swore your life to me." Her voice was small, fearful. "You swore to take me home to have my revenge. This is how you honor that promise?"

"I just need to prove they live," he said. "I did not say I would abandon you."

"Didn't you just bid me to go the ship alone?" She stole her hand back. "Are you so wrapped in your madness that you cannot remember? You must not chase ghosts. That way lies true madness."

"I saw them. I saw Alasdair with Valgerd, and by the gods I will make that woman tell me the truth."

"Valgerd was with me all along," Sophia said, the tears flowing down her cheeks. "You confuse dreams with life. You see things no one else sees. Hear the voices of your friends in every odd sound.

This land is no good for you. Too many ghosts haunt it. The ship leaves now. We must be aboard."

He looked back at the closed doors behind the grate. He had seen them. Beyond all possibility they had survived and somehow were now soldiers in the fortress at Pozzallo. Yet it made no sense. How could they have come to such a fate?

"It does seem impossible that they have become Roman soldiers in what cannot be more than a month."

"Of course it is impossible," Sophia said. She set her hands to his arm again, this time with a motherly touch. "There is no time with the ship leaving. Do not abandon me. You will break more than your promise if you do."

He looked into her glittering eyes. She was as pale as a spirit in the morning light. Perhaps she might fade away and never be seen again. He realized then that he could not bear leaving her side. He could not trade a real woman for the spirits of the dead.

"It's as you say," he said. "This land is haunted. I feel as if I am going mad."

"Let's board the ship," she said, smiling through her flowing tears. "We've a new life across the strait. You will have comfort at last. But we must go—now."

After a single, long stare up the wall, he gestured that Sophia should lead the way. She grabbed his hand and led him down the rut-filled path to the docks. The merchant ship's captain was short and thin, like a bent and rusted nail exposed to the weather. Yet he smiled and welcomed them both atop the gangplank.

The captain spoke a smattering of poor Norse, enough to give Thorfast orders to help with casting off the ship. Once he had aided the crewmen, brown-skinned and weather-beaten men stripped naked to their waists, he looked back at Pozzallo.

The fortress was already fading against the morning haze. The early sun cut sharp shadows into its walls. Thorfast stared after it, leaning on the rails.

Good-bye, my friends, he thought. I leave your ghosts here. But your memories I carry everywhere.

"I will return," he shouted across the waves. Some of the crew looked up, most ignored him. "You will be avenged, my brothers. This land will drown in the blood of our enemies. I swear it!"

So they sailed for a day and a night, and in the morning of the next day they came to a coast that looked the same as the one they had left.

Sophia, who had spent the short journey in the captain's company, now joined Thorfast at the rails where they both studied the approaching shore. Dozens of ships of every size and sail configuration slipped along the coast.

"There are so many ships here," he said. "It's like a sea battle with every ship trying to avoid a boarding."

"This is a major port," she said. "My cousin has married well, it seems. I should have attended her wedding. My father did, of course. So she should welcome me."

"You are not sure of our welcome?"

She shrugged. "What can I be sure of now? God will not help me in revenge, and the devil has no cause to aid the damned."

"But Odin would guide your blade if you call to him."

Sophia smiled and fingered the cross at her chest. "Call to him for me. A blessing on you is the same as one on me."

He looped his arm around her and gathered her close. She leaned in and together they watched the coast grow darker and clearer.

Thorfast aided in docking the ship while Sophia watched. She shared parting words with the short captain, who bowed to her as he indicated they should descend the gangplank. The captain raised a hand to Thorfast, and offered his few Norse words in parting.

"Far vel!"

Once their feet touched land again, Thorfast's single role was to stand close to Sophia with his hand on his sword hilt and glare at anyone she spoke to. He did not understand her conversations. He was glad Sophia had decided to go north with him. Learning to speak this Greek language would break all his teeth. He'd sooner learn to speak to walruses than these Romans. Still, men shrank from his glares and answered all of Sophia's questions as they moved from the dock to the start of the buildings.

They moved deeper into this port town, which was surrounded by high walls and towers patrolled by silhouettes of bowmen. The interior was filled with wretched stenches that conflicted with the freshness of the sea air that blew from the docks. Streets were too small and people too crowded.

"Cities everywhere are the same," he said. "People become herds of sheep that are kept in shit-filled pens."

"And where else are they to shit?" Sophia asked. They wove through crowds of people who thought nothing of them bumping or pushing along narrow lanes. Eventually, they came to wider streets that were free of sweaty, swift traffic.

Sophia asked several men directions. Soon she came to dirty, collapsing building where brown horses were lined up by carts painted in faded, flaking red paint. Men idled against the carts, arms folded and staring dejectedly at their boots.

"We will take a carriage to my cousin's estate."

Thorfast shrugged. "As long as he can offer us a hot meal. The captain was generous enough, but hardly had food to spare us."

"Now it must be a hot meal?" Sophia grinned at him. "Only a week ago you would have been glad for anything."

"A week ago I was not traveling with a rich princess. Standards change, my lady."

The so-called carriage was a fancy cart with worn-out pillows on the bench, worthless in Thorfast's judgement. They juddered and bounced along roads that led from the walled town into the countryside. He saw farmhouses that could have been picked off of Sicily and dropped here. He supposed Sophia had been right about Sicily belonging to Rome. The air was bracing and clean. The horse clopped along at a fair pace with the driver hardly offering more than a few clicks to goad the animal along. After an hour of quiet travel Sophia pointed at a walled estate of cream buildings and brown tile roofs.

"There it is," she said. "I have never seen it myself. But this is not far from my home."

"It's like Prince Kalim's palace," Thorfast said, sitting up straighter to see over the bored driver's shoulder. Sophia laughed.

They drove toward an open gate where two spearmen wore

impractically brilliant red and yellow tunics over padded armor. Their conical helmets caught the sunlight as their heads nodded. No doubt they were bored at their duty. Thorfast would certainly chafe at the life of a guardsman.

In a whirlwind of Greek conversations, Sophia paid the carriage driver, gained entrance to the palace—which Sophia called a villa—and then led them both to the doors of the main home. A servant met them, then vanished into the building to fetch his master.

Throughout, Thorfast stared like a countryside drunk who had wandered into a jarl's hall. He twice stumbled into Sophia while gawking at the number of buildings for what Sophia called a small family. The expansive yard contained diminutive trees in neat rows. A sweet scent flowed from these that stung Thorfast's nose. Everywhere was the sign of excess and waste. Servants crossing the yard dressed too richly. Two dogs were so fat and lazy that they lay on their sides in the grass, peering up with sad eyes as they passed. These animals did not work, it seemed. What purpose was there to a dog that did not work for his master? But beyond this, the home was in fastidious repair. Who had the time to fix every leak in the roof or gap in the wall? Yet the master of this place did not even allow grime on his walls. The brilliant cream color looked as if it had been just painted.

"My cousin does not speak anything but Greek. I'm not sure of her husband. So be careful of what you say," Sophia said as they waited at the doors.

"These doors don't look like they could keep out an ant." Thorfast ran his hand over the ornate designs. "Everything here is for show. Did you live in such a place?"

"My home was far bigger than this." Sophia raised her chin and scanned the yard with hooded eyes. "But this is still a wealthy man's home. Just be quiet and let me speak. You are posing as my servant and bodyguard, you'll remember."

"Posing? I'd call it a fact."

Sophia gave him a slight smile and brushed her hand against his. But before he could offer a witty retort, the doors swept open.

The woman who stood in the doorway wore a bright blue dress that dazzled Thorfast's vision. For a moment he saw nothing but a dress and a slice of pale flesh. The woman squealed in delight, which Sophia echoed. The two blue dresses, Sophia and the woman who must be her cousin, swept together in an embrace that seemed more contrived than natural.

They reviewed each other while still holding arms. No doubt they traded petty compliments as women often do. Thorfast now had a better look at the cousin. She was about Sophia's age, perhaps several years older. Where Sophia's hair was near white, her cousin's was raven dark. She seemed as soft as wool but moved with careful grace. Her smile radiated charm, and Thorfast decided he liked her.

The man appearing behind her, with the bony servant that had fetched him, was another matter.

He was no taller than Sophia'a cousin. His girth threatened to burst the silver buttons of his red shirt. His wedge-shaped head was emphasized by frizzy hair the color of driftwood that splayed out in a cone around his fat head. His eyes tried to be welcoming, but his fish-lips trembled on the verge of a sneer. He was either flushed or his wife had spent the last hour slapping his face. Thorfast could not tell. Neither did he like the man from his appearance alone.

Greetings flew back and forth. Thorfast heard his name mentioned, which followed up with a brief smile from Sophia's cousin and no acknowledgement from the man who must be her husband. All his effort was consumed in wrestling a thin smile that threatened to flee in the next breath.

They entered the home, which smelled of flowers. It was dark and rich and too spacious for Thorfast to resist staring. Surely only kings and gods lived like this. But now he stood amid more wealth than he could ever conceive.

Over the next month, he grew accustomed to such luxury.

Once Sophia had reeled out her story, with much heartfelt hand-holding from her cousin, they were provided rooms where they could stay.

"Indefinitely," Sophia had said. Thorfast thought this meant long enough for them to plot their next step. It turned out, however, that it meant Sophia spending tedious days of sipping wine with her cousin while he ostensibly stood guard. She put him to other uses as well.

He was most irritated whenever ordered to fetch her one of the dozen coats she seemed to have acquired without ever leaving the villa. He was no servant but resigned himself to the role, assuming it would end any day.

He had no one to talk to besides Sophia but rarely had time alone with her. For despite the horror of what happened to Sophia's family, she was still considered married to Quintus. Therefore, Thorfast had to sleep apart from her and "act properly" at all times.

He was going mad. He had allowed Sophia a period of adjustment. But weeks passed and she became more comfortable with her life. Her cousin seemed to encourage it, while her cousin's husband flashed smiles as faint and fleeting as melting frost. To Thorfast he shot hateful glares. He dared no reaction. Though he fattened up and his hair and beard filled in, his muscles slackened and his palms grew tender. He could stand no more of this act.

One month later, in the early morning while Sophia prepared in her room, he entered unannounced.

She startled, grabbing the small cross at her neck.

"Today we begin your revenge or my promise to you is done."

Sophia stared at him as if he had gone mad.

"I thought you were enjoying yourself?"

He snorted. "If this is how you live, then I prefer death. Yes, the food fills my belly and the wine warms my face. I want for nothing. But I am an eagle and you treat me as a caged hen."

"But we both needed to recover," she said.

He looked around her. The room was filled with furniture designed more for appearance than functionality. She sat on a low stool, padded to avoid any discomfort to the sitter, and ran a comb through her hair.

"Recover? How long do you need? Your cousin enjoys your company. Her husband, not as much. You steal her attention from him and his patience is ending."

"He is a fine man," she said, dragging the comb through her long hair. "We are not a burden to anyone. Besides, I am paying for our stay."

"Paying? I thought this was the hospitality of family?"

Sophia sniffed.

"Gods, woman, we need that coin to hire men to lead against Fausta. What are you thinking?"

"Lead men?" She clacked her comb against the table she sat before. "What are you here for? You will take me to Fausta, and I will see her dead. That's all we need."

Thorfast braced both hands against the side of his head. He closed his eyes until his breathing slowed. After a moment he knelt beside her and put his hand on her knee.

"You said an entire town was burned to the ground. That takes a war band. I think Fausta will be rather well guarded. We will at least need men to create a diversion so we can reach her without revealing ourselves."

Sophia pouted, staring at her comb.

"You still have your dagger?" She nodded. "Remember how you carried it close to your own skin? How you burned for revenge? Do you carry it now?"

She shook her head. Thorfast released a long breath.

"Fetch me your dagger. And don't glare at me. You've been ordering me about like your slave boy long enough. Get that dagger and put it against your skin."

"I cannot wear a dagger hidden on me while I'm here. What would they think?"

Yet she pulled the dagger from beside her bed, still in its sheath and the thin belt still looped through it.

"My sword is in my room. They trust us enough to allow that much. If they find a dagger on you, tell them the truth. Do they know what you intend? What have you even learned of your enemy?"

Sophia stared at the sheathed blade, then flopped it onto her lap.

"You are right," she said. "I let myself become tangled in a dream. After all I've been through, I just wanted my old life back. But that can never be, can it?

She smiled, though her lips trembled as if she might cry.

"Both of our old lives are lost," he said. "But so it is for everyone. Nothing remains unchanged but the moon and the sun. So our old lives are gone. What does it matter? We would lose them anyway.

Remember the life you have today. What will you do with it? Your bitterest enemy sits atop the ashes of your family and drinks wine. Will you stand for it? Will you not see justice done? If you sit in this room, combing your hair, preparing for another day of idle chatter, then that is a true sin."

Sophia took the dagger from her lap, planting the sheathed point against her palm and twisting it as she thought. Thorfast let his words dig into her. He stood and watched as she slipped the dagger's strap around her waist. Once it was fastened, she tucked it beneath her skirt.

"No one would ever suspect it," he said, hoping he had calmed the anger out of his voice.

"Quintus lives in the next town north of here. His groves stretch for miles, and his house, what I had called my own home until I learned better, is much like this one. Fausta would sleep with him in the upper rooms. She once had her own room when I was still his first wife. By now, I imagine they lie together."

"Then we find them as they sleep together. The gods make revenge easy for us."

Sophia adjusted the dagger and stood. She offered a repentant smile, then hugged him. She smelled like flowers.

"Such tenderness between us, yet we go to do murder. I am not sure I can do it."

"You can," he said, rubbing her arms. "Think of your father, your brothers, anyone you loved. Think of them burning. Think of them falling under ax and sword. Hear their screams as they died in fear and confusion. Your dagger will strike of its own will, I promise."

"I need to remember this," she said. "We have come so far."

"We've further to go," Thorfast said. "I must hang Prince Kalim's head from my ship's mast before I finally take you north with me. But first your revenge must be completed."

The door to the room slammed open. Sophia leapt out of Thorfast's arm, her face flushed red.

Her cousin stood in the door, face as white as milk contrasted with her raven hair. She stared in horror at Sophia.

Thorfast listened to the stream of Greek traded between them.

Sophia began to shake her head. Could their simple embrace be some offense against these Christian people? It seemed so.

Then the fat, wedge-faced husband appeared. He was shouting and cursing, and finally pulled back his wife so he stood in her place.

More tense words shot back and forth, and Thorfast's heart beat harder even though he did not understand.

Yet he had familiarized himself with Greek enough that sounds had begun to form into words. One was clear above all the others.

Quintus.

Sophia's eyes had gone as wide and blank as a dead fish. She looked up at him.

"Quintus is here. He has come to take me home."

23

Quintus appeared like a friendly, gray-haired seal in fine clothes. Thorfast thought to throw him a fish and laugh as he twisted through the waves begging for another. Yet he sat comfortably at the table where he and Sophia had eaten only the night before. She stood before him, head lowered while Quintus stared up in fascination.

Thorfast stood behind Sophia, desperately wishing he had his sword. He could gut Quintus the Seal, gut the wedge-headed husband for his treachery, then ride to take Fausta's head. There might be a few dozen soldiers to kill on the way in and out. No worries for him. The gods were laughing so heartily at this moment, they would never let him die. He was too entertaining to die.

But he did not have a sword. He could not truly fight his way out of the mess, and Quintus doubtlessly was not alone.

So he stood ready to snatch Sophia away. At the rear of the room, Sophia's cousin clamped her hand over her mouth in terror. Her shit-eating bastard of a husband held her by her shoulders as if she might fly through the ceiling. That man had to die, Thorfast thought. How else had Quintus learned of their arrival? The bastard had sent word.

Quintus spoke with reverence, and his seal-eyes were filling with tears. He stood slowly, taking Sophia's hands in his. She jolted back, but he pulled her still. Thorfast's hands flexed for the sword he did not have.

Guards hovered at the doors of the room. Thorfast noted their reaction to him. They carried short swords that would be better for fighting in such a closed space.

Not that he could fight.

Quintus did not even acknowledge him. He and Sophia spoke in strained and awkward cadences. Wedge-Head interjected from behind. Thorfast was truly going to twist that bastard's head from his shoulders.

Then Quintus gathered Sophia into his arms.

She squirmed and faced him. "Don't do anything. Ten men accompany him. He says you are no longer needed as a guard. Come find me—"

Quintus jerked her aside, and the friendly seal face now regarded Thorfast. The playful look never shifted, though his eyes reviewed him like he was no more than a basket of olives he planned to press. He gave a few words to Sophia's cousin then turned to leave. Sophia went with him, not looking back.

He wanted to call out, but remembered her warning that others might understand. So he watched with arms dangling at his side as she left.

Left?

The instant she slipped into the other room, he felt as if his entire word had gone with her. Despair and loneliness swept over him, though she must not even have been through the front door.

How could he survive here without her? He stared after her and heard the door beyond thump closed.

The husband appeared, his double chin pressed to his chest from his wide smirk. He had Thorfast's pack and sword.

With curt, angry words he dismissed him. The cousin began to weep and fled the room. But the fat husband, now with four guards behind him, would see him out.

The guards marched him to the gates, shoved him outside, and slammed the doors behind him. After straightening his clothes, he stared up the road. The column of men that Quintus led from a cart where Sophia sat beside him was about to mount a shallow rise.

"Well, I've got a sword," he said. "And I've a trail to follow. And I've been talking to myself for a month. So this is not so bad. Now I just have to beg Yngvar's ghost for a new plan. I'm sure it will all go smoothly."

If he followed too closely, Quintus might send men back to attack him. Yet if he delayed too long, he would lose their trail. He had no idea where he was. Not Sicily was the best he could say. He scratched his head and smiled.

"I probably should've been more curious."

He followed the road, which they would have to use as long as Quintus travelled by cart. He had set men to trail in the rear, but Thorfast stalked them from the cover of trees and bushes. The countryside was all farmland and groves. The same humid heat as Sicily pulled sweat into his clothes. He trailed Quintus until midday when they came to a so-called villa much like the one he had just left.

The cart vanished inside the walls and the gate closed after the rearguard gave one last glance around. These men were neither soldier nor warrior. Most likely they were thugs for hire. As such, their work was shoddy and one must have seen Thorfast pulling back behind bushes. But nothing came from it. When Thorfast again looked out, a small tower was all that overlooked the entrance.

"Now to get in there," he said. "What would be the most dangerous, unlikely plan?"

He sat amid the bushes and pulled off his boots. He fanned his sore and tired feet as he thought. Quintus's villa was not far from the sea. The salt air was masked with a heavier, more irritating scent from the olive groves stretching out everywhere. But his nose scented the ocean. He was not sure how that would aid him now. Perhaps it could be his escape route.

The road to Quintus's villa had been empty, but another road crossing before it seemed more active. Thorfast watched a distant group of travelers like black ants disappearing over a long and shallow hill. Green mountains were a backdrop to their passing.

Toward the direction of the sea, a group of men and three carts approached.

"So this land is heavily settled. That's not going to put me on the other side of those walls." He scratched his head, hoping he could shake out an idea. Sophia had her dagger. Once Quintus the Seal undressed her, she would be disarmed. Fausta would no doubt want to discover how her enemy had survived. He prayed Sophia would not reveal his role in it. While Quintus had a good look at him, he seemed to believe Thorfast was nothing more than a servant to be dismissed. Fausta was probably more calculating, and if she knew a Norseman had aided Sophia, then she would likely hunt him.

The group approaching from the sea drew closer while he sat. He studied the carts and the men accompanying them. To his surprise, the column pulled up to Quintus's gates.

"Of course," he said, sitting straighter to get a better view. "Deliveries will be coming and going all the time."

He watched the group shouting to two men atop the small guard tower. They directed the group around the side where Thorfast could not see. The carts turned with great effort. The shouts of the horse drivers echoed over the distance. The cart guards stood back and let the drivers do their work.

The plan formed in his mind. It was the flash that Yngvar had often spoken of. One moment he had no idea what to do, the next the complete plan leapt out at him. So it was now.

He thought of Yngvar and Alasdair, the first time since he believed he had seen them in Pozzallo. Perhaps he had seen other men who shared a resemblance. By now that memory was fading and he was not sure what he had seen. It had been a glimpse. He shook his head. That was not important now. But if they were here, their plan would be simpler. Alasdair would scale the wall at night then open the gates. Yngvar would storm the villa with a score of men while Aladsair located Sophia. Then all would be bandaging fresh cuts around a campfire far from this villa, but singing songs of victory.

His plan was different.

With only half a day left, he followed the road that led to the sea.

Judging from the salty scents, it could not be too distant. He was armed and his strength was back. Both gave him confidence to move alone among strangers. Better still, he had the few coins from Sergius that had not escaped the sack when he showered them over the Arabs.

The sight of a sprawling port city was no longer amazing to Thorfast. He had seen enough of these cities to say this one was a drab, dirty, and smelly clump of buildings where people shit on the same streets they walked. A typical city. He had arrived before nightfall, and the gates were open and still full of traffic. A dozen armored spearmen kept watch and more lined the walls. This was not a port city expecting peace. The guards wanted some form of payment to enter. He could not understand them. They guffawed when he paid a gold coin. Perhaps it was too much, but he had nothing else.

Once inside, he kept to side roads and lowered his head. He wished for a cloak with a hood, but he had only the plain clothes of a servant. At least he would not appear too rich, though more than one person stared at his sword as he wove among the people.

At last he found the docks and the scores of ships at bay. He roved among these until he found someone willing to make eye contact. Yet whenever he spoke, he found no one understood him. Two men kept pointing him down the long row of docks. Eventually he located a ship where the crew were settling down for the night. A bald-headed captain with a grizzled beard that flowed over his bare chest spoke Norse.

"A wolf without a pack, eh? That must be hard on you," the captain said after he and Thorfast exchanged greetings. He gave his name as Tariq. He spoke with a strong accent but his words flowed naturally.

"I alone survived the wreck of my ship. It has taken me too long to get my strength back. But I've a sword now, and with that I can gain everything I need."

Tariq laughed. "I don't doubt it. Right now I have a few Norsemen like you. Arabs, Berbers, and Greeks too. Over the years, I think every kind of man has walked this deck. But I have always found Norsemen the better sailors and fighters. So you are looking for work?"

Thorfast shook his head. "Not on a crew. I want to go inland. I escaped Ran's Bed once, and the whore goddess is still greedy for me. I fear to sail so soon or else she will pull me down to the sea bottom."

Tariq hissed. Two of his crew, likely the Norsemen he mentioned, stared curiously at him.

"Well, when your luck has changed find me again. I will be here for a while."

"There is an olive oil trade here," Thorfast said. "I think I would be better suited to guarding those wares. Are there any traders who could use a strong sword arm?"

Tariq tilted his head, but one of the other Norsemen answered for him.

"There is that Greek captain," he said, pointing down the docks. "Lost half his crew to a storm. He'll want to add to his escort for certain. He tried to recruit me."

"If I'd known that," Tariq said, "I'd have paid him to take you."

The men laughed, and Thorfast indulged a smile.

"And where does this Greek captain trade? Will he be buying olive oil?"

"Of course," Tariq said. "This is the best port for it, if that's your trade. It's not mine, though."

"Would you introduce me to this captain? I am eager to work again and have been too long on my own. Perhaps a good word from you would help me."

Tariq stroked his long beard, and suspicion seemed to enter his honey-colored eyes. "I can show you to him, but there is not much I can say about you."

"Of course there is." Thorfast fished out a gold coin and held it up between finger and thumb. "I am a strong, Norse warrior that is both loyal and hard-working. You heartily recommend me."

"That is the other thing I like about Norsemen," Tariq said, extending his hand for the coin. "They have a nose for gold."

Once the coin passed between them, Tariq and one of his Norse crewmen introduced him to the Greek captain. He was hired immediately.

"When your luck changes and you are ready for the sea, come find me. I am in this port all the time."

Tariq left him with his new crew, none of them capable of speaking any language he knew. This was especially fortunate, he thought. No one to pry at him and his plans.

He spent a night on the deck of their ship. The next morning, he was handed a cheap spear and marched out of the city with his new employer. The trusted guard sat in the cart with the coin box. He walked behind, at the rear of the column of nearly twenty men. They passed other carts and their guards headed toward the port. Greetings were made in passing. They never slowed, though the Greek snapped his head at every swaying branch or flight of birds. He was perhaps more accustomed to heavier guards. That coin box must be quite a prize, Thorfast thought.

Still before midday, they arrived at Quintus's villa.

The side gate was as busy as Thorfast had expected. It was only large enough to fit a single cart through. Its two red doors seemed flimsy for their purpose. Yet the villa walls were meant to keep out opportunistic bandits and not an army. By night a simple bolt would keep intruders at bay long enough for a guard to answer from the wall.

They followed the heavy ruts in the dirt track and passed through the gate. Immediately inside the gate, huge clay vases covered with leather sat in neat rows atop boards. Guards greeted them, and a merchant sat ready for business at a nearby table. The Greek captain started to make his deal and the box of coins was taken to be weighed. Confident of the trade, the captain ordered Thorfast and his fellows to begin moving the olive oil onto the cart. He put his spear down and joined the group shuffling toward the lines of containers.

They were too heavy for one person to move safely. While he worked with another dark-skinned man to lift one to the cart, he studied the villa. It was nearly the same as where he had lived the last month. Sophia would be upstairs in the main building, likely Fausta's reluctant guest. While he could reach her, he wondered at how to get her out. Small windows were not so high that leaping from one would cause injury. Though a man could break a leg simply walking an old path. The gods would have to favor him to avoid injury.

The gods would have to favor him no matter what. Standing amid the enemy, he felt his plans were as fragile as ice on a flower petal. Yet the gods would not favor inaction. He smiled to himself.

He and his partner set the heavy vase down in the cart. Thorfast looked at his partner. He pressed his knees together and cupped his crotch. Though no one would understand his words, perhaps one of Quintus's guards might.

"I've got to piss."

His partner rolled his eyes and yelled at him. Probably telling him to hold it.

Thorfast shrugged, then jumped down to the side of the cart and began to pull down his pants. His partner howled at him.

He understood the order to relieve himself outside the villa walls. Two of his other companions laughed as he danced around holding his crotch. His partner, however, waved him off in disgust and went to find another to help him.

Thorfast waddled toward the gate to the snickers of those he left behind. He slipped out, faced the wall and performed the motions of relieving himself, then slid back inside against the wall.

A routine trade conducted by routine customers. No one watched him carefully. His companions either huddled around the coin table where they weighed and counted payment or else they languidly moved olive oil onto the cart. Quintus's guards leaned on the walls and stared outside or else chatted with each other. None watched him.

He slipped along the villa wall into shadow. He imagined himself being like Alasdair and vanishing from sight. More likely, he was as obvious as a fat roach on a white wall. No one missed him just yet. Though soon his partner would learn he had slipped away. He needed to find Sophia before then.

He came to a side door for servants. He hid within decorative bushes that bordered the space, smelling the waste servants threw behind the bushes. He took a deep breath, considering what waited behind that door. Like rich men everywhere, Quintus would like his guards close but unseen. So Thorfast counted that they were all outside his home and only one or two might be inside. If it was otherwise, he was likely opening a door to death.

"Time to be a hero," he said as he put his hand around the iron loop.

He tugged it open with one hand and another on his dagger hilt. His sword would be useless inside the small rooms of the villa.

The dim light was impenetrable as he swept inside, drawing his dagger. Yet no one met him in the small room. This was the place where food was prepared. A dozen scents from sour to salty filled his nose. An archway led out of the room.

The layout was familiar to him. He crossed the largest room to sturdy wooden stairs without encountering anyone. He heard female voices from the other side of the house, but nothing moving toward him.

He bounded the stairs to the rooms above. The hallway led to a series of five doors. Sophia's was obvious. A small bar was set across it.

That meant no one was inside but her. His heart leapt at his fortune and he strode to the door. Planks creaked and bounced underfoot. But none of the other doors opened.

He pulled off the bar, careful to make no noise, and set it on the floor. Then he swept the door open.

As expected Sophia sat on a bed, light from an open window throwing a cream-colored rectangle around her. She was dressed in blue and white as she had been the day before.

"Sophia," he whispered. "Time to leave."

She faced him, then leaned back in shock. "How?"

"Let me sit with you and carefully explain how I got here. It should only take a few hours."

He rushed into the room, pulling the door nearly shut but not daring to clack it against its frame. His heart raced as he drew up beside her.

"We don't have time for that!"

He rolled his eyes, then pulled her by the arm from the bed.

"Of course not. If we hurry, I can get you out of the villa. No one is about. Escaping the yard will be another challenge."

Her smile was brighter than the light that framed her.

"I knew you would come for me."

"Don't be so glad yet. We haven't escaped. Do you have your dagger?"

She reached beneath her dress and drew the blade. Yellow light sparkled on its fresh edge.

"Quintus confined me here for the night. No one would think to search me for a weapon."

"If you don't care about surviving your revenge, then we could take it now." Thorfast held her by the wrist and raised her from the bed. "But I want to live long enough to kill Prince Kalim. So we should flee and take your revenge later."

Sophia nodded. "I know a place where we can hide."

They slipped into the upstairs hall. They passed closed doors and rounded to the stairs down. Thorfast's knuckles were white over the hilt of his dagger. His other hand wrapped around Sophia's wrist felt the wild throbbing of her pulse.

The commotion of heavy boots and the vibrations of male voices swelled at the bottom of the stairs. Before he could turn around, a half-dozen spearmen gathered at the bottom of the stairs. The whites of their eyes were bright in the dim light.

Behind them Quintus the Seal stared up in anger.

They shouted and began to charge up the stairs.

"Cornered again," he said, pushing Sophia back.

"What are we going to do?" She pulled free from his grip, dagger quivering in her other hand.

Then a baby began to cry from behind the door nearest them.

24

Thorfast whirled to the door where the infant cried then kicked it open. It slammed hard against the wall, blasting a wave of dust from the wood floor.

Inside a young woman with long braided hair held a baby wrapped in a red cloth. The baby wailed and his arms thrashed barely under his control.

Thorfast rushed at her. She was too young to be Fausta, he thought, but he knew the worth of the baby as Quintus's son.

Shouts came from beyond the door. Sophia rushed inside.

The girl turned the baby away from him, her voice trembling but defiant.

"Give me the child," he said, reaching for the baby, which cried harder. The girl cursed and struggled, but he tore the baby free.

The girl lunged at him.

He shielded the child in one arm as she scratched and pulled him. With his other hand he slammed the pommel of his dagger into her face. The young bones of her nose cracked as she screamed. She crumpled to the floor, and he kicked her aside.

"Get behind me," Thorfast said, lurching toward the door as Sophia stared wide-eyed.

He intercepted the guards, who had rushed around the corner

with their spears lowered into a bristling wall of blades. The length of the shafts, however, meant they could do nothing more than press forward. Still, they filled the door.

"Unless you back up," Thorfast said as he placed the dagger to the soft flesh of the crying baby, "you'll have a dead baby to explain to your master."

No one understood the words, but they did the situation. The guards pulled back their spears. The baby squirmed and wailed beneath the dagger. The nurse whimpered face-down on the floor.

Then Quintus pushed forward. His seal-like face shaded to purple and he stared murderously at Sophia.

"Explain to him we are leaving," Thorfast said. "But not empty-handed. We will trade his son for Fausta."

Sophia's mouth hung open. The baby redoubled its screams, kicking and thrashing.

"Now's not the time to lose courage," Thorfast said. "Your father and family are watching. Make your demand."

She swallowed hard, then nodded. Her pale face regained its color and she straightened her back. Then she sneered at Quintus.

Their exchange began as something terse, almost as if he were negotiating another sale. Yet their talk turned angry, violent, and accusatory. They pointed, raised fists. Quintus spit on the floor. Sophia made some sort of sign with her fingers that caused every man to fall back in terror, some making their own signs in return.

He would have laughed but for the screeching of the baby in his arm. Infants annoyed him even at their best behavior. A flailing, angry baby in his own arms made him wish to he could throw the little troll out the window. He eased back on the dagger, realizing he might be aggravating it. Holding an infant hostage was new to him. In most raids, infants were merely casualties that did not cry long.

At last Sophia and Quintus settled back to something more like real speech. She paused to explain.

"Fausta is not here," she said. "She is attending family business."

"Well, we've nothing more to do. We will hold his son hostage until he delivers his wife. Give us a cart and this broken-nosed slut crying at my feet. Someone has to keep this troll quiet. And I'll cut off one of the baby's limbs every time I catch someone following us. So do not test me."

Sophia touched the gold cross over her chest, leaning away with her lip curled.

"Revenge is bloody work," he said. "Tell him exactly what I said. He needs to fear us or we will not live to see tomorrow."

She spoke with care, and Quintus's eyes widened with every word. He glared at Thorfast, a curse hanging unspoken from his open mouth. But he acquiesced.

The villa cleared of guards, and both he and Sophia walked into the yard. The baby's crying waned but did not stop. His nurse followed along, hands cupping blood that flowed from her flattened nose.

A horse and cart awaited them. Every guard watched in silence. The Greek captain and his crew stood by their olive oil and gawked. The captain had gone as white as snow.

"You must drive," he said. "I dare not risk exchanging the child here. Do you know how to handle a cart?"

"I am a merchant's daughter. Of course I know."

Thorfast kept the baby in his arm while Quintus glowered in horror and rage. Sophia goaded the horse into drawing them forward through the main gates. The cart was small with loose wheels and creaking boards. Thorfast considered it a shrewd choice on Quintus's part. With luck the cart would break down within sight of his villa, opening them to capture.

Despite the number of people observing, the only sounds were the crying baby and the squeals of the cart's wheels.

Once they were out of the villa, Thorfast handed the baby to the nurse. She sat curled in a corner with her hands over her face. Her eyes had blackened and her chin and chest were splattered with blood.

"Keep this troll quiet," he said. Then he drew his sword and leveled it at her. "And you can't flee fast enough to escape this. So don't try."

She wiped her bloody hands on her skirt, then accepted the baby.

She avoided meeting his eyes. Instead she wrapped the baby tighter and whispered soothing words to him.

"As soon as you gain open road," he said, leaning over to Sophia on the driver's bench, "get this nag running as fast as the beast can go. The cart is going to fall apart soon. So let's get some distance and keep his men from sighting us."

"We can't take a cart to where I want to go anyway."

Sophia flicked her crop at the tired horse and built speed. Soon, she had the beast at a near gallop. The cart bounced and creaked. The nurse clutched the baby to her chest and pressed against the cart wall. The entire cart seemed it would fly apart. A wheel began to wobble and Thorfast called a halt.

"This is it," he said. "Any more and the cart will crash."

They rolled to a halt. In the distance, a group of travelers approached them.

"We go on foot from here," he said. "Send the horse ahead. An empty cart should draw enough curiosity from those on the road to let us slip away."

They disembarked and Sophia slapped the horse's rump to set it clopping ahead. The poor animal shined with sweat and seemed uninterested in more work. It only mattered that the cart stayed on the road long enough to delay traffic. The surrounding fields were wide open, though back from the road was what seemed like miles of olive tree groves.

"We're going in there," Sophia said. "By nightfall, we should reach an abandoned villa. It used to belong to a friend of my father. He and his family died of plague and the whole place fell to ruin."

"Quintus will not know of it?"

Sophia shrugged. "He has lived here longer than me. He must know. But it is not anyone's land. The place is cursed and no one goes there willingly. Seems as good a place as any to hide for a night."

The small group trudged into the groves. The shade of the trees relieved some of the heat from the back of Thorfast's neck. Yet what succor from the heat the groves provided was stolen by the heavy scents that stung his eyes and filled his nose with snot. By the time they had exited the far end of these groves, he thought he might never draw a full breath again.

"This place truly is cursed," he said, rubbing his watering eyes.

Sophia grinned, the first time since they had reunited in the villa. "You would feel much better if you could wash off. But I'm not sure of where to find water here."

"And my throat is already burning," he said. The nurse and the baby had also gone silent. They had paused only a brief time to allow the woman to nurse the baby. "At least our precious hostage is well fed."

They crossed wild fields under a sky deepening with night. Clouds had rolled in to obscure the splash of stars blinking over them. They walked half an hour and then came to a grove of dead trees. They were gray and skeletal claws that reached into the sky. The earth around them was full of weeds and patchy grass. The black ruins of a small villa lay ahead like shadows in the approaching night.

"Is this farm haunted?" he asked. "I've no means to fight with the dead."

"Evil spirts and evil men should have no trouble dwelling together," Sophia said. "It is only for a night. We can move on with the morning."

"We are the evil men?" Thorfast raised his brow at her as she returned a sardonic smile. He looked back to the nurse and the baby sleeping in her arms. Dark crusts of blood clung to her nose. Bruises had turned her face black. He shrugged.

"It's too bad about the girl and child. But Quintus and Fausta have earned their suffering. Anyone who serves a murderer should expect an ill-fate. I have no regrets for what we have done."

She stared at him, though her eyes revealed her thoughts were somewhere else. At last she nodded. "Neither do I. Let's gain the house before it is too dark to see our footing."

They threaded the dead groves. Black birds argued against their passage, bursting from their nests into the sky. Thorfast checked the villa first for the dens of any predators. He would have no good answer to any large animal, but he had seen no signs of danger. Satisfied that the villa was nothing more than collapsed piles of wood and stone, they made their place amid the ruins.

The nurse attended the child, which had wet himself and began to wail again. She tried to confer with Sophia, who screamed at the nurse and drove her off to solve the problem on her own. Sophia glared after her.

They found the shell of a building where they could sleep and guard the nurse against any treachery. She seemed a meek and broken thing. But Thorfast underestimated nothing and no one. Even a small cut could fester and bring death. This flaccid nurse with her broken nose might kill them all while they slept. Nothing was impossible.

Once they had cleared debris away for sleeping room, Thorfast sat with Sophia, drawn sword across his lap and his pack at his side. The nurse fed the baby once more. She was nothing but a milky gray slash of flesh showing in the shadows where she had been cornered.

"I still have coin," he said. "Too bad I cannot spend it. We must find drink by tomorrow."

Sophia nodded. She rested against a crumbling wall in the shell of the destroyed home. The space smelled of earth and dust, and of rot and mold farther inside where the sun never reached.

"Quintus had nothing to say to me," she said softly. "He collected me home as if I were a misplaced hammer. He had not even asked after where I had been. So he knew all along what happened to me."

"You thought he didn't know?" Thorfast leaned beside her, fingering the sharp edge of his sword. "Of course he knew everything, that bastard."

"I had hoped Fausta had just deceived him with a lie. That I had gone missing or else left him. But he knew. Fausta came to me last night as soon as I was thrown into that room. She tormented me with the details of what she did to my family."

The wind rushed through the dead trees surrounding the villa. Night turned the world to shades of gray. Sophia gathered the darkness to her like a mantle of sorrow. The satisfied suckling of Quintus's son was at odds with the sullen atmosphere that had descended on their space.

"You do not have to tell me what happened," Thorfast said, patting her knee. "But hold those memories to drive your revenge. You now stand over your enemy, your foot on her sword-arm and your blade at her throat. She will beg for mercy and you will show none. She has earned none. Cut her head from her body, drink the blood that flows from her neck. Rejoice in her death and know you have done the world good. For you have killed a poisonous snake that would surely kill others if left alive."

Sophia smiled mirthlessly. "I don't feel as if my foot is on anyone's neck. We are the ones cowering."

"This is not a retreat. We have shifted the battle to better ground. We cannot let the enemy choose where the fight happens. That way lies defeat. As long as we have that brat, we will alway be able to decide where the battle is fought. Trust me. Fausta and Quintus feel our threat more keenly than they ever imagined they would."

"What are we going to do next?" Her voice was soft and uncertain.

"Tomorrow we send the nurse to Quintus with instructions on where to meet us. Fausta comes alone. Once we have her, you will leave the baby for Quintus to retrieve. Fausta's family will have arranged for a killer to stalk us. Someone who will move like a ghost and cut our throats from the darkness. He will accompany her even though we will not see him. So let your revenge be swift and kill her on the spot. No time for torture."

"Torture," Sophia said, her eyes unfocusing. "It would be fitting."

"Fausta is her family's tie to Quintus's new power," Thorfast said. "They could claim something through the son. Perhaps they will let her die. Yet no matter what, they will avenge her. So we must flee as fast as possible. I met a man, Tariq, who I believe is a pirate trying to hide in plain sight. He can help us escape this land. He'll have a price too high to pay with the coin I carry. But we will persuade him that we can pay it. The gods will decide our fates, as they always do."

"Torture," Sophia repeated. "Fausta spent last night describing how her family tortured my father. He held out for days, beaten and starved. They had declared him dead in the attack, but held him Quintus's villa. My home. They forced him to sign documents to give over all his businesses and contracts to Quintus. He would not do it.

They told him I was a hostage. They showed him a finger they had cut from a hand and claimed it was mine. They promised my head next. He signed away everything, thinking he saved me. Then they killed him. Burned him alive in the ruins of his estate. Fausta watched and laughed. She laughed when she described how he screamed amid the ashes of his life."

Thorfast tucked his head down. Tears flowed from Sophia's eyes as she paused to recover her breath.

"The papers were acknowledged as legal. Fausta spared no detail of how her family bribed every official in ten miles. They must have spent their last coin on it. But they will now earn it back a hundredfold. All of it covered in my family's blood."

"If I ever doubted killing Fausta, you have eased my mind. Kill her soon, but cut her throat slowly. Let her suffer as she dies."

Sophia gave another bitter smile, wiping at her eyes with the back of her hand.

"And still I'm not sure I can do this. It is one thing to kill while defending yourself. But to kill a helpless person, even one as deserving as Fausta. I am not sure I can."

"I will guide your hand, if that helps. But we are now marked for death even if we were to set that baby free with his nurse."

"Will you take me north? I never want to see this land again. Will you make me a queen of snow and ice?"

He put his arm around her and she tucked into his shoulder. "It is not all snow and ice. There are green fields and heather. Mountains that reach to Valhalla and shelter the folk who live in their foothills. I will make you queen of such a place. You will never know danger again."

"I love you," she said, her voice a thin whisper.

He squeezed her tight. "Do not distract me before battle, woman. Do not tempt the gods. Let us rest. For by this time tomorrow the story will all be told. We will be running for our lives."

"Lives in the north?"

"Lives in the north."

25

The next morning Thorfast awakened to Sophia and the baby stirring beside him. His joints ached from the dampness of bare earth beneath him. Yet he had suffered worse in Prince Kalim's prison. A month of clean beds in a Roman villa had softened him.

Sophia sat leaning against the ruined wall. The baby rested on her lap. She studied its random kicks and jabs with a strange intensity. Her expression was trapped between hate and love. Thorfast was not certain he had ever seen such an expression on anyone. It was more than conflict. The tight lines on Sophia's face read as torment though she smiled.

The nurse hovered beside her. Her flattened nose was thick with scabs and dried snot, and her eyes were puffy with bruises. Even as Thorfast rose, she did not look at him. Instead she murmured to the baby, adjusting his red blanket as Sophia continued to stare down at him.

"Thank you for letting me sleep," he said. He had kept a watch until he could no longer lever his eyes open. Sophia had relieved him, holding his drawn sword which now rested in its sheath against the wall of the ruined building.

Birds sang from their hidden nests in the ruined villa. The heat roared back into the air now that the sun rose. The sky above was slate gray and full of wooly clouds.

Would the gods not see him through such cover, he wondered. If they were blinded then he could not count on their aid. His hand felt for Thor's hammer, which he had not worn in long months. He wished for one now. He needed the gods.

Sophia did not respond to his thanks. She did not stir at his rising. The nurse continued to soothe the baby, gently stroking his chest as she did. Her words were thick and nasal from her shattered nose.

"You know this land better than me. Pick a time and place to make the exchange. Let it be later in the evening, so that we will have the cover of night to make an escape." He stood, dusting off his pants, then strapped on his sword. Sophia still did not stir. He prodded her with his foot. "Are you asleep with your eyes open?"

"I have a place in mind." She continued to study the baby, her voice tired and distracted.

"Make it a woodlands, if you can." He adjusted his baldric and patted the comforting weight of the Frankish sword at his hip. "We must flee the moment we have Fausta with us. I will find something in these ruins to bind her hands. I'm sure she will bring a dagger under her skirts. Just need to keep her under control a short distance. Maybe we'll carry her head with us and toss it into a lake. Just so her ghost will never find it. Let her death be restless."

Sophia nodded without any enthusiasm. She stood, pulling away from the nurse. The two spoke in Greek, the nurse repeating her instructions to Sophia's satisfaction. She tried to see the baby once more, but Sophia pushed her away.

"Get running," he said, imposing himself before the nurse. "Or I'll hammer that nose through the other side of your head. Understand? Run!"

The nurse's eyes were lost behind black and swollen pouches, but she flinched away at Thorfast's shout. She ran and he followed. He chased her off the ruins into the dead olive trees until he was certain she would keep running to the road.

He stalked back to Sophia, who waited with the baby.

"You hold him," she said. "I cannot carry this child all day while we wait."

"I don't know anything about caring for a baby."

"I must be alone," she said, shoving the sleeping baby into his arms. "I will fetch you when it is time to leave. I must pray for forgiveness."

Thorfast accepted the warm, tiny child into his arms. He looked at him sleeping, a smear of thin black hair pasted to his head. A face like an apple that had been left to wrinkle in the sun. He was sweaty, likely from the blanket. But it seemed to comfort him. Sophia drifted off into the ruins.

"Don't go into any buildings," he said. "They could be dangerous."

She did not respond. He sat with the child in one arm. Each time he put the baby down, it cried. Holding it seemed the only chance at peace. By midday it was screaming for food.

"Be silent, boy! You'll be back with your nurse tonight. Too bad about your mother, but I expect I'm doing you a favor. A witch like her would probably make your life a misery."

Thorfast did not know what to do. The words had not comforted the baby, though he had not expected they would. Sophia was still away and he had nothing more to offer the baby. He set him down and walked off. The child would be safe enough.

At last by late afternoon, the baby had ceased crying and fallen asleep. Thorfast had rummaged through debris and found a length of rope that would serve as Fausta's binding. It was mostly rotten with a salvageable section. She would not need to be bound long. He found Sophia kneeling before a senseless pile of stones and rotting wood. Perhaps it had been a church, but Thorfast could not determine what the the debris had once been. She clasped her hands together in prayer. He left her alone and sat with the baby.

When the sun was drawing down to the western horizon, she rejoined him.

"It is time." Her voice was hard and resolved. Her eyes were focused again. "I will carry the baby."

She led them both through the dead olive trees back to where groves again occupied the landscape. They filed through these trees to the edge of a small wood. An uncovered well had been dug there, suggesting habitation nearby that Thorfast could not see. A well-trod path led away over a rise. Two figures, a man and woman, stood blocked out as shadows against the glare of setting sun through heavy clouds. A low wind fluttered through the hem of the woman's dress

"Stop here," he said. "Let's have a look around first."

Sophia pressed the baby to her chest. The boy began to cry again as if he sensed the approaching danger. Perhaps he felt it through Sophia. Her long pale hair flowed across her face. Taut lines drew down her brows as she glared at the distance.

Thorfast's own white hair now touched his collar and it too lifted with the breeze. He wished it provided relief from the heat. But it merely brushed over the glaze of sweat coating him, delivering only fleeting respite. As his heartbeat rose, he realized no wind could relieve him. He sweat from fear and worry.

Drawing his sword, he approached the well. He checked the perimeter and peered into the darkness of the well. A cool wetness reached up from it. He scanned the surroundings. To the front where the two shadows waited were scattered trees and a slope that obstructed the rest of the view. The enemy had the high ground after all. It did not matter in this fight. He was concerned for the trees behind him.

"A bucket would be welcomed," he muttered to himself, checking the well once again. Earlier he had found a brook near the ruined villa where he had drunk his fill. But he thirsted again.

Returning to Sophia's side, he rested his sword point in the grass.

"Quintus will have men hidden behind that rise. Someone might hide among the trees. I can't see anyone, but the evening gloom works against us in this." He paused, but Sophia simply nodded. The baby's crying grew stronger and it began to squirm.

"Don't crush the boy before you hand him over. Now, don't get any closer than the well. You wait there and demand they meet you. Don't bargain with them for the boy. The only thing of value they can offer in trade is Fausta. Send her back to me. Once I tie her hands, set the boy down and we will flee. The rest will be up to you."

Sophia gave him a long, blank look before smiling as if she had just recognized him.

"Thank you for keeping your word to me. I could not have come this far without you. I have prayed for you this day. Though I am a sinner, perhaps God will hear me anyway. He is merciful."

"I'd rather have him strike Quintus and the others dead than receive a smile from your god. Now do not waste time. Quintus's men will be moving to surround us even now."

She set the baby on her hip, then ran her hand over Thorfast's cheek. It was cold and trembling, though she seemed as serene as a new mother resting beside her hearth.

"An eye for an eye," she said.

Thorfast tilted his head at the statement. It was unlike her to be so poetic. The words did not sound like her own, but he understood the reference to revenge. He nodded in agreement.

She drifted toward the well, crying baby in her left arm while the right swung at her side. Her blue skirt skimmed over dirt and grass, lifting with the gentle gust of humid wind. She settled by the left side of the well, then called out.

"Fausta!"

The shadow of the woman looked to the man beside her, who must be Quintus. His corpulent outline was obscured by a heavy fur drape. Thorfast guessed if he could penetrate the shadow, he would see armor. The vision of his seal face atop a body clad in shining mail made Thorfast smile.

Fausta was a tall but frail woman. She had long black hair that ended in curls below her collarbone. Her head was also long and thin. She looked nothing like the demoness Thorfast had expected. He imagined someone stronger and more imposing. What he found was little more than an over-stretched wisp of a woman.

She too seemed to drift across the grass. She was dressed in a brilliant yellow skirt and bright blue blouse. Another shrewd choice, Thorfast thought. Trackers would see her easily among the trees. He shook his head at their hope. Her striking clothing would only help them find her headless corpse.

Sophia ordered her to stop out of arm's reach. Thorfast straightened up at this decision. But when Sophia began speaking, he realized this might be her only chance to curse her enemy. Once they had completed the exchange, there would be no time to enjoy twisting the dagger in Fausta's heart. So he rested both hands on the pommel of his sword and watched.

Fausta began to argue back. The baby cried harder. Sophia's words grew more urgent, more ragged. She shook her head, raised her fist, jabbed a pointing figure at her. Fausta crossed her arms and turned her head aside. She even laughed.

Across the field, Quintus tried to conceal his hand signals. But Thorfast guessed where he directed his men. They were filling along the opposite side of the slope to gain the edge of the woods. They would be in a fine position to cut off escape. But Thorfast was not going to oblige them. He would lead Sophia opposite their position and retain advantage.

For that instant of inattention, the scene with Sophia and Fausta had changed.

Fausta reached out with both hands, her mouth gaping with an unvoiced scream. Her eyes white with terror.

Sophia held the baby out with one arm.

With her free hand, she raised a dagger. The dagger she kept concealed beneath her skirt.

The baby screamed.

"Gods, no! Sophia!"

She plunged the dagger down. The baby's screaming ceased.

Fausta's scream erupted—a cracking, tattered wail. She leapt for the dagger-impaled baby in Sophia's arm.

Sophia's vehement curse blasted over Fausta. She then turned to the well and hurled the infant's body into it.

"Sophia!"

Thorfast's heart flipped. His hands shot through with cold terror.

First the snap of a bowstring.

Then an arrow sliced across the field, shot from where Thorfast had planned escape.

The shaft hit Sophia under her right arm. She slammed against the well, then flopped to the ground. Fausta threw herself across the well, hands reaching down for her murdered child. Her pained screams echoing back up at her.

Thorfast grabbed his sword.

Quintus roared out from the crest, rage and hatred and sorrow all rolling out like thunder. A dozen spearmen popped up from behind the rise, each looking dumbfounded at their leader.

Sophia did not move. He only saw her feet and calves peeking out from behind the well. She had been shot through her lungs.

She was dead.

Thorfast realized he would join her if he did not seize this moment.

Fausta remained hanging into the well, crying and screaming. Quintus held his head in both hands, bellowing his rage.

Thorfast ducked instinctively and an arrow grazed across his head. The air snapped in its wake, rippling his hair.

The near miss galvanized him. He charged into the trees to foil the archer's line of sight. Holding his sword in both hands, he wove among root and bush. Each step was like the leap of a stag that hurtled him toward the archer's position.

As if his sight were guided by the gods, he spotted the archer crouching on a heavy limb of a tall tree.

The fool took aim from his perch. Thorfast roared at him, but jinked behind a tree the moment the bowstring snapped. The arrow thumped hard against the wood. When he stepped out again, the archer had realized his mistake. He leapt off the limb and began running.

Filled with murderous rage, Thorfast sped like a wolf after a rabbit. The archer fled deeper into the trees. But Thorfast was now at his back. His brown hair and cloak flew behind him.

When he drew within arm's reach, Thorfast grabbed the flying cloak.

The archer fell back, slamming to the ground.

He had only a heartbeat to see the sword plunging down into his chest. Then he was squirming around the blade and coughing up blood.

Thorfast grabbed the bow and the quiver. He ran his hand over the archer's spasming body, searching for anything of use. The archer seized Thorfast's wrist and grimaced at him through bloody teeth.

"Die by your own arrow, you dog," he said. He fished one from the quiver, then rammed it into the soft flesh of the archer's neck.

He gasped then his hand dropped to his chest.

From behind, Thorfast heard more cursing and screaming. Fausta's wailing reached to the heavy clouds, smothering them all with heat and darkness.

He had time only to recover the bow and quiver. The archer had a hand ax tucked into his belt, which Thorfast also stole. Then he dashed into the trees.

Behind him, Quintus shouted orders.

Thorfast sped into the unknown woods, never slowing, never tripping.

And never looking back.

Sophia was dead and he was lost.

26

The shouts from behind Thorfast faded with the light. He wove among trees and bushes, heading toward the darkest points in the thin woods. Each leaping stride carried him toward the point where he hoped to lose his pursuers.

Brush and woodland debris clawed at him as he fled. Stinging sweat flowed into his eyes. Heat pressed on him.

Yet he did not stop until the calls from behind had faded.

He stumbled against a tree, resting against its smooth bark. He gulped for breath, used a sleeve to wipe his brow.

His sword weighed at his side. Against his opposite hip a small quiver with a half-dozen arrows slid forward. He held a bow in a sweat-slick hand.

All these weapons, he thought, but to what end?

He slumped down against the tree, too exhausted to continue. A dozen men were scouring this wood for him. He had no idea where he had run, but they would have no trouble following his path by daylight. His wild charge had left a trail a blind man could follow.

As the sun slid below the horizon, what scant light had penetrated the heavy clouds now vanished. The trees became darker shapes against the lighter gray of night skies. Bird song ended.

He heard nothing more than the crackle and rustle of wind through the trees.

They had abandoned the search. Likely they knew where to find him, and could capture him at any time. For the moment, they probably focused on retrieving the baby from the well. Yet even this would likely wait until sunrise.

The sun had set on death and tragedy.

His hands shook, he realized. Despite the heat and exertions, his fingers and toes were like ice. He tucked his hands underarm.

Sophia was dead.

He blinked hard as if it would erase the memory. But it did not. He still saw her collapsing with an arrow in her side. He still saw her white feet and calves splayed out from behind the well. She had made no sound.

She had fallen over and died.

Why did she kill the baby? Quintus's son was her only shield. As expected, the instant she had surrendered him she had been killed. She had to have expected this. He had told her as much.

His eyes stung not only from sweat. Hot tears clung to his lashes. He had not felt such pain since his sister had been murdered. Even so, that was at least an understandable result of war. Sophia did not have to die, at least not like this.

Why had she killed herself? That was what she had done, after all. Had he not promised to care for her, to give her a new home and family? Now he understood why she had been so distracted and distant. Why she never learned the baby's name or even wanted to hold it.

She had planned this from the start. Her revenge against Fausta was to kill her son. Thorfast understood the symbolism. She stole Fausta's family the way she had Sophia's.

But that was not the same. Fausta's family, the ones who should truly die, still lived. While Thorfast could not bring them justice now, he expected as he gained strength and power he would. He planned to topple Prince Kalim. How much harder would it be to destroy a Byzantine merchant family?

"That's not how you do revenge, woman."

His voice cracked and he sniffled.

Then he straightened up, blinking out the tears that clung to his eyes. He rolled his neck and set his jaw.

"I will show you how it's done." He collected the bow, then rose to his feet.

Finding the exit from the woods was simple. He followed the lighter spaces between trees until he returned to open fields. Cloud cover foiled hope of determining direction by the stars. He knew the rough direction of Quintus's villa. If he could arrive there in advance of Quintus, he could lay an ambush.

Yet the gods did not favor this plan. He set off toward where he expected to find the road again. However, he traveled for nearly an hour and the ground was becoming less hospitable and less like the fields he had crossed to reach the ruins. He turned back to his starting point. He walked past that point for another hour and then found the road.

Without stars or a moon to guide him, he had to guess the direction of the villa. He had half a chance to get it right.

No one traveled the roads at night, expect perhaps the bandits traders feared. He might encounter traders camped at the side of the road. Yet as he proceeded along the edge of the path, he found no one. Soon he spotted the orange light from the single tower overlooking Quintus's main gate.

He smiled up at Valhalla, silently thanking the gods. They expected entertainment this night and would not set his path away from danger.

Once within sight of the villa, he paused. Though it was not a fortress, it still had high walls and more guards than even a dozen men could defeat, never mind one. He crouched behind bushes that grew among mossy rocks off the main road. A well-worn path threaded past through open fields leading to the main gate.

His sword weighed heavy. It would be of little use to him inside the villa itself. Same for the strung bow he carried in hand. He patted the ax and dagger in his belt. These were his tools for tonight's work.

He studied the villa for activity. The tower was the main point of defense and orange light fluttered behind thin windows. The walls, from what he remembered, were not wide enough to be walked by defenders except over the main gate. The main gate was closed and the grate lowered. Something white hung over it.

"Sophia?"

Even at this distance, he was certain of Sophia's profile. Her corpse had been stripped naked then hung over the gate.

He clenched his teeth and tightened his grip on the bow. He could not see how she had been hung, but before the night was done, he would cut her down.

"Quintus's head will hang in your place," he said. "I swear it."

Though he felt as if a whole day had passed since Sophia's death, it was only early evening. He wanted to approach the villa in the deep of night, when the guards' vigilance inevitably waned.

When Fausta and Quintus both fell into exhausted sleep and their servants with them.

"Alasdair, if you are in your god's heaven, then see your old friend alone in this world. Be a good lad and show me how you move through fortress walls without being seen."

He waited from his hiding place. Anyone approaching from the road would spot him, but in the depth of night no one would come. He had learned how long an hour could feel during his stay in Prince Kalim's lightless prison. He figured the hours by the waxing and waning of light from the tower.

Yet as he waited, the clouds parted and a half-moon painted faint traces of silver over the villa. It was if the gods shined a light showing him the time to strike.

Keeping his back bent, he swept across the field toward the side gate where merchants made their trades. He recalled flimsy doors and piles of goods near it. While he did not plan to batter the door, he expected it would be the weakest entry point.

He found it unguarded, though he knew it was barred from the inside. The walls were as high as two men standing shoulder on shoulder. A companion could hoist him to the top of the wall. But lacking any help, he had to rely on his own wits.

Yngvar, you laugh at me from your bench in Valhalla, he thought.

I think I know what you would do. Fill your drinking horn and watch me, friend.

The side gate had a decorative lintel that protruded enough to provide a grip. With a running jump, he could reach the lintel and pull up to the top of the wall. If he had a plank or heavy tree limb, he could use it to ease his climb. But finding a suitable branch amid the distant trees was impractical in the darkness. He would have to jump or else waste precious hours searching for something he might not find.

His first attempt failed and his foot thumped against the door. He fled back into shadow, expecting guards. Yet none arrived. He realized his sword was too heavy. With a sigh, he set it against the wall and would return for it after.

Without the heavy weight of the iron sword, he succeeded on his next run. His fingers found the lintel and he used the momentum to get one hand on the wall. His foot still banged the door, but only once. He hung suspended for a moment, scrabbling to get a foot onto the lintel.

At last he found purchase and levered himself to the top of the wall.

He clung to it on his belly, the arrows in his quiver spilled and clattered inside the door. Closing his eyes against noise that sounded as loud as falling trees, he paused. But again no one answered.

With a soft thump, he landed on the opposite side of the gate. He collected the arrows. In case he needed to make a quick escape, he lifted the bar from the doors.

More olive oil had been prepared beside the gates, and he slipped behind these stacks into comforting shadow. From here, he had only to retrace his steps from the day before to find Quintus and Fausta.

He scanned the yard for his planned escape route. The stables directly across from him were the obvious choice. It was open to the air, with a tile roof providing shelter over the stalls. A half-dozen horses were stabled within. He could use one to escape. But he would never get the gates open from horseback. Next to it was a pen for animals, either goats or sheep. He could not determine from here. At least there were no dogs in the yard, which seemed odd to him.

One step at a time, he thought. First take revenge then see if you will survive it. After all, what am I escaping to? What life do I have left?

The side door into the kitchen was unlocked. He carefully pushed it open, knowing whoever worked the kitchens would likely sleep there as well.

His expectations were met. Two young girls curled up on a blanket in the corner. Their soft, rhythmical breathing indicated they slept. He stepped inside with exaggerated care. The door clicked behind him, but the girls did not stir.

Probably worked to exhaustion, Thorfast thought. Good thing for relentless masters.

He crept across the small kitchen filled with a miscellany of pots, jars, and sacks. He exited through the opposite archway then hugged the wall. He paused to get his bearings. The interior was darker than expected. With such heat, no one needed a hearth fire. Lamps were unlit, as no one would have cause to move through the house at night.

He lingered until his eyes were as adjusted to this darkness. Servants slept somewhere in here. Guards might be posted inside. From his time with Sophia's cousin, villa guards spent most of their days outside and not within the fine home of their master. Quintus should be the same.

As he waited, he heard a woman crying upstairs. The wailing ascended and descended as she expended her strength then recovered it.

Fausta, he thought. You will have something to cry for soon enough.

Feeling by hand, he followed the short hall toward the crying until he stumbled over a stair. Now he recalled the layout, and set his foot to the steps. They creaked and squealed underfoot. But he remained unworried.

He set the bow across his shoulder as he climbed. In his left hand he drew the dagger and in his right he carried the ax.

The woman cried behind a closed door at the end of the hall where Sophia had been held. Yet the heavy snoring of a man came from the half-opened door beside him. Further, a dull yellow light shined from it.

A hard lump stuck in his throat and his hands could freeze water. But he did not fear death. He feared not completing Sophia's revenge. If this was a guard, he might alert the entire villa.

He pushed open the door with his dagger hand.

Quintus lay sprawled on a bed. The beached seal laid out beneath an invisible sun. A candle had burned nearly to a stub on a table beside his bed, where an overturned mug and clay jug rested. The room reeked of sour wine.

And a dog raised its head at Thorfast's sudden arrival.

"Ah, there you are."

The beast snarled and scrambled to its feet. It began to bark.

Thorfast jumped at it. The dog leapt for his throat in the same instant. They slammed together.

The black dog was stocky and strong, yet unable to reach Thorfast's throat. The dog's bulk drove him back to crash amid another table and stool. What seemed a mountain of pottery crashed all around him. The dog snarled and snapped in a flurry of yellow fangs.

But Thorfast's dagger struck true. The beast took the dagger deep in its ribs even as it snapped at Thorfast's face.

It howled and yelped, and Thorfast kicked it aside. He leapt up, then slammed his ax into the beast's head. It gave a final yelp as it splayed out under the blow. Dark blood flowed out beneath it.

"Well, that should get some attention."

He whirled around at the sound of rustling bedding.

Quintus, red-faced and bleary-eyed, now stood beside the bed. He held a long, curving sword in one hand, and unsheathed it with the other. The motion nearly caused him to topple over his bed.

"A sword against my ax?" Thorfast smiled. "And you're drunker than a Yuletide skald. I'm disappointed you won't really understand your death."

For all his drunkenness, Quintus struck with smooth practice. Thorfast leapt back but slipped in the pieces of broken pottery. He crashed against the wall with a grunt.

Quintus roared curses Thorfast could not understand. He raised his sword in two hands to deliver a skull-splitting strike. In the tight confines of the room, Thorfast had no place to twist out of the blow.

The air hissed with the cut of the blade.

The wall shuddered as the sword plowed into it, jamming a hand's breadth over Thorfast's head.

He kicked Quintus in the crotch. The fat man stumbled back and Thorfast launched himself atop his enemy.

They crashed on the bed, sliding it to thud against the wall. Full of raging strength, Thorfast pinned Quintus to his bed. His dagger was still in the dog's side, but he held the edge of his ax to Quintus's neck.

"I won't waste my breath on you," he said. "You can't understand anyway."

Quintus's seal eyes widened with terror. He began to beg, his drunken voice quavering and weak. Thorfast shook his head and leaned by his ear.

"This is for Sophia."

He sawed across Quintus's fat neck. He gasped as the sharp blade opened the flesh to spray blood across Thorfast's face. Pushing harder, Quintus's throat lay opened. Blood jetted to strike the ceiling above. Thorfast leaned back, admiring the fat corpse of Sophia's husband.

Grabbing Quintus's head by the hair, he exposed the neck. He hacked four times until the head rolled free of the body. He held it up to his face.

"Olive oil tastes a bit bloody, doesn't it?"

He listened for the guards rushing toward him.

Nothing.

He strained to hear more.

Fausta continued to cry from down the hall, oblivious to the fight just two rooms away.

"I guess they expect you to rage and destroy your room," Thorfast said to Quintus's head. "No one's coming."

He set the head atop the blood-soaked body. He then retrieved his dagger from the dead dog, wiping it across its fur.

While he wanted to carry Quintus's head to the gate, he realized it was too ambitious a feat. Yngvar could pull off such a trick. He was not as talented. So he grabbed Quintus's severed head by the hair. Fausta could give it a final kiss before she met the same end.

He strode down the hall with confidence. If no one answered that storm of noise, then no one would come for Fausta's feeble screams. Blood from Quintus's neck dribbled behind him and pattered on the floorboards as he paused outside the door. He tested it to be sure it was not barred.

The door swung open.

A rectangular window was unshuttered and silver light flowed into the room. On the same bed where Sophia had sat the day before, Fausta now sat. Her brilliant yellow skirt and blue blouse were like a beacon in the low light. Her hands covered her face as she wept. She must have heard the door open, but did not react.

A table beside her bed held a candle with a flame about to die in the tallow stub. It seemed she had been offered the same wine as Quintus, but none of it had been touched.

She continued to sob as Thorfast's feet thumped against the floor-boards. Only when he stood over her, Quintus's head in his left hand and the dagger in his right, did she pause.

Her bony, pale hands slipped down her face and she stared confusedly at the blood puddling at her feet. Then she looked up.

Despite her bony and narrow head, she was not ugly. Her dark eyes were big and round, and these flew open in terror at the sight of Quintus's head dangling by his hair before her.

She did not scream, but fell back in breathless terror.

Thorfast threw the head at her feet, then leapt on her.

He pressed her frail body to the bed, clamping his hand over her mouth. She started to scream then, but it was muffled. Her free hand pounded at his shoulder until he collected it beneath him. Now with her fully prone, he put the bloody dagger to her neck.

She went still, pretty eyes wide with fear.

"Fausta," he said. "All across Sicily I heard about your evil. I've traveled a long way for this moment. Shame it's going to end so soon."

She shook her head beneath his hand. He smiled and traced the point of the dagger up her face to settle beside her eyes.

"Sophia should have killed you. Now the choice is in my hands. And you should know I'm not a forgiving man. I came here to do what Sophia did not. But as I think on it, I've got something better in mind."

Fausta struggled. Tears slicked her narrow face as it slid beneath Thorfast's palm. He pressed her head against the bed.

"You should live knowing you've been ruined. That your son and husband are dead. That's what Sophia wanted for you. Who am I to deny what she gave her life to do? But I have my own part in all of this. Let your dead son and dead husband be the last things you ever see."

Fausta began to buck against him, and he pressed harder as he leaned next to her ear.

"An eye for an eye."

He dragged the dagger across her eyes. She screamed and kicked as the blade sliced them open. The edge dragged across the bridge of her thin nose, cutting it to the bone. He sawed until her eyes were bloody ribbons.

She sobbed and screamed, but it was nothing more than she had been doing all night. Though she fought still, Thorfast leaned back to examine his work.

"That was for Sophia," he said. "This is for me."

He took the point of the dagger and began to carve her forehead. He etched the Norse rune that most fit Sophia's name in deep, bloody gouges. He held her by the chin as he worked. She hardly resisted, overcome by the agony of her blinding.

Fausta went flat. Tears, if they could even form, were nothing but lines of blood that seeped around her head to stain the bed beneath her.

He stood back, satisfied with this vengeance. He wiped the dagger on her skirt.

"Live with these scars," he said. "Wear your evil on your face for the rest of your days."

Then the sounds of shattering pottery echoed from he hall outside. A woman's voice shrieked in terror.

Outside the window, Thorfast saw the guard tower door open in response.

"About time someone came looking," he said. The woman at the end of the hall continued screaming, but it was receding as if she fled.

"I suppose I could've used my sword after all."

27

Fausta moaned and squirmed on the bed, hands pressed over her bloody eyes. Thorfast ignored her as he scanned the room. Quintus's severed head seemed to gloat at him from the floor, as if he had won after all.

Returning to the window, guards were assembling in the yard below. Three had already come out to answer the screaming girl. She appeared from beneath him now, running with hands atop her head.

"Well, I should've guessed," Thorfast said. The girl fleeing the villa was the broken-nosed nurse. She had probably come to check on Fausta then discovered the carnage in Quintus's room.

The nurse pointed toward the house. The three guards stood back in shock, all looking toward the villa.

Thorfast unslung the bow. The gods had given it to him with just a few arrows. They had not intended him to hold off an army with it. Now he understood its purpose.

He searched the open stables below. He spotted a pale horse's flank in the silver moonlight. The angle was difficult, but he nocked an arrow nonetheless.

The shaft sped across the night and struck the horse. It screamed and kicked in shock and pain. The horse's stable mates panicked in response, kicking against their pens.

The guards and the nurse did not know where Quintus's killer had gone. Now they all looked toward the stables. The guards drew their swords and the nurse fled in the opposite direction.

Thorfast smiled. He pulled back inside and slipped the bow over his shoulder again. He grabbed the iron candle holder, popping it out of the thick tallow.

"You won't need a candle ever again," he said to Fausta as she rolled in pain on her bed.

He lit the way down the hall, past the dead dog and Quintus's corpse. His feet left bloody tracks on the boards as he bounded down the stairs, gore-soaked ax in his belt and bloody dagger in hand.

At the bottom of the steps, he paused. Outside men were shouting. Horses screamed. He heard voices in the villa from other rooms, tentative and sleepy. He held the candle aloft and determined the room before him seemed full of things to burn. There was wood furniture, a rug, and a tapestry among many other useless things the rich people of this land collected.

A candle would not start the fire fast enough. Yet he entered the room and lit the few candles he found. Despite the urgency, he worked with precise calm. The panicking horses would create the delay he needed.

He returned to the kitchen where the two young girls were just waking up. Grabbing one by the leg, he dragged her forward.

"Time to wake up," he said. "I need your help."

The girl was thin and dark-skinned. She twisted like a worm in his hand. The other girl shot upright then covered her scream with two small hands.

"Flour," he said. "You people make bread. I want flour."

The girl he held stared in horror. The other girl backed against the wall and began to cry.

He looked for flour and found none. But a board had the white powder all over it. He released the girl and ran his hand through it. He shoved it into her face.

"Flour," he repeated, then pointed his thumb to his chest.

The other girl understood. She pointed at a sack covered in white handprints that rested by the door. He felt foolish, for it was obvious once he saw it.

"Well, run or burn to death," he said as he grabbed the flour sack. He nodded toward the opened door. He left them to decide, and returned to the room where he had lit the candles.

Two women servants stood in the room, amazed at the lit candles. Both were old and gray haired, but dressed in clean robes pinned at their shoulders. They screamed at Thorfast's arrival. Covered in gore, he must have seemed terrifying. He hoisted the bag of flour in his hand.

"Here's a trick I was shown as a boy in Frankia," he said. The two stared wide-eyed at him, backing slowly to the opposite door. "Terrible waste of good flour, though."

He scooped a handful of flour and flung it at the open flames of the candles. The powder exploded in a whoosh of fire. The two servants screamed and fled. The air smelled sour and ashes fluttered to the ground. But nothing had caught fire. He moved the candle beneath the tapestry, stood back and flung more flour.

This explosion spread fire to the tapestry. Now he had more to work with, flinging the flour until three more explosions had spread fire around the room.

He dumped the flour sack the moment the villa door opened. Without turning to see who had come, he sped out the kitchen door. The girls had also fled.

The new arrival began to shout.

Thorfast slipped out the side door and retuned to hide behind the olive oil. The tower guards were all running into the yard. The blaze inside the villa spilled yellow light out the front door. Fausta was screaming from the upstairs window. Across the yard a half-dozen guards had converged on the stables and panicked horses.

"You do good work," Thorfast said, smiling at the chaos he had created.

He waited until every man he counted had gone to the fire. They were forming a line from the well by the stables to the front door. No one could be spared when the main villa was burning up. Not only were their masters endangered but also their pay. Two men came running with a ladder to reach Fausta's window. Thorfast wished he could see their horrified reactions once they reached her. But he opened the side gate door enough to slide through. If Sophia had not been hung over the gate, he would be away. But he simply retrieved his sword and reentered the villa.

The fire had caught much better than he expected. Smoke and brilliant fire streaked into the night, from the side and back of the main building. Every guard and servant hauled sloshing buckets to valiantly fight the spread of fire. They would soon realize they could not win this battle, and Thorfast risked discovery when that happened.

He sped along the darkness of the walls. The flames cast an eerie golden light over everything, but also served to deepen the shadows by contrast. He reached the tower door, which hung open, masked in black shadow.

Peeking inside, he found no one present. The room contained the winch system to raise the outside gate. He took narrow wood steps up, dagger in hand, until he reached the top. He had cleared the tower of its guards.

Looking around, he found rough bunks, mugs and plates stacked on tables, bedding fallen to the floor. The guards had left in haste. A ladder stretched up to a square hatch in the ceiling. The exit would let him walk the wall over the gate. This was where Sophia had been hung.

He clambered up the ladder. Opening the hatch door, he put his hands through then pulled up onto the wall. He hugged the floor, careful to not reveal his profile against the moon. Looking across the yard, the fire had found the air and now raced up the side of the villa.

"If you could see this, Sophia," he said. "It's better than either of us expected."

As if in reflection of Thorfast's own plans, he saw men on a ladder carrying Fausta's writhing body from the window of her room while her villa yielded to flames. Her brilliant clothing was stained dark with gore.

Looking about this narrow wall section, he found a similar ladder. Of course, men would have placed one here to mount or dismount the wall with speed. Entering from the hatch would be inefficient during an emergency.

He fished the ladder down the front of the wall beside Sophia. Her naked body hung by a rope laced under her arms. Its ends were tied off to iron bolts hammered into the wood as if for this purpose. The arrow shaft in her side had broke down to a stub, likely snapped when they had stripped her.

Placing the iron dagger between his teeth, he tasted blood and metal. He set his feet on the rung and tested it. Even if he fell, he was not up so high that he risked death. So he descended to Sophia's level. He had to only cut one section of rope and she would disentangle. He scooped her to his side, her naked body cool but supple against his skin.

She should be stiff with death, he thought. Hours had passed.

She was cool but not cold.

She breathed, however shallow and ragged.

"You live?"

"I knew you would come for me," she said. Though her head hung limp and she made no movement at all. "I ... will not live long."

He sawed away the rope until it snapped, then took her onto his shoulder. He bounded down the ladder and leapt the final distance to the grass. Without hesitation, he ran for the concealment of the hiding place among the bushes by the road. He dared not speak, afraid that he had imagined all of this. Yet her body was pliant and her breath wheezed faintly by his ear. She was alive.

Laying her on the grass, he removed his own shirt and covered her with it. He glanced at the arrow wound. The shaft had gone deep. Surprisingly little blood had leaked from the wound. But there would be no way to remove that arrow without killing her. Judging from the rattling wheeze of her weak breathing, she was dying nonetheless— just in slow agony.

His tears fell across her face as he stared down at her. Her flesh was ashen and black rings formed around her eyes. They fluttered open as his tears splashed her cheeks.

"He said ... the birds would eat my eyes by sunrise. That I would rot on the walls until I was bone."

"Don't waste your breath on this," he said. "Listen, I have killed Quintus. I blinded Fausta and carved your name on her forehead. I burned their villa."

Her eyes widened then closed again. "Well, I picked the right man for revenge."

"That is Norse vengeance." He paused to marshal his voice. "Brutal and direct."

"I wanted to see the north. To become a hero's wife."

He took her pale hand and kissed it. "Why did you do it? You could have gone north with me. You could have lived if you had just followed our plan."

Her eyes opened again, and she gave a sad, feeble smile.

"Because you would not have me, dear Thorfast."

"That is not true. I would have only you."

She shook her head.

"I am a sinner. More than you know. I used you. I lied to you."

He sat back, setting her hand atop the shirt covering her torso. He tilted his head in confusion.

"How have you lied? Your family? Was this not true, the story of your father?"

"God, no." Sophia raised her hand as if to strike him, but it fell back to her body. "You have done a great thing for me. My family has been avenged. That is all truth. I have lied about your friends."

He stared at her, not understanding.

"Valgerd said two other Norsemen had joined my cousin at Pozzallo. She even fancied the one called Alasdair. I made her swear to hide this from you and from them. But your friends live. They serve my cousin as slave soldiers."

"Why?" His throat was tight and dry.

"Because they would prevent you from taking me here. Because they would steal you from me."

"No, I could have saved them. You could've convinced your cousin to release them. I would not have abandoned you. Why ..."

He choked back the awful words forming behind his teeth.

"Anyway, I forgive you for making a mistake."

She closed her eyes and shook her head. "Hear the anger in your voice? Your friends might've died in battle with the Arabs. Would you forgive me then? So you ask why I risked being killed. Now you know."

"That is no reason!" he shouted, and it carried across the fields. By now he cared not at all who might discover him.

"What is done is done," she said. "Go find your friends. Kill the Arab prince. Bury me beneath an olive tree. I will wait for you in hell, Thorfast."

He grabbed her hand again, putting it to his cheek where tears rolled over it.

"I love you, Sophia."

She smiled. Her head turned gently to the side. The rasp of her breathing stopped.

Sophia died and Thorfast knelt weeping over her body as the flames of the burning villa behind him stretched to the sky.

28

Thorfast patted the earth flat over Sophia's grave with a spade. He had paid the farmer a gold coin for the spade and permission to bury Sophia on his land. The old man did not understand him, but he understood the corpse and the gold and Thorfast's blood-splattered visage. He had dug through oppressive heat until his back ached. The old man and his son watched from a distance. The son waved at him when he looked up.

He raised a hand in return, and set the spade against an olive tree. For all of his time with Sophia, he did not understand what an olive was or what it tasted like. He swore he would never touch one or the oil made from one. Olives, to his mind, were covered in blood.

Picking his shirt and sword off the ground, he dressed then turned toward where the smell of the sea carried on the wind. He had no words to say over the grave, nor any more tears to cry.

Sophia had saved his life. He had repaid her as she had demanded. What else could he say for their relationship? They had slept together, shared danger together, and shared enough in common to form a bond. But death had separated them.

He decided she had been right about breaking his promise to her. Had he reunited with Yngvar and Alasdair, whatever she wanted would have faded from his mind. He might someday find a way to repay her aid. But she was correct to believe he would have been distracted from his duty to her.

Sophia had been a good woman. A beautiful woman.

But now she was a dead woman, and he could not linger on her.

Though he knew he would. When he dreamed, when his mind idled, he would always linger on her. He would always wonder what life could have been like with her at his side.

He walked out of the grove. Perhaps the old man would keep his promise and let Sophia's grave remain. More likely he would tell his wife and she would have it dug up and the grove blessed by holy men. No one wanted a ghost haunting their fields. If ever he returned and found the old man and his son had reneged on their promise, he would put them in the same grave.

He wandered toward the port town. He bathed in a stream along the way, though he could do little for the blood on his clothes. By the time the town walls neared, he realized he was better served throwing away the shirt. At least his dark pants did not show the blood stains as readily.

He searched his pouch. Five gold coins remained from the sack Sergius had given him. He guessed it would last him a few days while he waited to find Tariq and his crew again. He had to hold on to a few coins to pay his way into Tariq's crew. That bald-headed captain had left a good feeling with him, but Thorfast knew he would be trouble nonetheless.

He paid his entrance tax at the gates, and got nothing more than condescending grins at his ragged appearance. He eventually found his way to the docks to where Tariq's ship had been docked. But the berth was filled with another ship.

Rather than seek out Tariq, he sat in the shade of a palm tree and watched the workers along the docks. A guard patrol would likely chase him off, but for now he decided to rest.

What would he say to Yngvar and Alasdair? Would it be too much to believe Bjorn had survived as well? Truly Valhalla shook with the laughter of gods and heroes both.

But he had to return to Pozzallo as a lone man. If Yngvar and Alasdair had been made slaves, how much better would he fare? He patted his pouch, then withdrew not a coin.

Instead, he pulled out Sophia's gold cross. It was small and cool between his fingers. Her cousin had gifted it to her. Perhaps returning it to him, or at least making the offer, might mean something. Maybe Commander Staurakius would be grateful to him.

But then Sophia's other cousin had betrayed them to their enemy. How much could he trust these people, he wondered. Besides, there was an ocean to cross and warring Romans and Arabs to evade. A good deal of work lay ahead, and none of it seemed promising.

Once his back grew sore from sitting, he decided to walk the docks.

Halfway to the far end of the port, he spotted a Norse ship.

Not just a Norse ship.

His Norse ship.

"That is impossible," he said, all the while his pulse quickening.

He ran. Weaving and side-stepping the workers along the docks, he came to the ship.

It was the ship he had sailed into this land. A crew of unfamiliar faces worked it. Probably the men who had stolen it from the port of Licata.

He put his hand on his sword hilt and walked the final distance. Whoever was aboard that ship would learn a bit about its history and its captain would answer to him for stealing it.

The ship bobbed merrily at dock. Men ran along its length at their tasks.

Thorfast strode up to the side, then called out in Norse.

"Hey, who owns this ship? I'll have words with him."

The whole crew paused to stare.

Two figures in the prow pushed to the front of the crew.

Thorfast blinked, then tears burst from his eyes.

He faced Bjorn and Gyna.

AUTHOR'S NOTE

During the tenth century, Sicily was an Arab Emirate with the eastern coast marginally under control of the Byzantine Empire. By the end of that century the Byzantines would be gone for good. Throughout their stubborn occupation of the east end of Sicily, the Byzantines fomented revolution and discord throughout the island. Yet they never did better than to hold on to what they already had.

The Byzantine Greeks were fairly treated under Arab rule. In fact, Palermo would become one of the most prosperous cities of that time. Yet they saw themselves as continuous descendants of the Roman Empire and all the glory that entailed. So they were willing to fight for the land their ancestors had won in antiquity. The borders saw endless clashes and small actions, as well as some larger battles such as Messina in 965.

For the purposes of my story and to add a bit more drama, I have somewhat overstated the reality of Byzantine military presence in Sicily. Most of their real outposts were clustered around the northeast where the aforementioned Messina served as the center of Byzantine fighting strength. Pozzallo was more famous for its springs than any Byzantine military fort.

In contrast, the Arabs took a more reactive approach to their

Byzantine neighbors. In 912 they had negotiated a peace treaty with the Byzantine military governor (Strategoi) of Sicily which entailed an annual payment of 22,000 gold coins as tribute. As long as that payment was kept, the Emirate was happy to repel attacks and stifle rebellion when these arose. They controlled the majority of the island and knew time was on their side. Once they had decided to eject the Byzantines for good, they swept their enemies off the east coast forever.

The Arabs would one day be defeated by Normans, descendants of Norsemen who settled in France. However, long before this invasion, Norsemen could be found throughout the Byzantine Empire (and by extension, Sicily) as bodyguards, mercenaries, and raiders. The Norman invasion of Sicily had begun as innocuous visits by opportunistic Norsemen who would carry news of incredible lands and fabulous wealth back home with them.

Now we have seen Thorfast's harried journey through Sicily. We have seen the Wolves all still live. We know the gods have chosen to save their heroes. Now what challenges shall they set before them?

ALSO BY JERRY AUTIERI

Ulfrik Ormsson's Saga

Historical adventure stories set in 9th Century Europe and brimming with heroic combat. Witness the birth of a unified Norway, travel to the remote Faeroe Islands, then follow the Vikings on a siege of Paris and beyond. Walk in the footsteps of the Vikings and witness history through the eyes of Ulfrik Ormsson.

Fate's Needle

Islands in the Fog

Banners of the Northmen

Shield of Lies

The Storm God's Gift

Return of the Ravens

Sword Brothers

Grimwold and Lethos Trilogy

A sword and sorcery fantasy trilogy with a decidedly Norse flavor.

Deadman's Tide

Children of Urdis

Age of Blood

Printed in Great Britain
by Amazon

81964095R00144